Sacrifice

Corrupt Empire

Book Two

Sarah Bailey

Cover Art by V Designs

Published by Twisted Tree Publications
www.twistedtreepublications.com
info@twistedtreepublications.com

Paperback ISBN: 978-1-913217-01-3

This book is dedicated to Matthew Burroughs
You're an awesome reviewer and advocate of authors
Absolutely love reading all of your reviews on tehben.com
Thank you for being you

You can find Matt on Twitter at @MJBurroughs
He won my competition to have Sacrifice dedicated to him.
This one is for you!

Prologue

Avery

My heels clicked against the marble floor. The receptionist looked up at me, eyes going wide, but I ignored her. She knew who I was. Everyone knew my face. They just hadn't seen it around here since I went missing.

"Miss… Miss Daniels?"

I pressed the button for the lift.

"Miss Daniels?"

It dinged just as she came out from behind her desk. I smiled at her before getting in. I hit the button for the top floor. She hurried over to the lift.

"Don't tell him I'm coming," I said.

Her face was a picture of bewilderment as the doors closed in her face. Fifty floors later, I stepped out of the lift. I walked along the hallway, my footsteps muffled by the carpet. Arriving at the secretary's desk, she looked up.

"Hello, how can I… Oh my god," Clara said.

"Hello Clara. Is anyone in with him?"

She shook her head slowly.

"Good."

I walked towards the door to his office.

"Miss Daniels…?"

"It'll be fine, don't worry. Just don't let anyone disturb us."

I opened the office door and walked in. He stood by the window, looking out at the skyline with his hand glued to his ear.

"Yes… Yes… No, I understand… Well, just get it to me by next week. Right… Okay."

He clearly hadn't heard me come in.

"Yes… No… Okay, speak soon."

He let out a long sigh, his shoulders drooping.

"Fuck."

I took further steps into the room. His back stiffened, but I spoke before he could turn around.

"Hello Uncle Charlie."

Chapter One

Avery

1 slid down his front door, unable to go any further. My heart broke a thousand times over. I'd walked out on him. I'd walked out on the man I loved without a backwards glance and it killed me. I felt dead inside.

Aiden.

He'd successfully ripped out my soul and stamped all over it. I had no idea what I was doing or where I was going. I just knew I couldn't stay there with him. Not after what he said.

Stupid girl. Stupid, stupid girl.

Idiotic enough to believe he ever had my best interests at heart. He only had one goal. Destroy my family. And apparently, take down Frazier Shaw and his business in the process. Aiden wanted to dismantle it all. Use everything at his disposal. Including me.

Me.

The girl he professed to care about.

He had a fucking shitty way of showing it. How could he think I would ever say yes? He was fucking crazy.

But he's the fucking crazy guy you're in love with.

How had we come to this?

My day was well and truly ruined. The one day he promised me would be about me and him. Nothing else.

We'd both fucked it up royally.

I fingered the A on the necklace he'd given me. No matter what, I wouldn't take it off. It reminded me that despite what he'd done, Aiden felt something for me. Even if he hadn't wanted to. I knew it was stupid, but I couldn't let it go.

I had to get up. Had to move. I wasn't going back to Aiden, but I needed somewhere to go that wasn't my own flat. The police were still looking for me. I wasn't ready to face any of that yet.

I felt my pockets. Shit. I hadn't bought the burner phone with me. How the hell was I going to get anywhere? I had nothing. Literally nothing but the clothes on my back. And it was Christmas Day.

Who would I even contact anyway?

James.

The only person who knew where I was. And shit, did I need my best friend right at that moment. I hauled myself to my feet. Somehow, I'd find a way to get in contact with him.

I trudged over to the lift and rode down to the ground floor. Every step I took away from Aiden made me feel worse. I really thought I'd suffered enough pain, but my heart had other ideas. Loving him was physically painful. The sensation burnt in my chest, almost crippling me. I had to keep putting one foot in front of the other or I'd collapse and sob all over again.

When I got out on the street, there were a few people milling about. I really didn't want anyone to recognise me, but I had to call James somehow. I approached an older couple.

"Sorry, excuse me… I don't normally do this, but I'm in a serious bind."

The woman looked at me with distaste, but the man stopped and spoke to me.

"All alone on Christmas?"

"I guess. I just left my phone in a taxi and I really need to get in touch with my family. Could you by any chance let me borrow a phone at all, please?"

A blatant lie, but it was the first thing that came to mind. The woman continued to stare at me with annoyance. Not quite sure what her problem was considering I wasn't trying to hit on her partner or anything.

"Oh, sure." He pulled a phone out from his coat pocket. "Here. Sorry to hear you lost your phone."

I nodded at him in thanks and took it. Quickly dialling James number, I smiled at them as best I could. I took a step back so they wouldn't overhear my conversation. He picked up after the fifth ring.

"Hello?"

"James, it's Avery."

"Ave! Having a good Christmas with lover boy? Wait, why are you calling me off a different number?"

The mention of lover boy almost broke me. I could feel my chest constrict, the pain burning through me.

Aiden.

I took a deep breath, shoving those feelings back down.

"Um, I borrowed a stranger's phone. Listen, I know you're with your family, but can you come get me, please? I really hate to ask."

"What's wrong?"

"I'll tell you when you're here. Please, don't ask me now. I can't start crying in front of these people."

"Okay... I'll be as quick as I can. To be honest, I'll be fucking glad to get away. Dad is Dad. Dante is brooding. Jen and Fi keep wanting to play fucking charades. And don't get me started on the rest."

Jennifer and Fiona were James' twin sisters who were three years older than him.

"See you in a bit."

He hung up and I handed the phone back to the nice man.

"Thank you so much. I really appreciate this."

He smiled at me.

"Never hurts to help out a young girl on Christmas."

The woman huffed. I'd be glad to get away from her and her death stares.

"Okay, okay. Sorry, I promised her our little Christmas walk wouldn't be long."

I smiled at them and stepped away. He tipped an imaginary hat at me and they ambled off. Thankfully neither of them recognised me. I'd be well and truly screwed otherwise.

I stood outside Aiden's building, feeling awkward and cold. Daylight had faded and it was a cloudless sky. I wish I could've waited inside but there was no way I was ringing his doorbell. Doing that would tempt me into going back upstairs and letting him hold me. Letting him kiss me. Letting him fuck me so I could forget again. Shit. My back ached from him pounding me into the floor. The sex had been so raw. So brutal. All our feelings poured out and laid bare.

Stop thinking about it.

I fingered the necklace again. My heart burnt. I wanted him so much even though he'd hurt me. I craved Aiden with every breath I took. I wanted his smile. His touch. The way he smelt of cedarwood and pine. I missed him already. The only constant I had for the past few months.

Stop. You have to stop.

I couldn't. Aiden took up a permanent place in my mind. My heart. My soul. The screwed up, tattooed, avenging angel who'd completely ripped my life apart. He'd broken me and tried to put the pieces back together. Except those pieces were all muddled up. I no longer really knew who I was, but I did know I'd fallen for Aiden. Fallen so hard, I could no longer breathe air into my lungs properly because I wasn't right there with him. Now I had to find some semblance of who I was so I could move on. But moving on from Aiden would be impossible.

A fresh set of tears fell down my face.

Great. Now I'm crying in the street.

How long I stood there, I don't know. My fingers froze no matter how I tried to keep them warm. I shivered and kept moving back and forth. A few people gave me strange looks, but I stopped caring. I felt so lost and alone, nothing seemed to matter anymore.

James turned up in his black Mini Cooper. I dashed across the pavement, jumped inside and immediately whacked up the heating without saying hello.

"Cold?" he asked.

"Just a tad."

He set off. I glanced up at Aiden's floor. I could still see the Christmas tree lights twinkling in the window. It made my heart lurch and my chest ache. I fingered the necklace again.

Aiden.

I wanted to tell James to stop the car so I could run back to him. To be back in his arms where I felt safe. To let him kiss away my pain. To be with the man I loved so desperately. It took every ounce of self-control I had to keep my mouth shut.

"So... you want to tell me why you dragged me away from my super fun family Christmas?"

I turned to James, shaking myself out of my thoughts of Aiden.

"I'm so sorry."

"Hey, Ave... you know what they're like. It's bullshit. Back to mine?"

"Please."

"You got it."

He reached out, took my hand and gave it a squeeze.

"Shit, your fingers are like ice."

"I forgot to put gloves on."

"No shit."

He concentrated on navigating a roundabout before turning back to me. The look in his eyes said 'spill'.

"We had a fight. A huge fight."

"About...?"

I tried hard not to think about what he'd said to cause it, but the words rang in my ears.

"I need you to get engaged to Tristan Shaw. I need you to make his family trust you. And I need you to find all the evidence of your family's dirty dealings. There's more and I know Frazier has it. He has to. He would never destroy what he could use. I need you to get it for me so we can expose them for who they really are.

"We can't go to the police. We'll use public outcry against them. One by one, they'll fall and all that'll be left is a shell of a company for you to do what you want with. I need you to do this for me even though I hate the thought of you being near Tristan. Please, Avery. I hate it, but it's the only way. Please trust me. Please don't say no."

The only way? He was crazy. I hated Tristan. I'd known him since I was a kid. He was seriously messed up in the head. I once caught him trying to drown kittens the family cat had in the bath when I was around their house with my parents. When I pulled them out, I found he'd mutilated them already. Horrific.

I stayed away from him as much as possible. And now I knew how psycho Frazier really was, I hoped never to see either of them again.

How could Aiden think I would agree to such an idiotic plan? Tristan was well aware of my dislike and I can't say he's a fan of me either. It would never work. Never work in a million fucking years.

When my father told me they wanted us to get married and carry on the family business together, I just about lost it. Under no circumstances was I ever agreeing to it. He'd found another solution. One of my cousins would help me instead from behind the scenes. Only now I was realising it probably had everything to do with the other side of the business. Did everyone know about this except me? I felt sick all over again.

"Ave?"

I looked over at James, startled.

"Sorry… You asked what we fought about. Right. It's really hard to explain. There's so much fucked up shit I haven't told you about."

I crossed my arms over my chest, feeling as though it might explode at that moment. So conflicted.

Should I tell him or not?

"Between you and him?"

"Not exactly. More stuff about my family. The truth is awful. So fucking awful. I can't even… I don't know where to start."

It all felt too crazy. Too much to talk about. There were things I'd never reveal to anyone, but James was the only person in my life who might understand what I was going through. His own family was pretty fucked up. I could tell him a little of it, just enough so he'd understand what happened between Aiden and me.

James didn't reply. We sat in silence for the rest of the drive, almost as if he knew I needed time to work out how to tell him.

When we got in the flat, I stripped out of my coat, scarf and shoes.

"You're welcome to steal my clothes as usual," he said.

I smiled, giving him a nod.

"Well, you know where the bedroom is."

"Can we just go curl up?"

We'd slept in the same bed together so many times before. It was our thing. Curling up under the covers to talk when the world got too much. Aiden would hate it if he knew.

Enough. He needs to get out of my head.

"I'll fix us a drink then I'll be in."

I trudged into James' bedroom and went through his cupboards. I found a pair of jogging bottoms, a t-shirt and one of his jumpers. I stripped out of my own clothes, dressed and got under the covers. The sheets smelt like his Calvin Klein cologne. A scent I associated with him.

This felt so familiar. It reminded me of how much I missed the way Aiden smelt. Shit. I needed to get a grip. It'd been maybe a few hours since I'd seen him, yet thoughts of him consumed me. He'd etched himself on my heart. Permanently. Deep down, I knew I'd never be free of him. The kind of connection we shared wouldn't fade with time. It would remain. A bond forged for life.

When James came in, he was carrying two mugs. He gave one to me and set the other one down on the bedside table. He started stripping out of his own clothes, throwing them in his wash basket before pulling on a pair of shorts and a plain t-shirt.

We'd seen each other naked, so this wasn't weird, but it reminded me of how different James and Aiden were. My best friend was reasonably toned, but Aiden was ripped. He worked out daily and whenever he'd had a session with his boxing bag, he had me practically drooling over him.

Again. Stop. Just stop. You and Aiden are over. It's done.

Except it wasn't done at all.

"Mulled cider?" I asked.

"Yeah, didn't think you'd want wine."

I sipped at it. The spices warmed me. I smiled at him as he jumped into the bed and huddled under the covers next to me.

"So, now you're all wrapped up warm and comfortable, feel like spilling the beans?"

I sighed, taking another sip of the cider. There were things I couldn't say, but most of it I could. So I started at the beginning. Went right back to the night my parents were murdered. I didn't tell James I was there nor that Aiden kidnapped me and locked me up. I cried a few times. Talking about my family's dealings to someone other than Aiden made me feel worse about them. The shame tore at my soul.

He sat silently listening to me, not interjecting once.

"What he wants is impossible. I can't. You know Tristan isn't right in the head. No one would believe it, least of all Frazier."

He sat back against the headboard and took a sip of his own cider. He shook his head, his blue eyes meeting mine. I could see the shock and confusion in them.

"Holy fuck."

"Yeah, holy fuck is probably right."

"Ave, that shit is so fucked up, I don't even know where to start."

"And you think I did?"

He nudged his shoulder into mine.

"No. I was not expecting you to unload a whole can of 'what the fuck' on me though."

I half smiled.

"Least it wasn't a can of whoop-ass."

I mimicked the motion of whipping with my hand. He barked with laughter.

"Idiot."

Sacrifice

I sighed. Whilst it was all very well for us to make jokes, it really wasn't a laughing matter. What my family had done was sick. And what Aiden asked me to do was completely unreasonable.

"I'm sorry, Ave. All of that sucks. I mean the shit with your family and the company, don't have any clue how you're going to deal with it. You can't just do nothing, not when it's basically your company now. And the stuff with Aiden… I don't know him, but it sounds like he's got issues."

I hadn't told him everything about Aiden. I'd left out a lot. Mostly I spoke about how we'd spent weeks pussyfooting around our attraction to each other until we'd given in. I kept Aiden's not so vanilla desires to myself, as well as his real connection to my family.

"He does, but he's been through a lot of shit. I know he cares for me. We're more than just two people sleeping together."

"What do you mean?"

I'd left out something else. Something pretty important.

"I have feelings for him. It's real. It's like we're connected. And I know he has feelings too even if he's unwilling to admit them."

His eyes narrowed.

"Feelings… Are you…? Do you love him?"

I nodded. Hearing the words out loud made me feel weird. I'd told Aiden, but whether it really registered with him or not, I had no idea. I hadn't dared to look at him afterwards. Too worried it would ruin my resolve.

"Does he know?"

"I told him before I left. I don't know what he thought about it. It's so complicated, James. I feel like I'm breaking inside."

He took my mug from me, placing both on the bedside table. He shuffled down into the covers and pulled me with him, wrapping his arms around me. It didn't feel like when Aiden held me, but I was grateful.

"I don't want to cry anymore," I whispered.

"I know." He stroked my hair. "We're just going to lie here together until you fall asleep."

I didn't want to tell him I had no idea how I was going to sleep. All I could think about was how much I wanted Aiden. My soul called to his. And being away from him was so much worse than any of the things he'd done to hurt me.

Such an idiot. Stupid idiot.

Hours might have passed, I had no idea, but sleep eluded me. James was conked out next to me, his hair ruffled. He looked peaceful. I sat up and crawled out of the bed, careful not to wake him. I picked up his phone from the bedside table and went through into the living room.

I pulled off a blanket from the sofa and sat on the floor with my back to it. I pressed the button to illuminate the screen. Two in the morning. What I was about to do was incredibly stupid.

I unlocked the phone. James and I had always known each other's passcode. I scrolled through his contacts. My finger hovered over the name. I pressed down, putting the phone to my ear. It rang four times. Then he picked up.

"Hello?"

The rich, deep note of his voice broke me. I stifled a sob.

14

"Avery... Is that you?"

I put a hand over my mouth. Tears fell down my cheeks.

"Please tell me it's you. Fuck. Avery, please."

My hand dropped. Hearing his voice soothed me. It pieced together my broken heart.

You're so fucked up.

"It's me," I whispered.

"Fuck. Are you okay? Where are you?"

The relief mixed with concern in his voice crushed me. What the hell was I doing? Calling him was the stupidest idea I'd had all evening.

"I'm with James. And no, I'm not okay."

"I'm so sorry. Fuck. I've been worried sick since you left. Fucking hell. I hate this. I hate what I've done to you."

I took a breath, tears still cascading down my face.

"I can't sleep. I... I miss you, Aiden. I miss you so much." The words came tumbling out without me wanting them to.

It'd barely been six or seven hours since I'd left. Being away from him killed me.

"I miss you too. Let me come get you."

"No. I left for a reason and nothing has changed."

"Avery..."

"No, I shouldn't have called. This was stupid. I just... I needed to hear your voice. I hate that I still need you. I hate you so much."

And I loved him too. Such a fine line between the two warring emotions.

"Please don't say that. I'm sorry. Please, I need you. I fucking need you so much. I can't breathe without you."

"I have to go."

If I spoke to him any longer, I'd give in.

"Avery, please."

The agony in his voice destroyed me.

"I meant what I said. I can't keep letting you hurt me no matter how I feel about you."

"Avery—"

I hung up.

I felt worse and somehow better for hearing his voice. I wiped away the tears from my cheeks. Such an idiot. Was I so obsessed with him that I couldn't stay away? Had leaving even been the best idea? Couldn't I have worked it out with him? But Aiden wasn't the type to talk things through. Our relationship wasn't equal. He owned me.

Except I'd seen the look in his eyes when he realised I intended to leave him.

Despair.

Was he mine?

He had to be mine.

I had to know.

I looked down at the phone. If he could answer me that one question then maybe we could work it out.

Maybe.

So I rang him again.

"Princess."

His new nickname for me. Shit. It tore at me, but I had to stay focused.

"Just answer me one thing."

"Okay…"

"Are you mine?"

"What?"

16

"I'm yours, but are you mine?"

Silence. Seconds ticked by. They felt like hours, but it could've only been a minute.

"Who else's would I be?"

It wasn't exactly a yes, but it was more than I'd expected him to say.

"How am I supposed to know?"

"I told you, I never lied to you about how I feel. There is no one else. There has never been anyone else. I don't have relationships. I rarely even sleep with the same woman twice. You want honesty? I can't get enough of you. Every part of you. You are the only person I've ever wanted full stop. I know I've fucked things up between us. You have no idea how sorry I am. Please, let me come get you. I need you. I need you here. You belong with me. You said you're still mine. You said…"

I said I love him. His confession made my soul split in two.

"I'm not coming back tonight."

"Do you really… What you said when you left, is that how you feel about me?"

"I wouldn't have said it if I didn't mean it."

I didn't regret telling him I loved him. It was something I couldn't hold back any longer. I'd never been in love before. It was the only thing that made any sense in this fucked up situation. My heart belonged to Aiden and I knew on some level his belonged to me.

"Are you ever going to come back?"

"I don't know. I won't do what you need so how can I?"

"I don't fucking care about that. I can't live without you. Every fucking moment since you left has been agony. I know I've hurt you so much, but please, don't say this is over."

Was it over? My heart said no. I could hear the anguish in his voice. He'd suffered just as much as me. And right now, I couldn't hate him anymore. I was upset and angry, but that didn't change how much I cared. How much it broke me because he was hurting too.

"You know it'll never be over," I whispered. "I love you."

I hung up. The phone dropped onto the carpet and I buried my face in my knees.

Idiotic, naïve girl. How could you give him hope you'd return?

Because I knew I'd go back to him.

Because the stupid girl I was loved the broken, fucked up man who'd destroyed her world.

Chapter Two

Aiden

1 hadn't slept all night. I couldn't. Everything hurt. Her words on the phone rang in my ears.

"It'll never be over. I love you."

I didn't deserve her love, but I fucking hoped she meant it about us not being over. I couldn't stand the thought of it. Fuck all my plans. Fuck the shit with her family. I still wanted to tear them to pieces, but not at the expense of her and me. It wasn't until she walked out the door and didn't come back that it hit me.

I love her.

My heart belongs to her.

I am hers.

And I would fight with my dying breath to get her back. Just to have her here with me. There had to be another way. There always was.

I could still feel the phantom of her body against mine as I took her roughly against the floor. The way she'd cried and told me to fuck her. *Fuck. Avery.* I'd totally screwed up. Could she ever forgive me? Could she ever look at me the same way again? I didn't deserve it, but I loved her. I couldn't fucking live without her.

The buzzer for the door went. Fuck. I crawled out of bed and went into the hall. I didn't bother with the intercom, I pressed the button for the door. I went back into the bedroom and put some shorts and a t-shirt on.

When the knock on the door came, I went through and opened it.

"Merry Christmas…" Tina faltered. "Aiden, you look like shit."

I said nothing, stepping back so she could enter the flat. I closed the door behind her as she walked through into the kitchen. I followed her. It wasn't like she didn't know her way around. She flipped the kettle on.

"Where's Avery?"

Hearing her name tore at my fucking soul.

"Not here."

Tina turned to me.

"What do you mean she's not here?"

"She… she left me."

"What did you do?"

Tina knew it was my fault instantly. Knew me too fucking well. I couldn't take the look in her eyes. I walked away and threw myself into one of the kitchen table chairs, running a hand through my hair.

"I fucked it up."

She sighed and began pulling things out of my cupboards. When she'd made me a shake and herself a cup of tea, she sat down opposite me.

"Are you ready to admit you're in love with her?"

I nodded, taking a huge gulp of the shake she'd made me. I couldn't starve myself even though I had zero appetite.

"Have you told her?"

"No."

She shook her head, rolling her eyes.

"Why did she leave?"

"I told her what I wanted her to do. She unsurprisingly refused and told me she couldn't stay because I kept hurting her."

"And what exactly is this grand plan of yours?"

I looked away. Saying it out loud the first time made me realise how insane it sounded. Now I just felt ashamed. Telling Tina would only make it fucking worse.

"If she can get close to Frazier through Tristan, then I can get the evidence I need to take him down too."

"What exactly did you tell her she had to do?"

"Get engaged to him."

Tina stood up, leant over the table and cuffed me around the ear. I looked up at her, rubbing the side of my head.

"What was that for?"

She sat back down.

"You really don't understand women at all. How do you think that made her feel? Hmm? Do you think she wanted to hear you tell her to get engaged to another man?"

"Well no."

"Honestly, I really thought I taught you better than this."

She took a sip of her tea, looking up at the ceiling. I fiddled with my glass. She probably had taught me better, but I was fucked up and sick in the head. I'd never really spent this much time with a girl before. Never knew what it was like to want someone in the way I wanted Avery. So instead, I'd pushed her away.

"She said she loves me."

"And you didn't tell her you feel the same way?"

"She left before I could and when she said it again, she hung up on me. What was I supposed to do? I don't want to tell her when she's upset with me. She might think I'm just saying it to get her to come back."

She didn't respond for the longest time. I didn't know how to fix any of it. I no longer wanted Avery to go through with my stupid fucking plan. I just wanted her back. To hear her voice. I missed her scent. Coconut with a hint of vanilla. It wasn't even about how fucking amazing it felt when I was inside her. I missed her. Her presence in the flat.

"Did you sleep last night?"

"No."

"Aiden…"

"You know it's impossible. I really fucked up, Tina. All this time, having her with me made it all stop. And now, I don't know what will happen if I try to close my eyes."

Tina's expression betrayed her concern.

"You need to sleep. I don't want you getting into tro—"

"Don't bring that up. It's different now. I'll deal with it."

She raised an eyebrow.

"Will you? Or are you going to bury everything deep down like you always do?"

I really wished Tina had never seen me grow up sometimes. She saw me too clearly. She knew what I suffered with. How the nightmares drove me fucking crazy. The violent outbursts I'd had when I was younger because I couldn't deal with any of it. She didn't make excuses for my behaviour, just tried to help me. I'd rejected that help when I was a teenager. By the time I joined the army at eighteen, I was close to fucking breaking point. It was only the discipline I learnt in the forces that kept me from completely losing my mind. Discipline and control kept me focused.

"Aiden, she gave you peace, didn't she? I dare say she made you happy. Do you still want her marrying someone else?"

"No, I would've never let it get that far." I ran a hand through my hair. "I don't know how to fix me and her."

"Perhaps you might want to try a gesture that tells her you're serious about the two of you."

Gesture?

I couldn't think what she might be alluding to.

"Like what?"

She rolled her eyes and let out a long sigh.

"You've never called anyone your girlfriend before so why don't you start there?"

I stared at her.

Girlfriend?

"You want me to ask her out like we're teenagers?"

"No, I want you to be an adult and tell the girl you're in love with you want to have a real relationship with her. Is that too hard for you?"

I looked away, rubbing the back of my neck.

"No, I suppose not."

"And if you do this, you treat her right, Aiden. She needs to go back to the real world. You can't keep her hidden any more. Let her decide if she wants to help you deal with her family. Don't push her. Let her in. Let her help you. I hate seeing you like this. So fix it between you and fix it right. I want the Aiden I know is in there deep down back. The one I saw when he brought around the girl he wanted me to meet because she was special to him."

I knew she was right. The only way I'd get her back was if I proved I was serious. Whether I could really have a relationship with another person remained to be seen. Was I even capable of it? I'd spent so long alone keeping all my walls and my guard up. Then Avery came along and smashed through it all. Made me feel again.

I had to try, didn't I? Try for her.

"Okay. I get it."

"Good. Don't ruin it again if she gives you a second chance."

"I'll try not to."

And I would. For Avery, I was beginning to realise I'd do anything to keep her.

She's still mine.

I had to remind myself of that fact even though she wasn't here right now. I'd been a selfish arsehole to her. Keeping her locked up here where her mental state deteriorated. I had a lot of shit to make up to her. No fucking wonder she'd left me. I had to do better. Do right by her.

"Come on, you're going to try to get some sleep now and I'm going to sit with you. No excuses."

I didn't bother trying to get out of it. I did need sleep. Needed to function properly so I could work out how to get Avery back.

Tina followed me into the bedroom, made me get in bed whilst she pulled out her Kindle and sat with me. Fucking ridiculous really, me needing the woman who'd raised me to make sure I went to sleep.

I lay there for the longest time, trying to get thoughts of the girl I loved out of my head, but it proved fruitless. All I wanted was her here so I could wrap myself around her small frame and keep her safe. Take her pain away. I missed her so much.

And soon, I'd have her back again.

Tina left late evening after making sure I slept. We'd eaten lunch and dinner together whilst watching films. She reiterated I needed to sort my shit out before she left.

I felt listless, lying on the sofa with my arm slung over my face. Would she call again? I wasn't about to try ringing her since James might pick up. I wanted to hear her voice if I couldn't see her. How the fuck had things come to this? Here I was, pining after a girl. A fucking girl. I felt fucking pussy-whipped. She'd stripped away all my fucking walls and barriers and made me fucking helpless. I hadn't felt helpless since I was a kid.

Avery.

My whole entire world was that damn girl. Everything shifted. If only she knew the torment she brought on. My soul burnt for hers.

Mine. She's fucking mine. I fucking need her.

My phone rang. I fumbled for it on the coffee table, dropping my arm from my face. One name appeared on the screen.

James Benson.

It was after midnight so I knew it had to be her.

"Avery?"

"Hi," she whispered.

"You called."

The relief I felt at hearing her voice slammed into me with a force that took my breath away.

"Did you think I wouldn't?"

"I don't know what you're thinking or doing any more, princess."

I'd called her it as a joke that first time yesterday, but now it just fit. She was my princess.

"Well, I haven't done very much today. It was me, the sofa and the TV."

Were we just going to have a normal conversation? I supposed I should take what I could get.

"What did you watch?"

"Mostly cooking shows."

I smiled. She had a thing for those. I'd found her watching them on more than one occasion after I let her start using the TV.

"What about James?"

"He had to go back to his dad's. I would've called earlier, but he only just got back like an hour ago. He got in trouble for leaving yesterday. He didn't tell them about me obviously. Did Tina come over?"

"Yes, she was sad not to see you and gave me several lectures."

She giggled. Actually fucking giggled. The sound warmed my bones. Fuck. I wanted her here so badly.

"I can't imagine anyone giving you a lecture."

"You don't know what she's like."

Tina could bulldoze over all your arguments and basically make a tit out of you if she wanted. That woman was a force to be reckoned with despite her quiet demeanour.

"Were the lectures about me?"

I smiled again. Fuck. Why did this girl make me feel so… happy?

"Yes. She told me to fix things between us."

I wasn't sure why I decided to be honest. I guess I realised Avery needed that from me. Tina had been right. I had to let her in and honesty was the first place I could start.

"I don't know that we can be fixed, Aiden."

"Will you let me try?"

"It depends on what you're proposing to do."

Tina's words kept coming back to me. All of them. I knew what I had to do.

"Avery… I don't want to do this over the phone, but there are things I need to say to you. First and foremost, I'm sorry for everything. Everything I asked of you. Everything I did to you. I meant what I said last night. You are my world. I didn't give you a proper answer when you asked me if I'm yours, but I have a question of my own. Do you want me to be yours?"

She didn't immediately reply. I heard her shuffling about for a moment.

"Yes."

My heart contracted. Fuck. This girl. She made my whole fucking body sing.

"And if I asked you if you wanted to have a real relationship with me, what would your answer be?"

"Is that a real question, Aiden? Like do you actually mean it?"

"I suppose I do."

I did mean it. What was I saying? Why was this so difficult? Fuck. I wanted to see her face so much. To see her reaction. I hated doing this over the fucking phone.

"You suppose or you do?"

"I do mean it."

Silence. I heard her move again. What was she doing?

"Video call me and ask me again."

"What?"

"Just do it."

She hung up on me. What the fuck? Fine. If that's what she wanted, then I'd do it. Prove to her I was serious. She wasn't letting me get off lightly and I supposed I deserved it after everything I'd done.

I sat up, put my phone out in front of me and dialled. After a moment, she answered. Fuck. Seeing her face made my heart ache more. Her hair was braided down one side. She wore a blue t-shirt that looked far too big for her. Her doe eyes were bright with unshed tears. Fuck. Was that my doing?

She waved at me.

"Where are you?" I asked.

"On the sofa. James is asleep. I stole his phone again. He knows I spoke to you last night, but he's not judging. I told him everything, well, except for the whole murder and kidnapping business. I promised you it would stay between us. I don't intend to break any more of the promises I made to you."

The only one she'd broken was the promise not to leave me, but really, after what I'd done, that was justified. I couldn't blame her for it.

Fuck. My cock was rigid just seeing her through the screen. How did this girl manage to be so fucking alluring? Damn it. How could I fucking pay attention when all I wanted was her sweet pussy around my cock? Now was not the time to be thinking about fucking her.

"I miss you."

She smiled at me.

"I miss you too. I wasn't quite sure whether I could cope with seeing you, but shit, Aiden, I just... I needed to see your face. I want to know if you mean it."

"I do. I want you to be in my life. So fucking much. I want... I want a relationship with you."

I watched a tear fall down her cheek, which she quickly dashed away.

"You don't want me to get engaged to Tristan?"

"Fuck no. I don't want you to get engaged to anyone. I'm sorry I ever asked that of you. Honestly, right now, I couldn't care less about anything to do with the Shaws, your family or the company. The only thing that matters is you and me."

I ran a hand through my hair. We could work that shit out later when we'd got through this. And we could do that together. Her and me.

"You want me to... to be your girlfriend?"

Weirdly, that didn't feel wrong coming from her. I'd never wanted a girlfriend in my life and yet for Avery, I'd do just about anything.

"Yes."

"Are you mine?"

"Yes."

No hesitation. I was hers. Irrevocably hers.

Her eyes darted away to the side. Her expression conflicted. Was she going to say no? Fuck. I wanted this to be enough, but if she needed more, then I'd do more.

"Take me on a date then."

"What?"

"A date, Aiden. You know, dinner, movies, dancing, whatever. Just take me out somewhere. You want a relationship with me? Prove you're serious."

A date? Was she crazy? How could I take her out when she was considered missing by the police? Didn't she know how dangerous it would be? Fuck. She could've asked me to do anything, but that? That was fucking impossible. Until we'd worked out how to bring her back into the world, she'd have to stay hidden.

"You know that's not safe."

"I don't care. Work it out. Enlist James' help if you have to. Just do it for me. I rarely ask you for anything. I know how we work. I'm yours. You command. I obey. And that will continue when we're together, but this is non-negotiable."

The only thing that really registered was her telling me she was mine and we'd be together.

"Are you saying yes to us?"

"I'm saying if you take me out on a real date, then I'll come home and be with you."

I thought my heart might fucking stop. Home. Her home was with me. Fuck. Fuck. I had to do what she asked. I had no choice. Tina told me to fix it. Fix it between us.

"I'll take you on a date when I can work out how to do it safely, okay?"

Her fucking smile was radiant.

"Thank you. Can I make one small request?"

"Hmm?"

"Wear a suit."

I shook my head, smiling.

"Do you like me in a suit?"

Her cheeks stained red.

"Yes. It's hot."

My cock jerked again. Fuck. Knowing she found me just as attractive as I did her did things to me. I wanted her so fucking badly.

"What are you wearing?" I blurted out and immediately regretted it because her face, neck and ears began to match her cheeks.

"Nothing sexy."

"Show me."

"No. You'll get jealous because I'm wearing another man's clothes."

I didn't give a shit what she was wearing because I wanted her to take it off. I wanted to see her tits and have her touch herself for me. Fuck.

"Show me."

She tilted the phone down. The blue t-shirt came into view. I could see her tits straining against the material. She tilted it down lower. Jogging bottoms and a pair of boxers peeked out from the tops of them. Fuck. I didn't care if they were her friend's clothes. She looked fucking sexy to me.

I wanted her in my clothes and I'd fucking make her dress up in them when I got her back. I imagined her just wearing one of my shirts and nothing else. I ran my hand over my cock, unable to help myself. Seeing her body made me harder.

"Fuck. I want you."

She brought the phone back up to her face.

"You what?"

"I'm so hard for you. Do you want to see?"

Her eyes went wide.

"Wait, what?"

She didn't exactly answer the question about wanting to see me, but I didn't care. I tilted the phone down and showed her exactly what she did to me. I ran my hand over where my cock was straining against my shorts.

"What are you doing?"

"Showing you how much I want you in case you didn't believe me."

I checked the screen of my phone. She was shifting in her seat.

"Shit, Aiden, stop it. I believe you."

I did as she asked, bringing the phone back up to my face. I smiled at her. She was still blushing. Whilst she was open to new things with me, I guessed she was a bit uncomfortable talking about it with her friend asleep in the next room.

"Stop what?"

"I'm not doing… phone sex with you."

"No?"

"No. We're not doing any of that until you do what I asked."

We'd see about that. I wasn't sure how long I could wait to have her again. Not now she told me she'd come back. Shit, I wanted to get on my bike, ride over and fuck her on that sofa. I didn't care what time it was.

"So, you're just going to tease me with your body instead?"

"I wasn't… you asked to see. I told you it wasn't sexy."

"You're sexy whatever you wear."

She rolled her eyes.

"I wasn't trying to tease you. Do you ever think about anything else?"

"You should know by now I do. I think about your smile. The way you smell of coconut. How you get a dimple in your cheek when you're concentrating, which by the way is fucking cute."

She bit her lip.

"Aiden…"

"Hmm?"

"I'm still upset with you, but you're making it really hard for me to stay that way."

I was glad to hear it. I wanted her to forgive me so we could move beyond this.

"I'm going to make it up to you."

"I know you are."

"Good. I think you should get some sleep now."

"I hate sleeping without you."

I fucking hated it too.

"Soon, Avery. I promise."

"I'll hold you to that."

I smiled at her. She waved before ending the call.

And I had to go take care of myself because that fucking girl had made me so hard, I could barely fucking function.

Avery. When I get you back, I'm going to make sure you never leave me again.

Chapter Three

Avery

James and I spent the next couple of days discussing what we might do about my family and the company whilst watching movies and gorging on takeaways and junk food. We'd come up with a big fat load of nothing. I conceded we didn't have enough information and we needed Aiden's help. He was the one who'd told me everything in the first place. It only seemed right I'd work it out with him.

I'm not sure James was too impressed with me telling him I planned to go back to Aiden, but he'd made a concerted effort to help Aiden with this date. I knew he'd done it because it was me.

James grinned at me from the driver's seat.

"What are you smiling at?" I asked.

"I just can't wait to see Mr Tattoos' face when you take your coat off."

"Is that what you're calling him now?"

"It's like Beauty and the Beast."

"Ha bloody ha. He's not a beast."

Sarah Bailey

I did not like that analogy. It hit far too close to home. The whole kidnapping, keeping me prisoner, being kind of a dick to me? All that was more than a little bit comparable.

"Are you sure you're not his Disney Princess?"

I hit his arm.

"Shut your face, idiot."

"Aww, embarrassed? Don't you want to have a fairy-tale romance?"

"Oh my god, James, please. It's not a fairy-tale. Honestly, if you really knew Aiden, you wouldn't be saying that."

Not with his restraints and need to make me submit. The thought of it made me shift in my seat. I missed him. His touch and his voice most of all. I wanted him with such a desperation, it bordered on madness. I gave up pretending I wasn't obsessed with him. Aiden took up every inch of my brain. My heart physically hurt with longing for him.

"Mr Brooding and Mysterious? Yeah well, I'm glad it's you who knows him and not me."

"Okay, enough with the nicknames. Where are we going? You made me get proper dressed up for this, not that I don't appreciate the outfit."

"You'll see."

They'd both been very secretive. I hadn't spoken to Aiden much in the last few days and it killed me. Me leaving had probably been the best thing for us, but at the same time, I wished I hadn't. A knee jerk reaction instead of a well thought out decision. Things needed to change between us. Only time would tell if Aiden was really serious about being my boyfriend.

Boyfriend.

It didn't feel like the right word to describe him. He'd become not only my lover and my friend but the only person I couldn't be without. So boyfriend didn't quite cut it. Partner in crime perhaps? No. That sounded stupid and soppy as shit. Boyfriend would have to do.

"We're here," James announced.

I looked up at the building. It was one of those members only clubs with a very exclusive restaurant inside.

"Since when did you become a member of Black Night?"

"Since Aiden needed somewhere discreet to take you on a long overdue date. Now, keep your hood up until we reach him, remember?"

"Yeah, yeah, okay."

A doorman helped us out of the car and took James' keys. Apparently, they had valet service here, who knew? Parking in London sucked usually, which is why I didn't drive. That and I never learnt how.

James led me into the building and spoke to the front desk. None of the staff batted an eyelid at my hidden face. James took me upstairs to the members only dining room. Right in the back corner, near the fire exit, was a hidden booth.

When Aiden stood, my breath caught in my throat. Shit. He was in a dark grey suit, just like I asked, with a white shirt and a grey tie. He looked mouth-wateringly good. The days spent apart only fuelled my innate need for this man.

He walked over to me and unbuttoned my coat before flipping down my hood. He slipped the coat off my shoulders and set it down in the booth. Then he really looked at me.

The dress James had got for me was navy with a plunging neckline, floor length with a large slit up my right leg. I'd braided my hair down one side and had a smattering of makeup on. His eyes roamed over every inch of me, heat burning in those silver depths.

"You look stunning," he said, his deep voice low and seductive.

I felt my cheeks heat up. The way he was looking at me should really be reserved for when we were alone. James was standing right behind us.

Aiden took my hand and placed a kiss on my knuckles before helping me into the booth. My skin prickled at the contact. He slid in opposite me. I felt a little disappointed he was so far away. I wanted him close. I wanted Aiden full stop.

"Thank you for doing this," I said, only just about able to trust myself to speak.

"And your waiter for this evening… Yours truly," James said, taking a bow.

"Really?"

"Yes, after all, you're technically a missing person."

He tapped his nose. Aiden gave him a look which said, 'go away before I make you'. James grinned and retreated.

"So how exactly did the two of you swing this?" I asked.

"It's all about who you know and how much money you're willing to spend, princess."

That nickname again. Why did it make me feel all giddy inside?

Stop acting like a stupid girl whose crush just told her, he likes her.

I wasn't quite sure what to say. This whole thing felt strange. When I'd asked him for an actual date, I didn't really think he'd go through with it. I hadn't been sure Aiden was actually serious about this relationship thing with me. It seemed he was determined to prove that to me.

I picked up the menu. It was all very fancy. I ate out a lot in upper-end restaurants when I was with my parents, but with James and Gert, we mostly just made trips to Nandos.

James came over and took our order for drinks and food a few minutes later. I looked around at the booth, still feeling more than a little awkward. This place so wasn't an us place. I kind of saw Aiden and me in the back of some shitty bar whilst the music blared too loudly and we had to shout to hear each other talk.

"Um, so... god, I don't know how to do this, Aiden. This is way, way fancy and not really you and me, right?"

He smiled.

"I thought you wanted a real date."

"I know. It's just now we're here and I haven't seen you in days, it feels weird."

I reached across the table, putting my hand out to him. He hesitated for a moment before entwining my fingers with his. That simple touch steadied me. His palm radiated heat, seeping into mine.

"There's a lot we should really talk about," I continued. "The thing is I don't know where to start."

"We can start with I'm really sorry for what happened. It wasn't until you left that I realised how fucked up all of the shit I'd asked you to do was. I've been so focused on revenge, I didn't think about what it might be doing to you or how it would completely destroy what we have. This thing between us, it's real. I know that now. I never meant to hurt you, Avery. I'm just not good at this stuff."

James returned with drinks. He raised an eyebrow when he put down a beer for Aiden and a gin and tonic for me.

"I'll just be here," he said, pointing behind me.

I nodded and he disappeared from view. I fiddled with the glass.

"I know you didn't mean to. I want to put that behind us. I forgive you, okay?"

He nodded, squeezing my hand. I really had forgiven him. Whether that was stupid or not, I no longer cared. All I wanted was the man in front of me.

"Next time, I'll take you somewhere less pretentious, but getting to see you in that dress makes it worthwhile."

Next time?

The thought of more dates with him gave me butterflies. This was a side of Aiden I never imagined I'd see.

"This dress, huh? I thought you preferred it when I wasn't wearing anything."

His eyes darkened and his smile turned devious.

"And you said my mind is always in the gutter."

James turned up again with starters. I tugged my hand from his, shaking my head. My mind was definitely in the gutter after seeing him in that suit. Tonight wasn't supposed to be about sex, but shit, did I want him to undress me slowly and have his way with me.

When I glanced up at him, I could tell he was thinking the same thing. I very much doubted we'd be able to keep our hands off each other for long.

We remained on neutral topics whilst we ate. He told me more about Ben and some stories from his days in the army. Like the time they duct taped a fellow soldier to a flagpole during basic training, which they were all heavily reprimanded for. And I told him about the time Gert, James and I accidentally set off the sprinkler system at our school. It felt nice to have a normal conversation with Aiden that didn't consist of us arguing or talking about my family.

When we finished dessert, I was relaxed enough to play footsie with him under the table. Slipping off a heel, I ran my foot up his leg. His silver eyes burnt holes into mine. He caught my foot, holding it still before he ran his fingers along the inside arch. I tried to pull away, but he wouldn't let me.

"Stop it, that tickles," I hissed.

"Then behave yourself."

"Spoilsport."

He smiled and let go of my foot. I retracted it, scowling at him. Ruining my fun. I'd possibly had a bit too much to drink what with the two gin and tonics and the two large glasses of wine I'd consumed. I wasn't much of a big drinker.

I was just about to say something more to Aiden when James shoved his way into the booth next to me.

"We have a problem. A huge fucking problem," he said, his voice low.

Aiden looked on high alert immediately, his eyes darted out towards the restaurant. A moment later, his expression darkened.

"Frazier and Tristan are here," James continued.

"We need to leave," Aiden said.

"Yeah, you do because I think they might have seen me. If I'd known they were members, I'd have picked a different place."

"Don't worry about it. Not your fault. Put your coat on, princess," Aiden said, his eyes falling on me.

I complied immediately, not wanting to get caught by the Shaws. I wasn't embarrassed by Aiden calling me princess in front of James, but it did remind me of our conversation in the car. He was going to give me shit for it at a later date. He'd never let something like that go.

"Don't worry, I'll sort out the bill and all that business," James said, giving my arm a squeeze.

"Thank you," I said.

Aiden nodded at James before he eyed the room again. He put his hand out to me. I slid across the seat toward him. He wrapped an arm around me. James stayed where he was.

"We're going to go out the back, okay?" Aiden said.

"Okay."

Aiden looked out one last time and then he pulled me up with him. He tugged me towards the fire exit, which thankfully wasn't armed. We left the dining room without looking back and found ourselves in a hallway. He looked left and right before he dragged me towards where we could see a sign for a stairwell.

"Aiden… Where are we going?"

"As far away from those fuckers as possible."

He opened the door to the stairwell and we were hurrying down the stairs a moment later. At least I was trying to in four-inch heels whilst being tipsy. Not an easy feat at the pace Aiden set.

"Slow down, I'm in heels," I protested.

"For fuck's sake," he muttered.

Next thing I knew, he'd swept me up into his arms and carried me down the stairs at a light jog. I held onto his neck for dear life.

"Do you know what would happen if they saw us? We'd be fucked," he said.

I didn't reply because there wasn't any point saying anything. This whole thing had been my stupid idea in the first place. I'd put us in danger by insisting Aiden take me out on a date.

He set me on my feet when we reached the bottom, but then we were out the stairwell and moving through the ground floor of the club. The staff nodded at us.

Aiden stopped by the front desk and asked for something. I wasn't paying much attention to what he said. The attendant handed over two helmets. Aiden thrust one into my hands, picking up the other and tugging me out the door. I barely had time to register what was happening when we were out in the street and a few moments later, he ducked into an alleyway. There sat his fucking bike. I'd told him I was never getting on that thing with him.

"Are you crazy? How do you expect me to get on your bike in this dress?" I asked when he started sorting it out.

"Here."

He handed me a pair of my jeans and took the helmet from my hands, resting it on the seat. I stared at him for a long moment. He really was crazy.

When I didn't move, he started hitching my dress up for me until it sat on my hips. He took the jeans from my hands and helped me into them after I slipped off my heels. I tugged the dress further up so it bunched around my waist and zipped

43

the jeans up. Apparently, this was me suitably attired when it was freezing cold out. He put the helmet on my head and secured it before putting his own on. I slipped my heels back on whilst he got on the bike and started it.

The noise made my heart pound. He waved me over. I swung my leg over and sat down, wrapping my arms around his waist. I trusted Aiden to an extent, but this was a bike and I'd never, ever wanted to get on one.

He edged the bike out of the alleyway and then we were off. It was terrifying. He wasn't driving that fast, but I clung to him, my legs trembling. It was cold and I hated every moment of it. Perhaps if circumstances were different, I might have been okay, but knowing we could've been caught set me on edge.

Aiden didn't take us back to his flat. We drove into a car park in Holborn and he parked up. There was no one about and he helped me out of the jeans and pulled my dress back down. He tucked my jeans back into the seat of the bike. I was a little unsteady on my feet after the ride, but I didn't say anything about it to him. I was grateful he'd got us away from Frazier and Tristan.

"What are we doing here?" I asked as we walked out onto the street, hand in hand.

"I wanted to treat you."

I looked up at him, but he wasn't paying attention to me. A few minutes later, we stopped in front of a very expensive hotel. I found myself inside it the next moment.

"Are we staying here?" I asked.

"Yes."

He took me straight to the lifts and we went up two floors. When we stopped outside the room, he handed me his helmet before reaching in his pocket for the key card. I followed him inside. It was a rather large, very modern looking suite with plush furnishings. The bedroom was separated from the lounge area.

Aiden took the helmets from me and set them down on a side table. I looked around the room with interest before checking out the bathroom. A huge marble bathtub and a separate rainfall shower. *Holy shit.* This place was beautiful.

I walked back out and found Aiden waiting for me in the middle of the room.

"Do you like it?" he asked.

"It's lovely, but you didn't have to get us a hotel room."

I'd never seen Aiden look nervous or unsure of himself, but at that moment, he did. I slipped out of my heels and walked over to him. Staring up into those steel grey eyes, I wondered what he was thinking. And when he didn't reach for me, I couldn't help but need to know what was up with him.

"Can I kiss you?" he asked after a long moment.

Of all the things I thought he might say, that was not it. Since when did he ask permission to kiss me? Didn't he know how much I missed and needed him? Shit, it had barely been five days and yet a second without him felt like forever.

I went up on my tiptoes, wrapped my arms around his neck and pressed my lips to his ear.

"Aiden, you can do much more than just kiss me," I whispered. "I'm still yours. I told you, nothing has changed. I want your control. I crave it. I need you to tell me what to do."

Feeling his solid body pressed against mine sent tingles down my spine.

"You have my submission. Now. Always."

Chapter Four

Aiden

Her submission. Fuck. I didn't know why I was so fucking nervous about this. This whole dating thing was new to me. I hated how much I had to rely on her friend to tell me what was appropriate. I'd wanted to just take her somewhere simple, but the need to keep her hidden made that difficult. That's why we'd settled on a members only club where we could pay to make sure they were discreet.

The hotel had been my idea. I didn't want the first time we spent time together as a real couple to be tainted with the memories of what happened on Christmas Day. She deserved more. I really wanted it all to be special for her. And yet, here and now, standing with her, I was fucking terrified I'd not done enough. I needed Avery to come back to me. I couldn't fucking live without this girl. The light of my fucking life.

"Please, Aiden," she whispered, her lips brushing against my ear. "I've missed you. I want you to fuck me."

I could feel every inch of her pressed against me. It drove me fucking crazy. I'd been hard all night. That fucking dress did things to me. It showed off every curve she had. Fuck. What the hell was I waiting for? She'd just told me to fuck her.

I put my hands on her shoulders and pried her off me. Her doe eyes were wide, confusion in her expression. I'd remedy that. I needed her and she needed me.

"What are you wearing underneath that dress?"

She raised an eyebrow.

"Didn't you look when you helped me put my jeans on?"

"No."

I'd been too busy trying to get her on the bike so I could take her far away from the Shaws. I had no idea what the fuck we were going to do about that. It concerned me, but not enough right now to ruin our evening. I couldn't keep my hands off my girl for much longer.

"Why don't you take it off and then you can see?"

My cock jerked. Fuck. All her clothes needed to come off. I needed to see her.

"Turn around then."

She did as I asked. I took her coat off before I slowly unzipped the back of the dress. I slipped it off her shoulders and down her body. It pooled at her feet. She turned back to me. Fuck. You could barely call that underwear. The black lace just about covered her hard nipples and the matching set of underwear did little to conceal her pussy from me. I swallowed.

Reaching for her, I grabbed her waist with one hand and ran my fingers down her sternum with the other. I felt her tremble. Fuck. I'd missed her. The way she responded to me was incredible. This fucking girl.

I cupped her breast, running my thumb over her lace covered nipple. She shuddered, letting out a quiet moan.

Would she still do as I wanted? I needed to test what she'd said. Did I really have her submission?

"Princess, you're so fucking sexy. As much as I appreciate this little set here, I want you to take it off, lie on the bed and spread your legs for me."

"I want you to kiss me."

"I will. Just do as I say."

I let go of her. She looked up at me for a moment before stepping around me and walking towards the bedroom. I turned to find her tugging off the bra and stepping out of the underwear. She got on the bed, lay down and opened her legs for me.

Fucking hell.

I shrugged out of my suit jacket and loosened my tie. Walking over to her, I smiled.

"Put your hands above your head."

She did it without objection. I used my tie, looping it around her wrists and tying them together. I kicked off my shoes and unbuttoned my shirt. I let her watch me strip down until I was bare before her. My cock was rock hard and pulsating. Her tongue darted out of her mouth, running over her bottom lip.

"How hard do you want me to fuck you, Avery?"

"Make me scream."

I crawled on the bed and settled over her. Our bodies weren't quite touching. The anticipation of being inside her almost had me losing control, but I wouldn't.

The only thing Avery had left on her body was the necklace I'd given her. I ran a finger over the A on the silver chain.

"I haven't taken it off," she said.

"No?"

Her doe eyes met mine.

"It reminds me of what we have with each other and that I belong to you."

I leant down and brushed my lips against hers. Her taste intoxicated me immediately. I gripped her braid with one hand and kissed her, hard. Her tongue danced with mine.

When I pulled away, she was breathless, eyes wide with lust. I shifted, running my tongue down her chest until I met a nipple. I took it between my teeth, biting down as I stroked the other one. She arched against me, moaning.

"Teasing isn't fair."

I looked up at her from where I was nestled between her shapely breasts.

"What do you want?"

"I want your cock inside me - and don't tell me you don't want that too."

I grinned. Of course I fucking wanted to be inside her. My cock ached for her.

"Mmm? Are you sure you're ready for me?"

She nodded.

"Check if you don't believe me."

I didn't strictly need to since I knew she'd be fucking wet for me. Still, any reason to touch her pussy. I reached down and ran my finger across her entrance. Dripping. Fuck. I could continue to make her wait, but this was about her. I'd give her what she wanted.

"Aiden, please."

I grabbed hold of both her legs and pressed them upwards into her chest. I wanted to fuck her deep. I needed it. I shifted up and held my cock, running it up and down her pussy, across her swollen clit. She whimpered in response.

"I'm going to make you come all over my cock."

I pressed inside her. Her pussy was just as hot and tight as I remembered. Fuck.

"Aiden," she groaned.

She felt so good. So fucking good. I missed her. Everything about her. Especially this. When we were together like this. My cock buried in her heat. Our souls fucking joined.

"So tight, fuck," I grunted.

Her doe eyes stared up at me, mouth parted as I thrust into her. It was really the most beautiful sight. Her hands tied up, knees against her chest. So open for me. Mine. All mine. And even though that was true, there were still things I needed to prove it. To make sure she wouldn't leave again. Whether she agreed or not remained to be seen. It wasn't the time to push her. Not when I'd just got her back.

Her delicate skin was flushed. Her moaning became louder as I slammed into her. So fucking responsive. No one else felt or sounded like her. No one else gave me happiness and contentment. She belonged to me and I to her. I loved this girl with every part of me. She just didn't know it yet.

I pulled out of her, reached up and untied her hands. Grabbing her by the waist, I flipped her up onto her hands and knees. She looked back at me, eyes wide with affection and desire. So fucking perfect. I gripped a hip, guiding myself back inside her pussy. I took hold of her braid with my other hand and held onto it as I fucked her. Harder. Faster.

"Touch yourself."

Her hand snaked between her legs. No hesitation. Fuck. So compliant. So submissive. In this room, I controlled her. Outside of the bedroom, I knew things had to change. This was a real relationship which meant I had to start treating her as my equal. She was, but the need to control her outweighed everything else at times. Somehow, we'd work it out. We'd do it together.

Together.

The word bound itself around my heart.

I am hers and she is mine.

I looked down at her luscious behind which I was currently slapping up against. Fuck. I slowed, letting go of her hair and running my hand over it. I wished at that moment I'd actually thought to bring the necessary with me. I wanted her there so fucking much. It would have to wait. And she'd not said yes yet even though she'd enjoyed the toys. I needed her to come around in her own time. When she did, I'd be gentle. Make sure I didn't hurt her. I wanted it to feel good for her too.

"Harder, Aiden, I'm so close."

Her words brought me back to the here and now. I gripped both of her hips and fucked her deeper and harder, just like she wanted.

Avery let out a loud moan when she came apart around my cock. Her body trembled and she gripped the sheets. I rode out her orgasm until I couldn't hold back any longer. Her pussy clenched around me like a vice, tipping me right over the edge. Fuck. My cock pulsated as it tore through me. No one else made me come so fucking hard every time we had sex. Avery was like fucking magic.

Both of us panted when we were spent. I leant over, kissing her neck and running my fingers down her sides. Her perfect skin felt so fucking good under my hands.

"I missed you, Avery… I missed you so fucking much."

"You have me now," she said, her voice a little breathy.

"You're perfect. Don't ever change. I need you."

She craned her head back.

"I need you too."

I gripped her face and kissed her. This angle was awkward. I wanted her facing me so I could devour her mouth. I released her and pulled back. Within moments, my cum started to run down her leg. *Shit.* I shifted off the bed and grabbed the complimentary box of tissues off the bedside table. Walking back around, I cleaned her up as much as I could. She gave me a nod before slipping away into the bathroom. I cleaned myself up before lying down on the bed.

The release and the knowledge she was back calmed me. I'd been on edge for days whilst James and I organised this date for her. It had taken a lot of fucking negotiation to get the club to agree to our stipulations. That, name-dropping his father and a hefty sum. Money wasn't an object. As much as it grated on me, I was glad of her best friend's help. I wouldn't have been able to do this for her without him.

She came out of the bathroom and crawled onto the bed, settling down next to me. Her doe eyes were bright and happiness radiated from her.

"Was this enough for you, princess? I mean the date and this…"

She put a finger over my lips.

"Yes, stop worrying. I'm here. I don't need you to prove anything else to me."

I pulled her hand away, rolled on my side and dragged her into me. Cupping her face, I kissed her. I'd missed her lips. Just the simple act of being able to hold her and have her close was more than enough. Fuck. My girl. Mine.

When she pulled away, she smiled and stroked my cheek.

"Aiden… I…"

"Hmm?"

"I love you."

I couldn't breathe. She'd said it before, but this time, she was actually saying it to my face. My heart constricted. Fuck. How did she manage to tie me up in knots all the time? I wanted to say it back, but the words stuck in my throat. I'd not said that to anyone. Not since my mother. Not even Tina and I loved her like she was family.

I couldn't keep staring at her like I was a fucking deer in headlights or something. I took her hand and pressed it against my chest, right above my heart. Her brows knit together. I should be able to just fucking say those three words.

Fuck. Why was it so hard?

I saw the moment it dawned on her exactly what I was trying to say but failing miserably. She met my eyes again. Hers told me she understood. I wished I could be fucking better for her, but right now, I'd just about got my head around the fact she was actually my girl. That this was a relationship.

"I need time, princess."

She leant forward and kissed me again.

"It's okay. I don't need you to say anything."

I still felt like I didn't deserve Avery at all. After everything I'd put her through, she was understanding and accepting. I had to make it up to her somehow. I'd give her anything she asked for.

"I'm sorry."

"I don't need you to apologise. This is new. There's no rush. All I want is you and me together."

"You and me belong together."

Her eyes lit up. I entwined my fingers with hers. Beautiful. Perfect. And mine.

My phone rang. I cursed. Totally just ruined the moment between us. I rolled away, got off the bed and tugged it out of my jacket pocket.

"Hello James."

"Not interrupting, am I?"

I chose not to rise to the suggestive note in his voice. He had definitely interrupted, but at least we weren't fucking. I sat back down on the bed, running my fingers along Avery's arm.

"Did you have any trouble from the Shaws?"

"No. I slipped out the back too. Couldn't come up with an excuse for why I was there. Bill is settled, so we're good."

"Hopefully Frazier won't think anything of it but can't be too careful."

"Did you two kiss and make up?"

I rolled my eyes.

"You can ask her that yourself."

I pulled the phone from my ear and put it on speaker.

"Hi James," Avery said.

"Did that little number I got work?"

"James!"

"Did he put it on speaker?"

Her face went red. I wasn't sure whether to be annoyed he bought her underwear or amused by the exchange between them.

"What do you think?"

James laughed.

"I'm not even sorry."

"You're such a dick."

"And yet, you still keep coming back."

"I'll make him hang up if you don't behave."

She looked up at me. I still didn't like how close they were, but Tina's reminder that I couldn't keep her away from her world any longer kept me from commenting.

"Okay, okay. You're all good, right?"

"Yes, I promise. Thank you for everything you did."

"Ah, it was nothing really. You know I just want you to be happy."

She smiled, edging closer to me.

"I am."

"I won't keep you. Enjoy the rest of your evening."

"Bye dickhead."

"Bye Disney Princess."

He hung up. I looked at her, but she was scowling.

"What was that about?" I asked.

"Oh god, he was being a dick in the car and going on about how we're Beauty and the Beast. I told him to shut up, but you calling me princess in front of him has clearly made it worse."

I raised an eyebrow. Beauty and the Beast? That wasn't far off what we were.

"Do you not want me to call you that?"

Her face fell.

"No, no. I do. It makes me feel special. He just likes to wind me up."

I wrapped an arm around her.

"Special, huh?"

Her ears went pink.

"Am I not your princess?"

I cupped her face, running my thumb over her lip.

"Mmm, you are. The most beautiful princess in all the lands."

She frowned.

"Don't you start too."

I grinned. She walked into that one. Fuck. This felt so right. Being here with her. Making jokes like we were normal.

Except we weren't normal.

I'd got her back, but the road ahead would be paved with problems. There was so much we still had to do. So much to overcome.

I would let her have these few precious moments before we ran into trouble.

She needed them.

I needed them.

I hoped together we'd be okay.

But things always have a way of falling apart around me.

I pressed her down on the bed and kissed her. Letting our passion and need for each other eclipse everything else.

Because soon, there would be a world of shit coming our way when Avery went back out into the real world.

And I, for one, was not fucking prepared for the fallout.

Chapter Five

Avery

hen we got back to the flat the next day, Aiden announced we were having a New Year's Eve get together. He'd already bought things for dinner, snacks and drinks. When I asked who was coming, he said James, but there was a glint in his eye which told me he was keeping a secret. And when he made me set four places at the table, I knew I was right to be suspicious.

Who else is coming? Why is he being so secretive?

I was about to ask when the buzzer for the door went. Aiden didn't let me get it.

"Go wait in the living room, princess."

I did as he said, sitting down on the sofa and staring at the TV. Whilst our relationship was different now, I knew Aiden and his issues with control. There was no point fighting him on this.

Voices filtered down through the hallway. I couldn't see who was at the door because Aiden's bulk hid them from view.

"This is Aiden."

That was James' voice. It was what came next that made me freeze.

"Hi, it's nice to meet you."

Is that…?

"Perhaps it's best if you come in," Aiden said, stepping back.

My heart stopped dead. Standing just beyond the threshold was the one person I'd missed almost as much as James.

"I don't know why you had to be so secretive, James," she hissed. "What are we doing here?"

"You'll see," James replied as the two of them walked in.

I stood up, hopping from foot to foot. Aiden told me to stay here, but I wanted to run down the hallway. He led them down towards me and as soon as they all entered the room, her eyes went wide.

"A… Avery?"

It'd been far too long. Gert, my red-haired, blue-eyed best friend, stood there in her trademark black jeans and black boots. I walked around the coffee table and straight into her arms.

"Hi," I whispered.

"Where the hell have you been?" she whispered back.

"Here with Aiden."

"Who is he?"

"I'll explain later."

She pulled away and gave me a searching look. I shook my head. I turned to Aiden and James.

"I can't believe you two. Is this really okay?"

James grinned and Aiden nodded. Shit. I didn't know what to say. Having Gert here meant the world to me. I'd have words with both of them later. They shouldn't have kept it from me, but I was also glad they had. I hustled her over to the sofa. Aiden left the room to get drinks sorted and James sat with us.

"Seriously, what happened to you, Avery?"

I sighed. This wasn't exactly the conversation I expected to have on New Year's.

"A lot of things happened. Mostly I just couldn't deal with my parents being gone. I'm sorry I disappeared."

"And you've been staying with that... sex god all this time?" Gert asked, her voice low.

"Not you as well," James muttered.

"What do you mean?"

James sniggered and my face burnt. I could hardly blame Gert for thinking Aiden was hot. He basically screamed sex, lust, power and danger. Not to mention how beautiful he was to look at. And the stunning artwork covering the skin beneath his shirt. I almost couldn't believe he was real and mine.

"Aiden is my boyfriend," I said.

"Excuse me? He's your what?"

"The man she's shacking up with and fucking, Gertie," James said.

I put my head in my hands. Trust James to make a comment like that. He had no tact when we were alone. There was a cough from Gert. I looked up.

Oh for fuck's sake.

Aiden stood there with two wine glasses in his hands and a raised eyebrow.

Can the ground swallow me up right now?

I got up and went over to him, taking the glasses from his hands.

"Sorry about that," I whispered.

He reached up, cupping my face.

"He's not wrong about the fucking part," he replied, his voice too low for the other two to hear.

"I swear you and James are making it your mission to embarrass me."

He leant down, kissing my forehead.

"So innocent, princess."

Before I could retort, he walked away back towards the kitchen. I went over to James and Gert, handing them a glass of wine each.

"Oh, god, you two are so cute," Gert said, sighing.

I wouldn't exactly describe Aiden as cute. Dangerous, yes. Cute, definitely not.

She turned to me, eyes wide.

"Hold on, what about Peter?"

"You did see me publicly say it wasn't going to happen between me and him, right?" I said.

"Well, I can hardly blame you. Shit babe, you did good."

I gave her a warning look as Aiden came back. He handed me a glass before sitting on the arm of the sofa next to me, his hand curling around the back of my neck. His touch sent tingles down my spine.

"So... you're the one who's been hiding my best friend then?" Gert said.

"You could say that," Aiden replied.

I eyed James who shook his head. We weren't going to tell her the truth.

"I asked him to, so blame me," I said.

"And when did this happen?"

She pointed between us.

Can't she ask me that later when we're alone?

Talking about my relationship with the man next to me was all kinds of complicated.

"Only recently," Aiden said for me.

I looked up at him. His grey eyes were cautious but when they met mine, they softened.

Well shit.

My heart hammered wildly in my chest. His fingers traced lines along my neck. If my friends weren't here, I would've kissed him. Except being affectionate in front of people wasn't my thing. Especially not with the fire that burnt between Aiden and me.

Thankfully the conversation turned away from our relationship and as the night wore on, dinner was a great success. Aiden let me talk to my friends with minimum interruption. It felt like old times except I was different now. Some of my innocence stripped back. My knowledge of the world was tainted.

We were all standing by the window waiting for the fireworks with the TV on for the countdown. Aiden wrapped his arm around my waist and leant down to me.

"Do I get a kiss at midnight?" he whispered.

"You can have as many as you want."

I may have had too much wine. The thought of kissing him in front of my friends no longer seemed like such a big deal.

In fact, I wanted it.

"I'll hold you to that."

A few minutes later, whilst Gert and James chanted the countdown, Aiden turned me towards him and tilted my face up. The affection and desire rolling off him hit me like a tidal wave. I drowned in those molten silver eyes.

"Five. Four. Three. Two. One. Happy New Year," James and Gert shouted in unison.

Aiden leant down and captured my mouth, stealing away all my thoughts. My body arched into his, hands falling on his chest. His kiss was slow and deep, drawing out every inch of desire and causing it to pulsate through my veins. Fuck did I want him.

"All aboard the PDA train." James' voice broke through my lust filled haze.

Aiden pulled away, glaring in James' direction over the top of my head.

"Leave them alone," Gert said.

I heard the popping sound of fireworks and turned to the window. We had a relatively clear view from Aiden's flat. I lay my head against his chest and his arms wrapped around me.

"Happy New Year, princess," he whispered.

"I hope we have more moments like these."

"Like these?"

"Yes, ones where I don't feel like my world is crumbling before my eyes."

He clutched me tighter.

"I'll try make sure we do. I just want you to be happy."

The fireworks continued to go off. The display was always centred around the wheel.

"You make me happy most of the time."

The rumble of his chest vibrated through me as he chuckled.

"Most of the time?"

"Yes, you also make me mad."

He stroked my hair, fingers tangling in it.

"You're a little infuriating too."

"We're even then."

Perhaps it was the alcohol which loosened my tongue. He didn't seem to mind my honesty. No one was perfect, but the two of us were it for each other. We belonged together like he said last night. So what if we occasionally pissed the other off? Our arguments always resulted in explosive endings. Ones which made my toes curl. Fire flooded my veins. And now I really wanted my friends to be anywhere but here.

We hadn't had sex since last night. This morning we'd had breakfast in the suite, but Aiden had been a little preoccupied with something to do with my uncle who'd rang him first thing. Now, being pressed up against his solid form, I couldn't help but need to feel him everywhere.

It would have to wait. We still had guests. I pulled away and looked up at him as the last of the fireworks finished. His grey eyes glinted with affection. *Shit.* I loved this man so damn much. My heart ached, the intensity of my feelings slamming into my chest all at once. And there was something I desperately wanted to give him. When we were alone, I'd tell him.

"Drinking games?" James said.

I turned to him, frowning. There was no way we were doing that. I was already at my limit, any more and I'd be on the floor.

"Christ, you're always trying to get us drunk," Gert said. "Hell no. You'll end up making us spill about Avery's embarrassing stories and I'm sure she'd rather us not divulge that information."

"Yes, Avery would like you to keep those to yourselves," I added.

"I'd like to hear them," Aiden said.

"And that's exactly why we're not going to indulge in drinking games."

Two hours later, James and Gert had fallen asleep on the sofa. We'd put a film on and they'd continued drinking. Aiden and I abstained, too busy cuddling.

I wrapped a blanket around them and followed Aiden into the bedroom. The moment the door closed, I pounced on him. I wrapped my arms around his neck and kissed him. He responded at first, but after a moment, he pulled back. I let out a little mewl of frustration.

"Aren't you tired?" he asked.

"No."

My fingers went to the buttons of his shirt. He let me undo them one by one.

"Aiden… I want something from you."

"And what would that be?"

I ran my fingers over his chest, tracing the outline of his tattoos.

"I want you to take something from me which I'm giving willingly."

"You're not making any sense."

The alcohol was playing havoc with my mind. My inhibitions were gone. And now it was time. I was ready.

"Take my virginity."

He frowned.

"What?"

"I want it. You know what I'm talking about."

His eyes widened.

"What? Right now?"

"Yes."

"You're drunk, Avery."

I shook my head. Who cares if I had too much to drink? I knew what I wanted.

"I wanted to tell you last night, but I was too nervous. Please don't say no."

"You know I want that, but not like this."

"Why not?"

"For one, your friends are in the next room and I'm not going to fuck you there when you're drunk."

He cupped my face.

"But Aiden…"

"No. We're not doing this. Go get in bed. You need to sleep it off."

I couldn't quite believe my ears.

"So what, you won't even have sex with me at all?"

"I didn't say that."

I pulled away from him and stomped towards the bed. Now I was just pissed off and a little embarrassed. I'd asked him for the thing he wanted in the first place and he rejected me. How could I feel anything but hurt and shame? Why had it only taken a day for us to get into an idiotic fight?

"Avery…"

"Don't. Just don't. I'm going to bed like you told me to."

I pulled off my clothes and heard the bedroom door open. When I looked around, he was gone. I put on a t-shirt, not bothering with shorts and crawled in bed. How the fuck was I going to sleep when I was mad as hell, horny and hurt? Damn Aiden. He drove me insane.

A minute later, I heard the door close again and his footsteps. He put a glass of water next to me on the bedside table. He shuffled around the room before he got into bed next to me. My back was to him, the covers over my head. I really didn't want to see or speak to him.

When I felt him reach for me, I stiffened. He curled himself around my back, his hand resting on my stomach. His breath tickled my ear.

"Princess, please don't be angry with me."

I didn't respond. He could beg for all I cared. He'd successfully made me feel like shit so he could just do one right then.

His fingers found their way under my t-shirt, brushing up my side. I tried not to respond to his touch, but my body craved him. It was a traitor.

"Please, Avery. Don't ruin tonight."

How the hell did I ruin tonight? He was the one who ruined it by refusing. He cupped my breast, running his thumb over the nipple.

"Don't you want me to fuck you?" he asked.

"No."

"Are you sure?" He ground his cock against me. "Don't you want my cock here?"

"Stop it, Aiden. I'm not in the mood any more."

"I don't believe you. I know you're wet. You've wanted me all night. Don't think I haven't seen the way you've been looking at me."

Fuck him. I really hated him being right. His hand left my breast. He tugged at my underwear, pulling it down enough so it bunched up on the tops of my thighs. His hand fell in between us and he ran his finger along my entrance. I bucked involuntarily.

"Stop it," I whispered.

"You asked me to take your virginity, so that's what's going to happen."

It took a moment for it to register and by that time, I felt his finger at my other entrance, pressing against it. Since he'd done this more than once before, it slipped in easily. I jerked in surprise.

"So tight," he whispered. "It's going to feel so fucking good, princess."

"Aiden…"

"Shh, let me take care of you."

My voice was stolen as he pressed deeper. Was this actually happening? Why had I said I wanted this? But it was Aiden and he meant everything to me. I wanted him to have all of me so much.

"I don't want you to hurt me," I whispered.

"I won't. I'll make sure you're ready. Are you sure you still want this?"

My brain whirled with the alcohol-fuelled haze, my fear that it might hurt and my need to have Aiden fuck me. Right now, I needed him in me. If that meant anal, then so be it. I enjoyed the toys more than I thought I was going to. There was no reason I couldn't take this final step with him.

"I want you to."

He growled in my ear before he pulled away. The next sound I heard was him popping the cap on a bottle. When he curled around me, he did what he'd done several times before, opened me up to him. Except this time, after he'd used two fingers, he inserted a third one. That stung a little. I winced.

"Relax, princess."

I was trying. I took a deep breath, needing oxygen in my lungs. I trusted Aiden, but even with the alcohol bolstering me, I was still nervous. He moved his fingers, stretching me further. I bit down on the covers. It didn't hurt, it just felt different. A few minutes later, he pulled out of me.

"I'm going to fuck you now, last chance to change your mind."

He shifted back. I didn't want to stop. We'd come this far. He pressed more lube inside me before I felt his cock. He gripped my hip with one hand and pressed against me. My body locked up against the intrusion.

"Avery, you need to breathe."

I hadn't realised I was holding my breath. When I released it, everything happened at once. The sharp sting as he slipped inside me. His grunt a mixture of pleasure and pain. And my yelp as I gripped the covers.

I gulped down oxygen.

Holy hell.

"It feels weird," I whispered.

"Are you in pain?"

"No."

It didn't hurt, not really. I always expected it to, but he'd taken care of me. Made sure I was ready first. His breath fanned across my face as he moved closer and kissed my cheek.

"Thank you, princess."

"For what?"

"For letting me fuck you here. For coming home. For caring for me and most of all, for loving me."

My heart felt so tight. All my emotions threatened to burst out. I reached down and put my hand over where his was on my hip.

"We belong together."

He kissed my cheek again, pressing a little deeper inside me. He let me adjust to it each time as he gave me more. I felt so full. Aiden wasn't exactly small. I had no idea if I could take it all.

"You're so fucking tight."

He pulled back a little before thrusting in again and starting to build a slow, steady pace. My hand and his fell between my legs. His fingers circled my clit, eliciting a moan from me.

Whilst the sensation of him fucking me there was still a little strange, I couldn't help but press back.

"Aiden," I groaned. "Fuck me harder."

I could feel his cock pressing deeper as he did as I asked. The pleasure began to overtake everything else. I thrust back against him, needing more.

"Do you like this?"

"Yes. Don't stop."

"Mmm, look at you taking it so well. You feel incredible."

His fingers left my clit and instead, he plunged them inside my pussy. I bucked against him.

"So fucking wet. I can tell you're enjoying this, aren't you?"

I moaned. His cock pressed deeper and harder along with his fingers.

"Tell me."

My voice stuck in my throat.

"Tell me, princess. I want to hear how much you love this."

"Aiden…"

"Say it."

"I love you fucking me there. Please don't stop."

He growled, biting down on my earlobe. The heel of Aiden's palm rubbed against my clit as he fucked my pussy with his fingers.

It all exploded inside me at once. I cried out. He cursed. I rode the wave of pleasure, clenching around him. It fizzled in my blood, spreading through my veins.

Holy fuck.

The overload of sensations made it impossible to breathe. I could've sworn sparks formed in my vision. It was almost like an out of body experience except I could feel every single one of my nerves tingling.

He grunted. I felt his cock pulsating and him press deeper as he came too.

My world changed in that moment. Our hearts beat as one. Our souls bonded together. All of our feelings exposed and raw. Perhaps it was the alcohol or maybe it was just happiness,

I didn't really care. All I knew is Aiden gave me something no one else had. Freedom and acceptance for who I really was inside. The girl who needed to give the man she loved everything because she'd chosen to submit herself entirely to him. Aiden saw me before I knew who I really was. And I fell deeper in love with him. He was a permanent mark on my heart. One I'd never be free of.

When I finally took a breath, my heart raced out of control and if I hadn't already been lying down, I would've collapsed. My body felt like jelly. I could hear his harsh breath on my ear as he panted.

"That was…"

"Fucking amazing," he finished for me.

Despite how wonderful he'd made it feel, there was a nagging question in the back of my mind.

"Why did you change your mind?"

"I'm finding it increasingly difficult to say no to you, princess. And I'll be honest, I wanted you so fucking much. I hated not being able to touch you in the ways I wanted with your friends being here."

I smiled. I wasn't the only one suffering from the need to fuck. Aiden was like drugs. I was well and truly addicted to the feelings he gave me.

"I'm sleepy now."

He chuckled, pulling away. I crawled out of bed, very unsteady on my feet and made it to the bathroom. On the way back, I realised I was more than a little sore. Whilst he'd been careful, both of us had gotten a little carried away in the moment.

Crawling back into bed, Aiden held me close and kissed me.

"I love you," I whispered.

"My heart is yours, princess."

In his own way, Aiden just told me he loved me too.

I didn't need those three words.

All I needed was him and me.

Always.

Chapter Six

Aiden

"Hello Uncle Charlie."

The fact she was even alone with that cocksucker made my skin itch and my blood boil. Avery was my fucking woman and if that prick ever tried to lay a hand on her again, he'd find himself minus a limb.

I wanted to throw the laptop out the car window, but I wouldn't. I promised her I'd be with her every step of the way. Not physically but watching over her. Making sure if anything happened, I could be there to protect her.

The aching need to have her in my arms almost overrode all my senses. She'd given me everything. New Year's had cemented us together completely. She'd given me the last part of her innocence, her virginity. And I fucking loved her even more for it.

I remembered the way it felt to be inside her. The heat. The tightness. How she'd told me to fuck her harder. And most of all, how we'd both come apart entirely together. There were no more places to hide. I saw her and she saw me.

I still hadn't managed to tell her I loved her, but I'd given her my heart all the same. She knew how I felt without words. And that's exactly why she felt safe knowing I had my eyes on her and Chuck.

Fucking Chuck.

Her uncle stared at her as the colour seeped out of his skin. I could see them from three different angles and the tiny camera Avery wore in the pin on the lapel of her blazer.

She stood tall and proud, facing down her uncle like he was her adversary. And in a way, that's exactly what he was. Killer heels, a black skirt which hugged her figure, a navy blouse under her black blazer. Her dark hair tied back in a low bun. Every inch the businesswoman she needed to be. And the sight of her made me shift uncomfortably in the car seat, my cock straining against my trousers. I wanted to bend her over her uncle's desk, pull up her skirt and fuck her senseless.

Whilst we'd finally had anal on New Year's, she'd yet to agree to it again. I knew she'd been sore afterwards. I saw it in her eyes. I didn't want to hurt her but being inside her and her pleas to fuck her made me abandon my gentleness. Whilst Avery, my beautiful, strong and effortlessly sexy girlfriend, didn't resent me for it, I knew she needed time. And I wasn't being a dick and taking what I wanted. I was trying to be a better man for her. Only for her.

We'd discussed what to do about her family over and over. We didn't have a solid plan, but she had to accept her place as the head of the company she had come to despise. She had to go back out into the real world. I couldn't keep her hidden away any longer. I took what Tina said to me seriously. I'd asked Avery what she wanted to do. I told her she was under no obligation to help me with her family. Avery wanted to go after them. She wanted to fix this mess.

My original plan wouldn't work now she knew everything. I'd taken out Mitchell so that made things easier. They were all on edge because of it. Whilst our plan wasn't solid, we had to start by making sure we kept Chuck in line. And that began with this conversation.

"You're back," Chuck said.

"Yes. I'm here to take what belongs to me."

"So, you think after being missing for three months, you can waltz back in here and demand the company be handed over to you?"

Avery didn't flinch. She stared at Chuck with unnerving intensity. Just as she had done to me in the first days when I'd kept her in the cell.

"Legally speaking, it belongs to me. I suggest you don't make this hard on yourself."

"Where the fuck have you been all this time?"

"Where? Did Dad not tell you what he had installed in my house?"

That little piece of knowledge she'd granted me when we'd come up with a story to explain her disappearance.

Chuck raised an eyebrow, his brown eyes full of unconcealed irritation. He wasn't happy with his niece's reappearance, nor the way she was speaking to him.

"No. Are you going to enlighten me?"

"The basement contains a bunker or you could call it a panic room. Either way, it has supplies to last a year. Don't be disappointed you didn't know, it isn't on the building plans. As far as the world knows, it doesn't exist."

She was more resourceful than I gave her credit for. We'd visited her house together last week. She lived on the ground floor and there was a tenant above her. One who happened to be out of the country. And that bunker was very real. Her father had spared no expense in protecting his daughter. It was a fortress. Impenetrable. And full of everything she could need to live comfortably.

Chuck's eyebrows knitted together.

"And how did you manage that little stunt with the video?"

At least he hadn't questioned the bunker. He knew Mitchell would never have left his daughter vulnerable. Despite their power, they had enemies too.

"I paid someone in cash to help me. How they managed to make it go viral is a question I didn't ask."

My princess knew exactly what Chuck would ask. She had the answers. The truth woven into the lies she told.

Where the fuck had she been all my life? The very thing I never knew I needed or wanted. I'd been right about her helping me tear down her family. My secret weapon. I just hadn't realised it would be something we did together as partners. I still controlled so many aspects of our relationship, but this was different. This was about righting wrongs. And she'd be the face of their destruction whilst I orchestrated their downfall from the shadows.

Chuck shifted, walking over to his desk and sitting down. Avery stayed where she was, watching her uncle expressionlessly. I saw the fire in her eyes. The hatred. He wouldn't read it because he didn't know her like I did.

"Have you informed the police?"

"No. You're welcome to call them. If they want me to explain myself, they can come here and ask me. In the meantime, I want a meeting with the board and the company transferred into my hands."

"What makes you think I will answer to your demands?"

She splayed out her hands.

"Firstly, the company is mine by law. You know Dad made it ironclad. And secondly, if you don't, it will only take one interview from me to ruin you entirely."

His face fell.

"You wouldn't."

"Wouldn't I, Uncle Charlie? I don't care if the world knows your sick twisted fantasies."

His fist curled on the desk. I froze. He better not fucking lay a hand on her.

"You're bluffing."

"Are you sure you want to test that theory? Or do you want the world to know you like little girls?"

Seconds ticked by as niece and uncle stared at each other. A battle of wills. I knew who'd break.

"Fine. I'll call the board and the police."

"Thank you."

He rolled his eyes, flattening his palm on the desk.

"You have to do one thing for me."

"What would that be?"

He rose from the desk, walking around it and coming to stand in front of her. He was half a head taller than her even in her heels. He gripped her by the chin and turned her head to the side. Rage boiled inside me.

How fucking dare he touch her. I would fucking rip his balls off.

"Explain to me how the fuck you came to have a tattoo of an A behind your ear."

Avery took a step back, wrenching out of his grasp. She put her hand over the back of her neck, covering it from view.

The still-healing tattoo. The one which marked her as mine. My cock jerked at the knowledge I'd branded her and sent her out in the world to be my weapon.

She wore the mark of their enemy.

Just as I'd given her the necklace with an A, which she never took off, I gave her this too.

And no one would know because she shared something with me.

My initial.

Two Weeks Prior

I held her hand as we walked up the street. She didn't know where we were going. Our breath misted in the cold air. I'd made sure she wrapped up warm, her face hidden within her jacket hood.

I was equal parts nervous and happy about what would happen next. Avery needed to do something for me, but I wasn't quite sure if she'd say yes. Even after what we'd shared together only a few days ago.

I gave her a chance to see her other best friend. And she'd finally allowed me to have what I'd coveted from the moment I knew I wanted her. Now, I needed to take another first from her.

Reaching the shop, I pushed open the door before she had a chance to look up at the sign. She'd know soon enough.

Ben looked up from where he was perched on his stool. A grin spread across his face.

"Shithead."

"All right?" I replied, smiling back.

Avery flipped down her hood and looked between us, realisation dawning on her face.

Ben stood up and took a few steps toward us. I let go of Avery's hand and half hugged him. When we drew apart, his eyes fell on my girl.

"Ben, this is Avery."

He stuck his hand out to her.

"Nice to meet you."

She shook his hand.

"You too."

Then she turned to me, eyes narrowing.

"Why didn't you tell me?"

I shrugged. I meant to, but I liked surprising her. Besides, I'd only just worked up the courage to actually introduce her to my best friend and the man I thought of as family. And telling him I had a girlfriend had been a conversation that landed me with a tirade of abuse about how I'd always told him I never wanted to be shackled to a woman. We'd both laughed it off, but I hoped he saw what I did when I looked at Avery. She offered me the world and I wanted to bow at her feet. My goddess who I really didn't deserve. None of that mattered. I was hers and she was mine.

Ben grinned, shrugging.

"He keeps everyone in the dark. I wouldn't worry too much about it."

"How's Skye and bump?" I asked.

"Honestly, mate, I'm glad to be out of the house. Pregnancy has made her grumpy as fuck."

I stifled a laugh. Skye was formidable enough as it was. She had to be to put up with Ben day in, day out.

"When is she due?" Avery asked.

"A month or so. If it was anyone else but Aiden, I doubt she'd let me come to the shop today."

Avery's eyes screamed 'why are we at his tattoo shop rather than visiting their house' at me. I reached for her hand.

"You want to ask me something?"

She let me take it, moving closer. Ben sat back on his stool and started fiddling with the ink pots and his gun. The bastard knew I hadn't asked her yet. We were here for me, but also for her.

"You... I know what you want and you should've asked me long before we came here," she hissed.

"Princess, don't be upset."

I knew it was the wrong thing to say the moment her doe eyes flashed with anger.

"I tolerate a lot of things from you, but not telling me you want me to get a tattoo, that crosses a line."

Tolerate? Did she think that was acceptable to say to me? Fucking hell. Sometimes she really pushed my fucking buttons.

I tugged her further away from Ben.

"What the fuck does that mean?" I said, keeping my voice low.

"It means you put me through a lot of crap, Aiden, and I accept it, but you can't order me to permanently mark my skin for you."

I hadn't even told her what I wanted yet. It wasn't what she thought. I took a breath. Getting into a fight wasn't needed today and especially not in front of Ben. I really wished she'd stop testing me all the time. I supposed it was my own fault for falling in love with a girl with such a deadly temper on her. One which matched my own.

"If you let me explain…"

"Fine. Just don't expect me to say yes."

I'd upset her. Even though I knew she appreciated me introducing her to someone important to me, she was pissed as hell too. I didn't blame her, even though it grated on me she immediately got annoyed before I'd even had a chance to tell her exactly what I wanted. I pushed her just as hard as she pushed me.

"I want us to wear each other's initial, princess. Just a single A. You choose where I wear yours and I decide where you wear mine. This isn't about me wanting to mark you. It's about us. Together. As a couple."

Her doe eyes searched mine for the longest time. She looked confused at first but then her features morphed into understanding.

She turned my hand upwards in hers. Her fingers traced a line over my right wrist which wasn't yet inked.

"Here."

My heart slammed against my ribcage. I didn't care where she wanted it. I'd gladly wear her name on my skin. I belonged to her.

"You want it there?"

She nodded. Agreement. She just fucking said yes to me yet again. Every time I thought I asked too much, she always managed to surprise me with her acceptance of my needs. My desires. How much more would I take from this girl?

Everything because she is yours, a voice whispered.

"Where do you want to mark me?"

I'd known the moment I'd decided she needed to wear my initial. I reached up and tucked her hair behind her ear before caressing the skin there. She sucked in a breath.

"Behind my ear?"

"Yes, it might be hidden by your hair, but it tells everyone you're mine even though most will assume it stands for Avery. You and I know the truth."

Those doe eyes I adored so much burnt with love and acceptance.

"Okay."

And with that, I led her back over to Ben. I sat in the chair and she sat on one of the other stools. I wanted to show her I was willing to have her etched on my skin before she did the same for me. Just like she was etched on my heart.

Ben made small talk as he prepared the necessary. He'd touch up my other arm in the process. He showed Avery the A he'd designed to go on our skin. The swirling calligraphy was a little feminine, but I didn't care. This was for her.

She nodded her approval. I was fucking glad of it. I'd seen it before when I'd talked it over with him on New Year's Day.

Ben stencilled my skin before he picked up the gun and started. Avery watched with rapt interest. She asked Ben questions about his design process and the two of them spoke in length. I hadn't told Ben about Avery's artistic skills. He seemed very interested in her drawings and asked her to make me send him photos.

When he finished, he wrapped it before shifting around so he could touch up the words on my other arm. Avery held my hand and looked over the freshly inked A on my wrist visible through the cling film. I was so used to being tattooed, I barely registered the pain of the needle.

"It's lucky both our names start with A," she said.

"Not fate?"

"I don't believe in crap like that."

I smiled. She was exactly like me in that respect. Fate and destinies were for deluded souls who believed in miracles. Avery and I weren't destined. We just belonged to each other. We'd made a choice. There was always a need to possess and take everything from each other, but we'd still made the decision to give in. She submitted and I gave her freedom. That was who we were.

"Maybe Avery can design your next piece?" Ben piped up.

I glanced at him. His head was still bowed, but a smile played on his lips. Cheeky fucker.

"I know what I'd choose," she said.

I knew too.

"What's that?"

"Something to do with angels and wings," I said before she could answer.

Ben looked up at her, the gun stopping for a moment.

"Really now?"

"He's not wrong," she replied, shrugging.

"There's a story there you two aren't telling me."

"Mind your own fucking business," I grunted.

Ben grinned and set back to work again.

A few minutes later, he was done. I traded places with Avery whilst Ben prepared new needles and ink for her. She gripped my hand, tensing when Ben laid the stencil behind her ear. He made me check the placement before he picked up the gun.

"Ready?" he asked.

Her eyes met mine. Her fingers tightened. I knew she was scared, but I'd be here for her for every moment.

"Yes," she replied.

She winced when the needle pricked her skin, her eyes closing against the pain I knew she was experiencing. Yet she didn't utter a sound. My girl. So strong. I'd broken her, but now she'd found her way back.

"You could've picked a less painful place, Aiden," Ben said.

"She's okay, aren't you, princess?"

Her hand tensed, her eyes flying open. She wasn't supposed to move her neck. Her eyes told me she was dealing with it even though she was in pain.

Ben's eyebrow raised at my term of endearment for her. I shot him a warning glare. If he even fucking brought that up like James constantly did, I'd kick the shit out of him.

Ben knew better than to mess with me. I tolerated her friend winding her up about it, but she was my fucking princess. She gave me peace.

When I looked into those doe eyes, I saw a future. One that wasn't about revenge, betrayals or family secrets. It was just me and her together.

That's what we had to fight for.

Us.

Even when we were fighting each other, it was because of our intense connection and love for one another. Love that threatened to consume or tear us apart.

"Don't worry, Avery, it'll be over soon."

She remained still and mute, her eyes fixed on me. She had no idea what this meant to me. The letter A bound us together. Her skin and mine.

When I took her home later, I'd worship her. Make sure she knew just how much I cared for her. All of her. The beautiful, dark-haired girl with doe eyes who'd given me so much more than I ever deserved.

Ben finished up her tattoo and sat back. He smiled at the lines he'd created.

"What do you think?" he asked me.

She let go of my hand as I stood up and walked around the chair. Fuck. Seeing the black ink stark against her white skin did things to me.

"Perfect."

"Perhaps we should let her decide whether she likes it."

I rolled my eyes. Avery sat up, wincing a little and hopped off the chair. Ben pointed at the mirror a few feet away. She walked over and turned her head to the side. Her brow furrowed. I realised she couldn't see it properly.

I walked over, picking up the handheld mirror from the counter and held it up behind her. Only then did her expression change. She bit her lip.

"I like it."

"You do?"

She nodded, turning to me and lacing her fingers with mine.

"I'm yours and you're mine."

I smiled, putting down the mirror so I could cup her face.

"Thank you, princess."

Forgetting entirely my best friend was watching us, I kissed her. Her tongue melded with mine, intoxicating me. I only released her when I heard the shuffling of bits and pieces behind us.

"Let me clean up and we can go for a drink, maybe?" Ben said.

"She can't go out in public yet," I replied.

"You're right, I forgot. Back to yours perhaps then?"

I looked at Avery who gave me a nod.

"Will Skye get mad if you stay out late?"

"If she does, fuck it. We've not seen each other in months and I would like to see first-hand just how talented your girlfriend is."

Said girlfriend flushed. I smiled, running a thumb across her cheek. Then I pressed her towards Ben so he could wrap her neck.

Our tattoos symbolised so much between us.

Hers. Mine.

Together. Bound.

Forever.

Chapter Seven

Avery

I stared at my uncle, not sure how to answer the question about my tattoo. Aiden had taken care of it daily for me as well as his own. He'd been careful when washing my hair and had a delicate touch when he put cream on it. It itched like mad on occasion, but I could deal with it.

I dropped my hand and steeled my expression. There was no need for Uncle Charlie to understand the truth.

"So what if I got a tattoo? I'm almost twenty-one. What difference does it make to you?"

"Not very professional of you to get it on your fucking neck," he replied.

"It's my body."

"Christ, you really are a brat when you want to be. No wonder Mitch laid down the law about the company with you."

I stiffened. I didn't want to talk about my father with him. He was dead. And he was also dead to me. I no longer mourned him. He wasn't worthy of it.

"Regardless of your personal opinion of me, the company is still mine and Dad is gone."

"Yes, he is. You don't happen to know anything about that, do you?"

I should've expected that question. Me disappearing right after they died was always going to be suspicious.

"Why would I?"

"Your phone was in their penthouse and that little boyfriend of yours told the police you were there for dinner."

I flinched. Peter was not my boyfriend and that reminded me I still needed to talk to him. It would have to wait. Also, I doubted my actual boyfriend would let me do so.

Aiden.

I knew he was watching every moment of this encounter between me and my uncle. Just like I knew it would have driven him crazy when Uncle Charlie touched my face. It'd made my skin crawl. I hated him being close to me, but I would stand my ground. I was not going to show weakness.

"I'm sure the police can ask me if they're interested, but I had nothing to do with their deaths."

"No, I'm sure you didn't, but you know something about it. Why else would you have gone missing for this long?"

"They were murdered. How did you expect me to feel?"

Anger boiled inside me, threatening to burst out. Even if Aiden hadn't taken me, I'd still seen them die. That would fuck anyone up.

"So you do know something."

"I merely forgot my phone there after I had an argument with Dad and by the time I realised, it was too late. So no, I don't know who killed them or why. What does it matter? They're gone."

My uncle narrowed his eyes.

"That still doesn't explain why you disappeared."

"You wouldn't understand. You enjoy the spotlight. I hate it. All that media scrutiny? I couldn't deal with it. So yes, I hid away from the world until I felt ready to face it again. Believe me or don't. I'm going to Dad's office."

I turned on my heel and strode out of the room. He didn't call after me. I wouldn't have answered or stopped if he had. I kept my expression neutral as I walked by his secretary. I could break down later when I had Aiden next to me. He'd kiss away the pain. Make me whole again.

When I reached my dad's office, I hesitated with my hand on the door handle.

Was I really ready to face this?

I pushed the door open and walked inside. The huge office almost seemed to take a breath as if no one had been in here since my dad died and it finally had an occupant. The door closed softly behind me.

"I wish you were here with me," I said to the empty room.

Really, I was speaking to Aiden, but no one would know that. Perhaps if anyone viewed the footage, they'd think I was speaking to my dad. A moment later, the phone in my bag buzzed. I pulled it out.

AIDEN: I am here.

ME: You say that, but I still feel alone.

I walked further into the room and stood by my father's desk. I dropped my bag down onto it as my phone buzzed in my hand.

AIDEN: You handled Chuck well. I'm proud of you.

I smiled. Knowing I did good made this a little easier.

AIDEN: Princess, you're so much stronger than you think.

ME: Flatterer.

I slipped off my blazer as I walked around the desk and hung it over the back of the chair before sitting down. This felt strange, being in his office. I should really say my office now.

I opened the top drawer of his desk, rifling through the contents. Nothing particularly interesting. A few pens, memory sticks and other bits and bobs. The second drawer had various unimportant documents. The third was locked. I tugged my bag closer and pulled out something Aiden had given me. A lockpick. He'd taught me the basics.

I managed to get it unlocked within a few minutes and pulled open the drawer. I rifled through the contents and froze when my hand landed on a photo. I picked it up, staring down at it with horror. There was a girl who could've been no older than sixteen. That wasn't the reason it made me feel sick. It was her eyes. Eyes which belonged to the man I loved. I knew immediately who this was. What I didn't know is why the fuck my father had a photo of her in his desk.

My phone buzzed again. The photo slipped from my fingers.

AIDEN: What did you find?

I shook my head. I couldn't bring myself to say the words. I closed the drawer abruptly. The photo remained on the floor. I could hardly breathe. I gripped the arms of the chair, trying to calm down. So many implications. So many reasons why he had this photo. I couldn't. I just couldn't.

My phone buzzed, but this time he was calling me. I reached out and picked it up.

"Princess, what's wrong? Do you need me to come get you?"

I took a deep breath.

"No, don't do that."

"What did you find?"

"I can't talk about this right now. I'll show you later."

"Avery…"

"Please, don't. You know it will ruin everything."

Aiden would come if I asked him to. We couldn't afford that. Not when the company wasn't in my hands. I had to make sure my relationship with him stayed under the radar whilst we took down my family and Frazier Shaw. There was no doubt in my mind he needed to be stopped too. No matter how much he terrified me to my very core. Just another monster who deserved nothing but punishment for the pain he'd inflicted on others.

"You promise you'll show me?"

"Yes, I should go before he comes in here."

"Okay, remember I'm here."

"I know."

I hung up and put the phone back on the desk. Bending over, I picked up the photo from the floor and slipped it in my bag. He told me he didn't talk about her, but this was a conversation we needed to have. He had to tell me what happened. That photo meant my father had something to do with his mother.

"Funny, Mitchell, you lost the right to negotiate the moment you took something that never belonged to you."

93

The memory of the night Aiden murdered my parents slammed into me like a thousand shards of glass cutting into my skin.

Did my father have something to do with why Aiden's mother was dead?

I wanted to throw up.

The world spun around me, twirling until I could barely see straight.

I had to get it together and fast. Spiralling out of control was not an option for me. My uncle would be in here soon and likely the police too. I had questions which needed answering, but not now. I had to stay strong. I couldn't break down.

Taking several deep breaths, I sat up straighter.

I had to be Avery Daniels. The new owner of Daniels Holdings.

And she wouldn't fall apart.

Not now.

Not ever.

I trudged back to where Aiden had parked the car. The rest of the day had been long and drawn out. As predicted, the police detectives had interrogated me when they arrived. I'd given them the exact same story as I had to my uncle.

I didn't know who killed my parents. I didn't know how the video I'd made went viral. And yes, I'd spent most of my time locked away in my bunker.

I gave them no reason to suspect my story. I kept calm and answered everything. They had no choice but to believe me. I had to go down the station tomorrow to give them an official statement.

A board meeting had been scheduled for two weeks' time. Now, all I wanted was to curl up with Aiden and forget this had happened, but the matter of that photo couldn't wait.

I got in the car, tucking my bag in the footwell and kicking off my heels before I looked at my boyfriend. His grey eyes spoke volumes. He reached over, cupped the back of my head and his mouth crashed against mine. It wasn't a sweet kiss. His fingers curled into my hair, holding me in place whilst he took his fill of me. Devoured my mouth like he was starving. The last couple of weeks we hadn't spent a day apart.

He pulled away, resting his forehead against mine.

"I missed you," he breathed.

"You saw me all day."

"That's different to having you right here next to me where I can touch you."

I smiled. He was right. Us being near each other set off fireworks and explosions.

"Did he call you?"

"Chuck? Yes. He's pissed as fuck about you being back suddenly, but we knew that would happen."

"Can we go home? I'm exhausted."

He stroked my cheek and kissed me again before he leant back into the driver's seat. I would show him the photograph, but only when we were back at the flat.

I didn't speak to him until we got home, lost in my own thoughts. I slumped on the sofa after kicking off my heels, not wanting to get up. This outfit was uncomfortable. I hated wearing restrictive clothing.

"Do you fancy helping me take this off?" I asked.

He smirked, dropping to his knees by my feet and running his hands up my thighs.

"If I take your clothes off now, I cannot guarantee you won't get fucked before dinner."

I raised an eyebrow.

"Is that so?"

He leant down, kissing my thigh just above my knee. I shivered.

"Yes."

As much as I wanted him to touch me and melt away the tension from my body, I couldn't.

"We need to talk about something."

He stiffened, raising his head.

"Is this about what you found in his office?"

I nodded. He sat back, releasing his grasp on me. I reached into my bag with trembling fingers. Pulling out the photo, I handed it to him. Aiden's expression turned dark immediately. Dark and closed off. He shut down entirely, his whole body tensing and curling in on itself.

I waited for him to say something, but minutes ticked by as he stared down at the photo in his hands. Shit. I shouldn't have given him that. It clearly hurt him to see her.

I leant towards him, putting my hand on his shoulder. He jerked in response.

"Aiden... I know who it is, but what I don't understand is why he would have a photo of her."

His mouth opened and closed twice. Then he looked up at me. His expression was cold. I felt the icy chill of it on my skin.

"Because he was obsessed with her."

The tone of his voice sent a shiver of dread down my spine. My father was obsessed with his mother. Of all the fucked up and terrible things I'd imagined, that was not one of them.

"What do you mean?"

"I won't explain it. I told you, I don't talk about her."

"You can't tell me my father was obsessed with her and then shut me out. That's not fair."

He shrugged my hand off his shoulder, stood up and walked away. Walked the fuck away from me. I wrapped my arms around myself, trying to keep my racing heart in my chest. It burnt with pain. The sting of his refusal to say anything further bit into my skin.

"The truth is worse than you can ever imagine, Avery. It's better that you don't know."

His voice came from behind me. I turned. He was standing by the window, looking out over the twinkling lights of the city. The photo was still in his hand at his side.

"And you just get to decide that, do you?"

"Yes."

I stood on shaky legs. Not only had I endured the worst day possible from the confrontation with my uncle and the police, I was now faced with this. Him. Cold and unreachable.

Why had I gone through my dad's desk? This would've never happened if I hadn't found that photo.

"I don't accept that."

"You don't have a fucking choice."

I wanted to get angry with him, but I couldn't. I was exhausted. He was being unreasonable and quite frankly, he could fuck off if he was going to behave like that towards me.

"We're back to that now, are we? You know what, fine. I don't have the energy to deal with you right now."

I strode from the room. I no longer cared about dinner. All I cared about was getting out of these stupid clothes and going to bed. I shut the bedroom door behind me and tore off the blazer, throwing it on the floor. Next came my blouse followed by the damn restrictive pencil skirt. My bra joined them.

I knew very well it would wind him up further that I'd left all my clothes on the floor. The threat of his anger wasn't enough to make me pick them up.

I crawled into bed. I hadn't bothered to turn the lights on so there was nothing left for me to do but sleep.

I stared at the empty side of the bed where he'd normally be. I felt so fucking alone. My heart felt tight. My body ached with need. The need to be comforted. The need to feel him against me.

I was crazy over that goddamn man. I couldn't live without Aiden, but right now, I couldn't live with him either. Maybe it would be better if I went back to my own home. Perhaps we needed space from each other.

The thought of going back to my empty flat filled me with dread. I wasn't safe there. I was only safe here, with him. Where he could protect me if anyone tried to come after me.

Now I'd gone back out into the real world, that was a very real possibility. What if my uncle decided he wanted me gone?

I was a problem for him. I always had been and especially now I'd threatened him to keep him in line.

I waited, but Aiden didn't come to bed. I hadn't heard a peep from anywhere else in the flat. Had he even moved away from the window? Why did I even care when he was being such a dick?

Because you love him.

Thanks brain. Loving him was sometimes incredibly frustrating. He was so bloody stubborn and unyielding.

I rolled over and crawled out of bed. Not caring that I was only wearing skimpy knickers, I wrenched open the bedroom door and prowled the flat in search of him.

My assumption about him not having moved was correct. He stood staring out the living room window. For fuck's sake, I really had no fucking willpower when it came to him.

I walked around the sofa and pressed myself against his back, wrapping my arms around his waist, my hands splayed out across his stomach.

Aiden," I whispered. "Please don't shut me out. I love you so much."

Chapter Eight

Aiden

*H*er whispered plea sent my pulse skittering. I hadn't meant to get angry with her. I really hadn't meant to shut her out. That fucking photo ruined everything. Reminding me of just how much I hated her father and all the things he'd done to hurt my mother. All the times he'd raped and beaten her whilst Kathleen watched.

Fuck.

I didn't need reminders of those fucking awful memories. It killed me. Mitchell having a photo of her from a time when she was still innocent. Sixteen and fucking clueless. The fucker hadn't even met her then. It would still be four years before he laid eyes on her. By that time, she'd already been raped, beaten and abused beyond what anyone should ever have to go through. And she'd had me.

"She keeps disobeying you," the woman's voice drifted down the hallway.

I opened my bedroom door a little wider, poking my head out. Mummy told me to stay in here, but I couldn't help it.

"Then I'll just have to remind her who her master is," the man said.

"Please, Sir. I didn't mean to do anything wrong," Mummy whimpered.

She told me they weren't meant to be here this evening. That this was her night to be with me, but they'd come knocking and she shoved me in my room before letting them in. I didn't understand why she had these people here all the time. The ones who hurt her.

"Shut the fuck up. You will not talk unless spoken to," the man shouted.

I heard the distinct sound of someone falling on the floor with a thump and a cry of pain. I clenched my fists. All they did was hurt her. Tina wasn't here this evening. I had to take care of her when they were gone. I'd wipe away her tears.

Mummy didn't deserve any of this. I vowed to be stronger for her. To make sure that one day, I'd avenge her. A stupid promise for a seven year old kid, but I'd do it anyway.

For her.

Avery clutched me tighter, reminding me she was on my side. That she loved me without conditions or restraints.

"I'm sorry, princess."

And I was.

"I won't ask any questions. I just need you."

The claws pulled at me, but I shut down the past. Nothing would change it. What I had now was more important.

Her.

I pulled her arms from my waist and turned around. My eyes fell on her almost naked body. Fuck. Despite what just happened, my cock went hard at the sight of her. Fuck it. Her body called to me. Always did.

I tugged her towards me and my mouth crashed down on hers, stealing away anything she'd been about to say. I gave her no choice but to kiss me back. I touched her wherever I could, running my fingers across her skin. She made everything seem less crazy and fucked up.

"Ever since he saw her, he wanted her," I told her between kisses. "She was twenty and I was three when they first met. It'd take another four years for everything to go to shit and then she was dead."

Avery's hands were on me, unbuttoning my shirt.

"Was she one of my family's girls?"

"Yes, but she wasn't like the others. Not after she had me."

"Why?"

I cupped her breast, running my thumb over the nub. She gasped, arching into me. Touching her helped me talk about this.

"The man who raped her and gave her me, he made sure she was given more to raise me. Don't ask me anything else about him."

She pushed off my shirt and ran her hands over my chest. I shuddered.

"I know why Dad had to die, but not Mum."

I wished I didn't have to tell her this.

"She liked to watch the abuse."

Avery froze, her eyes catching mine.

"That's... oh god."

"Shh, princess, concentrate on me. Listen to me and touch me."

Slowly her body relaxed and her hands resumed their progress to my belt.

"Good girl."

I ran my fingers down lower and hooked them into her underwear, tugging them off. She stepped out of them, closer to me.

"I knew their voices, but I only discovered who they were after Chuck introduced me to them. That's when I knew I had to destroy everything. They beat, abused and raped her whilst I was in the same flat. I heard it all. I saw it at times. Never saw your parents, but other men. I found evidence when I dug into her past with your father."

She undid my belt and trousers, pushing them off my hips. Her fingers ran over my cock. It jumped in her hold. Fuck. I needed in her. Needed her to take the painful memories away.

"I'm so sorry."

"It's okay, princess. Now you understand why I couldn't allow them to live."

She nodded. I tucked my hands under her bum and hoisted her up onto my hips. She wrapped her legs around me. I turned, pressing her against the window as I kissed her again.

"I fucking need you so much, Avery. You make it better."

"Then fuck me and let me take your pain away."

I reached between us, pulled out my cock, kicking off my boxers and sunk into her. Fuck. She felt so good. Wet and hot.

She moaned when I thrust inside her, not giving her much time to adjust.

"Princess, fuck. I can't begin to tell you how much you mean to me."

She grabbed a hold of my face and kissed me like she was drowning in me. I pounded into her harder.

"There's something else you should know."

Her doe eyes were wide.

"What?" she asked.

"One day, the man who gave me life might come after me and by extension, you. I'll protect you, but you can't trust anyone but me and your friends, okay?"

She nodded. I expected her to ask me why, but it seemed she'd taken what I said about not asking questions about him seriously. It was when I investigated my mother, I discovered who he really was and that knowledge kept me up at night for weeks afterwards. If it came to it, I'd tell her for her own safety, but right now, we only needed to worry about her family and the Shaws. They were our priority.

I buried my face in her neck, breathing in the scent of coconut. Fuck, she smelt amazing. Always did. Her fingers threaded in my hair, her other hand clutching my shoulder.

"Harder," she moaned.

I'd never fucked a girl against a window before. Lucky we weren't near the ground floor, but if anyone looked up, they'd be able to see what I was doing to her. Possibly not such a brilliant idea.

I pulled her away from it and carried her towards the sofa. I shoved her down on it and settled between her legs. Slipping inside her heat, I stared down at her. Beautiful. Precious. This girl really was everything to me.

"Princess, I… fuck… Avery, I love you."

She froze. The shock in her face told me she wasn't prepared for me to say it.

"You… I… Oh."

She looked away from me, fear flashing across her features. Why the hell was she scared?

"Aiden… I need to tell you something."

It was my turn to freeze. What the fuck? Why would she be acting like this the moment I tell her I love her? She'd told me I could take my time, but I needed to say it. I had to get it out.

"I don't want to keep this from you anymore."

"Keep what? Avery, what's going on?"

Her eyes met mine.

"I love you so much. I'm so happy you feel the same way, please don't think I'm not."

I cupped her face. What was she so afraid of?

"Please, don't. I know this really is the worst possible time. I'm so sorry, Aiden."

Now I really was fucking concerned. I pulled away from her. She scrambled back and tucked her legs into her chest.

"Princess…"

She put a hand up.

"I have to get this out. I have to…"

Horror and abject misery crossed her face.

"You're going to hate me and him."

Him?

"How do I even explain this? I told myself I'd never reveal this to you, but it's so unfair of me. Do you remember when I told you not to ask me about my friendship with James?"

The world stopped. My heartbeat pounded in my ears. I knew what she was going to tell me and I didn't want to hear it. I'd suspected for so long, but now, now I didn't want my suspicions confirmed at all.

"For two years, James and I... We used to sleep together before I dated Peter."

My fists clenched. How the fuck could she keep this from me?

"The pressure of our families and everything else got to us. Gert didn't understand. We only had each other to talk to and talking sometimes wasn't enough. It just happened and then it kept happening. I don't know why or what the hell we thought we were doing but it's how we coped."

I got up, pacing away. I couldn't look at her.

"I'm sorry. I know I should've told you. I didn't want you to get angry with me or him. It's in the past. It stopped six months ago. I promise."

Three months before we met. She might not want me to be angry, but I was. Pissed off that she'd kept such a vital piece of information about their friendship from me.

"You said there were three. Who were the other two?"

"A stupid drunken night with a boy I met in Jamaica and a boy from school. Both only happened once."

Did she not understand what that meant? The most significant man in her life had been and was still her best friend.

"Never had a boyfriend, Avery? That's fucking bullshit. What the fuck else do you call your relationship with him?"

I heard her get up from the sofa.

"It wasn't like that."

"No? You're deluding yourself if you think that wasn't a relationship between you. I've seen the way you are together. I'm not stupid or blind."

"It wasn't about sex. It was just about the need to feel close to someone when all else seemed like it was falling apart. I needed someone. He needed someone."

I turned on her. Fuck. Her eyes filled with tears. Her body language told me she was sorry and in no small amount of emotional pain.

"And you think it's okay to fucking tell me this now? Right after I told you something I've never said to anyone before."

This entire day had been fucking shit for both of us and tonight made it so much worse. I strode towards her, taking her by the shoulders and shaking her.

"I love you, Avery. I love you so fucking much. Do you understand that?"

She nodded, tears slipping down her cheeks.

"Why would you keep this from me?"

"I didn't want you to hate me or hurt him," she sobbed.

Hurt him? Why the fuck would I do that?

"You thought I'd hurt him for something you did before we even met? What the hell kind of person do you take me for?"

Then I saw it. She was terrified of me. She might love me, but she was scared of how I'd react to things. Scared of me blowing up at her. And I hadn't given her any reason to think otherwise.

I released her, taking a step back and putting a hand to my mouth. I kept telling her I'd hurt anyone who touched her. I'd made her fear me since the day we'd met. Fuck. How could I ever make her trust me fully? No wonder she hadn't told me. Fuck. I hated myself so much. I knew having a relationship with someone was going to be almost impossible for me, but this, this was much worse than I ever imagined.

I ruined us before we even started.

I destroyed us the moment I took her parents lives.

The moment we fucking met.

Why had I been stupid enough to think this wouldn't end badly? I wasn't capable of being the sort of man she needed. I thought I could make up for what I'd done to her. All I did was bring her more pain and misery.

"You're scared of me."

She frowned, tears still falling down her cheeks.

"What?"

"You. You're scared of how I'll react to things. That's why you keep things from me."

"I'm not."

"You would've told me the truth before, so yes, you are."

She closed the distance between us, reached up and tugged my face down to her level.

"I'm scared of the side of you which takes lives without a second thought. The cold, calculating side." She pointed at my chest. "But you, Aiden, I'm not scared of who you are in here. I know you. I trust you. I love you."

And then she captured my mouth in hers. My body bent to her will. I tugged her into my arms, holding her against me. Fuck, she felt so right. I might never be the man she deserved, but I was the one she chose. I vowed then to try to be worthy of the trust she bestowed on me.

Pulling her down on the sofa with me, she straddled my lap and sunk onto my cock. Despite our fight, I was still rock hard and she was deliciously wet. Our discussion about her revelation was far from over, but sex always brought us back to each other.

"I love you," she whispered, rising and falling on me at an increased pace.

I gripped her hips, encouraging her to keep going.

"I love you too."

Now I'd said it once, the words fell from my lips easily. I adored, worshipped and loved the ground she walked on. Avery was mine. I wouldn't let her go no matter what we'd done in the past nor what was to come in the future. She was the one. My soul and hers were right for each other. Whatever decreed that I neither knew nor cared. With her was where I belonged.

Neither of us spoke again. She rode my cock harder, her fingers gripping my shoulders. My fingers trailed up her inner thigh. I knew her body. What made her tick. How to give her the most satisfying climax. The subtle ways she'd taught me to read her. Just as I had taught her what pleased me.

Avery was the only girl I enjoyed vanilla sex with. The deeper I fell in love with her, the less I needed the restraints. I had her submission and that was more important than tying her down.

Her head fell back when I strummed her clit, a soft moan escaping her lips. Fuck. Seeing her lost in me was always such a fucking turn on. I thrust back against her. I wanted her to let go and give into the sweetest ecstasy. And when she did finally come, she panted, her body trembling and clenching around me. I let myself go with her. Needing to find the heaven she floated in.

She leant her forehead against mine when we stopped breathing so hard. Her fingers curled around my neck.

"I'm tired of fighting and secrets. Can't we just have one day where it's just you, me and nothing else?"

Her words fucking tore at me. I was still pissed off she'd kept things from me. She was right though. We fought too much. My need to control her got worse as the days went on and she bore the brunt of my frustration with myself.

"I'm so sorry, princess."

"Shh, don't. I know this is hard for you. I never expected anything else. I haven't made it easier. I push you too much, but you have to stop shutting me out. It makes me so afraid I'm losing you when you do that."

I cupped her face with both hands.

"I'm not going anywhere. You and I belong together, remember? I'm trying to be better for you."

She shook her head.

"I don't want you to change. I need you." She placed a hand on my heart. "I'll always crave your control. It feeds me just as much as it does you. Don't ever forget that even when we fight."

Could I love this girl any more right now?

I kissed her forehead before releasing her.

"I think I owe you dinner, then I'm going to run you a bath."

She smiled, her doe eyes twinkling.

"Sounds perfect."

She shifted off me and ran to the bathroom to clean up. I found my boxers and tugged them on. Walking into the kitchen, I pulled out a few things to make her a quick pasta dish. I knew she was tired after today. Having to deal with Chuck and the police can't have been easy on her, then me going off the deep end over the photo of my mother and her revelation didn't help matters.

I doubted I'd ever be okay with her having had a sexual relationship with James. Knowing he'd touched her and seen her naked fuelled the violence inside me I usually kept at bay.

Mine. Mine. Mine.

I needed to get a grip. She was right to be worried. I wanted to hurt him. Except I wouldn't. Being an adult about this situation was the only way forward.

Her arms banded around my stomach. Her lips pressed against my back. She'd put a t-shirt on. I could feel the fabric against my skin.

"You know there's nothing sexier than a shirtless man cooking for his girlfriend, especially this tattooed one right here."

I chuckled. She'd successfully pulled me out of my dark mood with that sentence.

"Is that so?"

"Mmm, you make my panties wet."

I snorted, running my hand over hers.

"Are you trying to compliment or flatter me?"

"I'm trying to make you smile, but obviously what I said is true. You do make me wet with a single look sometimes."

I stowed that little detail away for future use.

"Go sit at the table."

She kissed my back again before she let go. I turned to watch her walk over, pull out a chair and sit down. She rested her chin on her hands and looked at me with a grin. The tension between us had evaporated completely. I had more shit to make up to her. And I would because I loved her.

"I'm just going to sit here and admire my boyfriend. Is that okay with him?"

"Look all you want, princess. No one else gets this view."

"I should hope not."

I winked at her whilst I put pasta in boiling water.

"Do I detect a hint of possessiveness in your tone? Are you going to start a catfight if you catch a girl looking my way?"

She scowled.

"You are mine."

The way she said it made my heart tighten.

"Are you quite sure about that?"

"Don't you start with me, Aiden, unless you want me to demonstrate the fact to you."

Now I was intrigued by how she would go about doing that.

"Maybe I do."

"Later. Hurry up and feed me."

I laughed. I dumped out the water and finished it up with pesto and parmesan. I placed both plates on the table and got her a glass of water. She dug in straight away, mumbling 'thank you' with a mouthful of food.

As promised, I ran her a bubble bath when she finished. She gratefully sunk into the water. I kissed her forehead and left her to it. I still had things to do. Not least of which was to make sure Chuck didn't try to pull any shit now she was back. And we still had Frazier Shaw to worry about.

What would happen when he found out Avery had returned ready to take over the company?

It would likely be nothing good.

She and I had a lot to prepare for.

And I vowed to keep her safe.

Even if it cost us everything.

Because to me, Avery was worth losing it all for.

Chapter Nine

Avery

The board meeting might be in a couple of weeks, but that didn't stop some of the members coming to see me. I'd been polite and courteous to each one of them. I couldn't work out who knew about the dark side of the business and who didn't.

Until they hired me a secretary, Clara was helping me, much to Uncle Charlie's annoyance. And when she buzzed to say Frazier Shaw was waiting, I wanted to tell her to inform him he had to make an appointment. Except I couldn't. He was the firm's solicitor. I had to deal with the man whether I wanted to or not.

I asked her to send him in whilst I fired off a quick text.

ME: Frazier is here.

AIDEN: What the fuck?

ME: I'll let you know how it goes.

I popped my phone on the desk as he walked in. Frazier Shaw was dressed in a grey pinstripe suit with a cravat. *So pretentious.* His grey hair was slicked back and he appraised me with dark eyes.

"Hello Avery."

"Good afternoon Mr Shaw, what can I do for you?"

He strolled toward me.

"There's no need to be so formal. I have known you since you were in the cradle."

His eyes roamed over me, a deadly smile appearing on his face. I straightened my spine.

"What brings you here?"

"I heard you were back. I wanted to see for myself. Chuck says you're ready to take over. The papers are being drawn up as we speak. You are the irrefutable heir after all."

"Well, as you can see, I'm here. I assure you, I'm prepared for my role."

He cocked his head to the side.

"Yes… well, if you require anything else of Shaw Associates, you will let me know. I do hope we can begin a successful working relationship together."

I swallowed back the bile rising in my throat. I wanted to tell him to get the fuck out of my office and never darken my door again. I remembered the video Aiden showed me of him. I tried not to think about the wild look in his eyes when he'd lowered the drill to that girl's leg.

"Of course, I have every intention of continuing business with your company."

It killed me to say that. I wanted another firm who were far more reputable and not involved in the horrors my family had committed, but I couldn't. I had to keep up appearances.

None of them could know, I knew the truth. The role I had to play would be key.

I wished I had Aiden right here with me. I didn't feel safe in Frazier's presence. He wouldn't do anything in the office because there were cameras in here. I was in no doubt he was aware of that fact.

I was going to have my father's office redecorated so I'd taken another one, closer to my uncle. I hated relying on him for help with the business, but the reality was I had no idea what I was doing.

"I'm glad to hear it. I'm sorry about your parents. Mitch and Kath were my closest friends. I do hope the murderer is brought to justice."

I shuddered. I didn't want Aiden arrested for it. Yes, what he'd done was wrong, but my parents deserved it. Especially knowing what my dad had done to his mother. It sickened me. The more I discovered about my father, the harder it got to see him as anything other than a monster hidden behind a well-constructed mask. My love for my parents was a pile of ashes at my feet. When the wind blew, they'd scatter, never to be seen again.

"Thank you. It's been difficult, but I'm sure the police will discover the truth."

He paced away a few steps.

"Tell me, Avery, do you know why someone wanted them dead?"

I shrugged. I knew all right.

"No. Did they have enemies?"

"Everyone in a position of power has enemies."

His eyes met mine. I could see the warning in them. The one which told me not to cross him. Not to make him into an enemy. Problem was, he was already on my shit list. His time in this world was limited. Aiden would see to that. My boyfriend. The stone cold killer with a heart that only beat for me.

"You'd do well not to rock the boat any time soon. You're going to be in charge and that's a big responsibility to put on a twenty-year-old girl with no knowledge of how big business works."

I didn't move an inch or change my expression. Inside, I raged at his words. I might only be twenty, but I knew how sick and evil he was. I was walking a dangerous line when I agreed to take up my place as head of Daniels Holdings. So much rested on my ability to convince them I was capable and had no idea about what other shit they got up to.

"I'm sure it will be a steep learning curve, but with my uncle's guidance, the company will continue to thrive."

I had to become proficient in the art of bullshitting. I intended to destroy it all so they couldn't hurt anyone else.

Aiden and I could've washed our hands of all of this. I was within my rights to appoint someone else to run the company and not be involved myself. Except I had a responsibility. I had to finish what Aiden had started. Together, we'd make sure they all crashed and burned for what they'd done.

"Of course, your uncle worked closely with your father." He paused, his dark eyes appraising me. "I know you and your father discussed having one of your cousins work closely with you. Have you perhaps reconsidered my son for the role?"

I locked my muscles in place so I wouldn't react. I should've known he'd bring that shit up, but I wasn't prepared for it. It made me ill, sickness coiling in my stomach. Not only did it remind me of what Aiden originally wanted me to do, but I didn't want to be anywhere near his son. Tristan was just as disturbed as his father.

"I've already decided to have Ed come work with me."

I hadn't, but he was the obvious choice. Dad kept mentioning him as the perfect candidate. It left me with the distinct impression my cousin knew about the human trafficking and sex ring my family kept under wraps.

Edward Daniels was my father's cousin, Troy's son. He was four years older than me. His sister, Lindsay, was only sixteen and not yet out of school. My cousins were all nice enough, but I had a tainted view of my family now. I couldn't exactly see Ed in the same light any longer.

If Frazier was annoyed by me choosing my cousin over his son, he didn't show it. He smiled at me, a gleam in his eye.

"A fine young man. He will be an asset to you."

Ed knows. He has to know.

"I'm sure."

I wanted Frazier to leave. He didn't have any other reason to be here. My phone buzzed on the desk. I eyed it. Aiden sent me another message. I didn't move to touch it.

"Well, I shall leave you to your day. The paperwork will be delivered before the board meeting," he said.

"Thank you."

He gave me a sharp nod before turning on his heel and striding out of my office. I let out a sigh of relief as soon as the door closed behind him. I pulled my phone off the desk.

AIDEN: Call me.

I sighed, leaning back in my desk chair. I was already rattled by Frazier's presence. I didn't need Aiden going off the deep end too. Things were already weird between us after I'd told him about James. A few days had passed and I was beginning to worry. Outwardly, nothing had changed, but I knew Aiden and his moods. It would grate on him. It was a question of when this would blow up in my face again, not if.

He'd get pissed off if I didn't call him, but I also needed to call my cousin and speak to Uncle Charlie. I decided my boyfriend could wait. I was at work and that meant concentrating on doing the necessary. I stood, slipping my phone in my trouser pocket and walked out of my office.

Clara nodded at me when I stepped up to Uncle Charlie's door.

"He's free," she said.

I turned the handle and walked in. He looked up from his computer, a frown immediately appearing on his face.

"Frazier was just here," I said, walking over to the window and looking out.

Our offices were located on the top floor of the building. The views of the city spanned far and wide. The city of secrets and lies.

"Checking up on you no doubt," my uncle replied.

I still felt uncomfortable in his presence, but it didn't matter. I had to work with him.

"Dad told me Ed would be best placed to help me with the business when we discussed it. I think he was right."

I eyed my uncle out of the corner of my eye. His eyes lit up.

"Accepting you need help now, are you?"

I resisted the urge to curse him for his sarcastic tone.

"Unless you want me to call Frazier and tell him I'm happy to have Tristan here…"

He paled. His reaction piqued my curiosity. Did he hate Frazier and Tristan as much as I did?

"Ed will do just fine. Do you want me to speak to him?"

I shook my head. It was better coming from me. I hadn't seen any of my extended family for a long while, but the world knew I'd returned to the public eye.

I refused any interviews. The police had given a statement regarding my reappearance yesterday after they'd got my official statement. Now, we had the paparazzi camped outside the building. I wasn't sure how I'd get out of here without being snapped and followed. Aiden wasn't coming to pick me up for that very reason. We still had to keep our relationship a secret.

"I'll do it. Got to start somewhere."

My uncle didn't respond. I turned to him. He was staring at his phone, his expression dark.

"Is everything okay?"

He waved me away.

"Yes, yes. Go speak to your cousin."

I wondered what he'd received. There was no point me trying to snoop. I could get Aiden to do that for me. The reminder of him caused my pulse to spike. He wasn't going to be happy with me for not calling him straight away.

I walked out of my uncle's office and left him to it. No point sticking around. I didn't need his approval to appoint Ed but keeping him onside was more important in the long run. If I ran things by him before I did them, he'd think I trusted him.

Sitting back in my office chair, I tugged out my phone. Aiden had texted me again, but I decided not to look at them. Instead, I dialled my cousin's number. He answered it on the fifth ring.

"Hello little cousin. Long-time no speak."

"Hi Ed."

"I'm sorry about your parents. Shitty business."

"Thanks. It's been difficult, but I'm back now. Trying to get things in order."

My phone vibrated against my ear. More texts from Aiden no doubt.

"Of course, Dad told me you are at the office. I'm sure you'll see him at some point."

Troy worked on one of the lower floors. I was surprised he'd not popped up to see me, but I wasn't particularly close to my dad's cousins.

"I'm actually calling because I'd like to see you."

"Me?"

"Yes, I want to discuss you coming to work with me. I can't make a formal appointment until the company is signed over to me, but no harm lining things up."

Ed was silent for a long moment.

"I can come to the office now if you're free."

"You're not busy?"

I knew he was working somewhere in the city, so I was a little surprised.

"Little cousin, for you, never. I'll be there in half an hour."

He hung up before I could say any more. I didn't expect him to drop everything to speak to me. Perhaps he'd been expecting this. My dad had told me several times he'd discuss it with Troy and Ed. Maybe he had done so already and not told me. I'd never know.

True to his word, Ed arrived in my office half an hour later. His dark hair was tousled, brown eyes glinting.

"Avery."

I smiled, standing up and coming around the desk. He enveloped me in a warm embrace. When he released me, he gripped my arms.

"You look good."

"Thanks. You want a drink?" I replied.

"A cuppa would be divine right now."

I walked around to my desk and sat back in my chair, pressing down on the intercom button.

"Clara, can you make Ed and I tea please?"

"Of course, Miss Daniels," she said.

I released the button and indicated the chair in front of my desk to Ed. He folded his long legs into the seat, unbuttoning his suit jacket.

"How's Linds and Aunt Penny?" I asked.

"Both doing well. We missed you at the funeral."

I looked at my hands.

"I'm sorry I missed it. Grief does funny things to people sometimes."

When my eyes met Ed's, they were full of sympathy. I forgot for a moment that my cousin likely knew my family were a bunch of sick bastards.

"It's okay. It came as a shock to us all, but we don't need to talk about that. I am here to discuss the future after all."

I gave him a half smile.

"You're right. Shall we start with my plans?"

He nodded, inching his chair closer to the desk whilst I flipped around the tablet laying on there.

Ed and I spoke for the rest of the afternoon, going over various details until we'd hashed everything out. I was pleased. He knew a lot more about the property industry than I did. His knowledge would prove useful, although he was likely groomed to work in the family business. I should keep my guard up with him, but I found I couldn't. Ed had always been sweet to me.

I looked at my phone when he left. There were four missed calls and twelve text messages from Aiden. I sighed, checking through them. They all pretty much said the same thing as his original message. He was desperate to speak to me.

ME: I'm leaving the office now. Please don't be mad. Love you x

I hoped it was enough. I didn't feel like having it out with him over the phone. The thought of it exhausted me.

Except Aiden was having none of my text message. As soon as I'd seen he'd read it, my phone started ringing.

"Hi," I answered.

"Avery, you need to go back to your own flat tonight."

I frowned. He didn't sound mad at all. Just concerned.

"Why?"

"Chuck has a man on your place. If you don't turn up there, he's going to start wondering where you're staying. He's suspicious enough as it is."

My uncle had a man watching my house. This was absolute bullshit. I wanted to storm into his office and demand he call his dogs off. That would not be a smart move, so I settled for inwardly seething instead.

"How do you know?"

"He told me. I expected him to keep tabs on you. I know the guy, he won't harm you."

I stuck my head out of my office door.

"Hang on… Clara, can you call a driver to take me home, please?"

Clara looked up from her desk. I really didn't want to deal with the paparazzi camped outside our office.

"No problem, Miss Daniels. I'll ask him to wait in the lobby for you," she said, smiling at me.

I nodded, ducking back into the office.

"Will I see you tonight?" I asked Aiden when the door closed behind me.

The thought of spending time apart made my heart ache. I'd not spent a night without him since I'd gone back to him. I couldn't imagine falling asleep without Aiden's bulk wrapped around my back.

"Was that ever in doubt?"

"Bring supplies and dinner."

"I take it you'll be wanting me to make said dinner."

I smiled, snagging my coat and scarf from the stand in the corner of the room.

"No, I'll do it."

"I'll see you soon, princess."

He hung up without waiting for my response. I put my coat, scarf and gloves on, stuffing my phone in my bag. I headed out the door, waving to Clara before getting in the lift. I rode down to the lobby. No one else got in, which I could only be grateful for. I was in no mood for small talk with random employees.

The driver was waiting in the lobby. He gave me a nod when I approached him.

"This way, Miss Daniels," he said.

I recognised him as my dad's driver from when he was alive.

"Thank you, Davis."

The reporters were on us, shouting various questions as soon as we were out the door. I ignored them all, focusing on keeping one foot in front of the other. Davis shielded me from them all the way to the car and got me situated in the back. We were off when he got in the front and pulled away from the curb. I sat back, watching the city pass us by. I'd only been to my flat once since Aiden took me. We'd had the locks changed as a precaution.

It felt weird to return to what should be my home. Aiden's felt like home to me now, but I did miss my studio. I'd converted the second bedroom since it was just me living there. It had everything I could ever need, although I wouldn't have much time for drawing with running the family business.

When we pulled up, I thanked Davis as he came around and opened my door. He walked me up to the front door.

"You have a good night, Miss Daniels," he said, giving me a nod as he descended the steps again.

I looked up and down the street, wondering where on earth this guy Uncle Charlie had on me was. I supposed if he was doing his job properly, I wouldn't be able to see him. I let myself in the front door and then into my flat on the ground floor. It was freezing cold.

Sighing, I didn't take my coat off as I went through into the kitchen at the back. I dug around in the boiler cupboard, turning it on and then adjusted the thermostat. Next, I went into my bedroom, changing my work clothes for warm pyjamas and a dressing gown, stuffing my feet into my novelty sheep slippers. Not particularly sexy, but I was too cold to care much about my appearance.

I had an entirely new wardrobe courtesy of Aiden. It felt strange to see all my old clothes. It just felt plain wrong to be in here in the first place. I wanted to be back at Aiden's where everything smelt of him and I felt safe. There was no point lamenting over the fact I had to stay in my own home.

Walking across the hallway, I went into my studio, running my hands over the various half-finished drawings on my desk. I looked at my easel where the painting I'd been working on before Aiden took me sat. It was a half-finished portrait of my dad. Seeing it brought tears to my eyes. I'd started it for his birthday which would've been next week.

I had no idea what to do with it. Finishing it seemed wrong but leaving it here would be a painful reminder of the man I had mixed feelings about. I turned away, clicked the light off, walked out of the room and shut the door. That was something I didn't want to deal with.

I went back into the kitchen and almost jumped out of my skin. Standing at the patio doors, half hidden in shadow was Aiden. I knew it was him from the way my heart thumped uncontrollably and the gleam of his silver eyes. I unlocked the door and stood aside for him. He walked in, dumped a bag down by the door and set two more on the kitchen counter.

"Shit it's cold in here," he muttered.

"The boiler was turned off. It'll warm up soon."

I shut the patio doors and locked them again. Him coming through the back had been unexpected, but with the house being watched, I could understand why.

He gave me a half smile. I promptly bundled myself up in his arms, resting my head against his solid chest. Neither of us moved or said anything for several minutes. The tension in my limbs faded away. Aiden made the world seem right again. His presence calmed me.

"Did you watch my conversation with Frazier?" I asked, unable to hold back the question.

"Yes. You didn't tell me about your cousin before."

"Frazier put me on the spot, but it's the right decision. He knows the industry and business. Plus, I'm eighty per cent sure he's aware of the other side of things."

I pulled away from him, going over to the shopping bags he'd brought and started pulling out things. Last time we were here, we'd emptied my fridge out, so it was bare. I noted he'd bought me stuff he knew I liked to cook.

"Angling for Mexican tonight?" I asked, holding up the soft taco shells he'd bought.

He didn't say anything. Instead, he grabbed me by the waist and pressed me against the counter. Untying my dressing gown, his hands slipped under my t-shirt. His fingers were like ice on my skin. I shuddered.

"I don't trust anyone in your family. Don't let your guard down."

He bit down on my earlobe.

"And I don't want dinner right now, princess. I want you."

Chapter Ten

Aiden

*I*t made me so fucking mad that she decided to involve another family member without consulting me. I was already struggling with the knowledge she'd had a sexual relationship with James. This was the icing on the cake. I tried so hard to keep my need to control her at bay. I was failing her on so many levels. This fucking girl really was going to be the death of me.

"Strip. Bedroom. Now."

I stepped back from her. She turned to me, eyes wide.

"I've been in the office all day. Can't we eat first?"

I held back from grabbing her and forcing her in the bedroom. One of my hands curled into a fist at my side. Her eyes went to it.

"Aiden, what's wrong?"

I really was being a fucking dick. How many times had I told myself I needed to be better for her? Here I was, losing my shit all over again.

I walked away, shrugging off my coat and planting myself in one of her dining table chairs.

Get a fucking grip.

"Nothing. We can eat first."

My fingers itched to be on her. My need to have Avery at my mercy returned with full force. Battling with my darker urges was always a fucking problem.

She walked over to me and ran her fingers through my hair. I almost growled in response. Her hands on me didn't help my rapidly disintegrating control.

"I don't believe you."

"Just make dinner."

Her fingers stilled at my tone. She retracted her hand, instead, pressing it to my shoulder as she got down on her knees in front of me. Her hand dropped, running up my thigh. I didn't stop her when it reached my throbbing cock. Her eyes met mine, something dark simmering in those hazel depths.

"How about you feed me this instead?"

Her fingers made quick work of my jeans. My mouth went dry when she pulled my cock out and ran her hand along its length. Instead of her being at my mercy, I was currently utterly at hers.

I groaned when she ran her tongue around the crown of my cock. Fuck. She really knew how to drive me crazy. I barely had time to breathe when she took me in her mouth. She wasn't gentle. Her teeth grazed my skin and I jolted upwards, shoving more in her mouth. My hand immediately went to her hair, fingers digging into her scalp.

"Fuck. Fuck. Don't stop, Avery, please. Fuck."

She kept going, taking more until I hit the back of her throat. Her small hand wrapped around the base of me. I wanted more. I needed fucking more. I wanted her to take everything. She was fucking mine.

She didn't stop. A minute later, my cock was buried down her throat and I was in heaven. I stared down at the top of her head bobbing up and down. For a girl who'd never sucked cock before we met, she certainly knew how to work her mouth. I was so fucking close to blowing my load already.

My eyes fell on my wrist where her initial was branded onto my skin. The reminder I was hers just as much as she was mine. It sent me over the edge. I grunted, my cock spurting hot, sticky streams down her throat. She didn't move away until I dropped my hand to my thigh.

She got up off the floor, swallowed and kissed my cheek before walking towards the kitchen. She washed her hands and proceeded to pull out a chopping board and a knife.

"How long do you think Uncle Charlie will have someone watching my house? I don't really feel at home here."

I blinked, staring at her. My girl had just sucked my cock and now she was calmly chopping up chicken and talking to me like nothing happened. What the fuck did I do to deserve her?

"You don't feel at home here?"

"No, yours is home now."

I didn't know what to say to that. On the one hand, I was happy she knew she belonged with me. On the other, her being at mine came with added danger now she was back in the world.

"We just have to give it a few days."

I tucked myself back in my boxers and jeans, aware that I was still half hard for her. Would this attraction ever dampen down? The need to fuck my girlfriend until she was a panting mess on the floor.

I watched her prepare dinner in silence as she hummed to herself. She looked cute all wrapped up in her dressing gown and fluffy slippers. I knew underneath there, a curvaceous body I craved with every waking moment was waiting for me.

My control was slipping again. I reminded myself she needed to eat and then I could fuck her. And fuck her I would. I eyed my bag as if I could see what I'd stashed in there before I left my flat sitting in amongst a change of clothes.

What would she think when I showed her? It's not like she hadn't seen what was in the box under my bed. She knew my desires. Except we hadn't exactly used anything from there since she'd come back to me. There was no way she'd be expecting this.

She brought dinner over to the table a few minutes later. Spicy chicken tacos. She'd made these for me before. Avery had a thing about Mexican food.

She told me about her day whilst we ate. I hadn't had time to watch her with her cousin because I'd been busy with a job for Chuck. It involved chasing up some of his dealers. Always messy work.

"I mentioned to Ed about the charities I want the company to sponsor. He didn't bat an eyelid when I spoke about women's refuges," she said.

"Why would he? He doesn't think you know about their shit. They all think you're playing right into their hands."

"I suppose so. I guess I wanted to get a reaction, to see if he is actually innocent or not."

"If he is innocent, then what?"

She rubbed her forehead.

"I don't know, Aiden. I guess I just don't like the thought of wiping out my entire family if some of them don't know about the shit the others have gotten up to."

I was certain some of her cousins had no idea what was going on behind closed doors. I wasn't after them. The ones on my shit list were Chuck, Troy and Troy's younger brother, Arthur. And all the other men who paid handsomely for her family's services, including Frazier fucking Shaw. That sick cunt was fast approaching top of the list after his visit to Avery today.

"I don't kill innocents. You, of all people, should know that."

She looked at her plate, her doe eyes flashing with pain. I hated reminding her of the day I'd taken her. It was a fucked up start to our relationship.

"I know you don't."

I knew in the eyes of the law, I was a murderer. A cold-hearted killer. The girl in front of me had witnessed that first hand. And she'd fallen in love with me anyway. Avery saw my other sides. She knew the real me behind all the fucked up shit I'd done.

I reached over the table and grasped her hand, stroking my thumb down the back of it.

"Princess, if they don't know about it, they're safe, okay? I promise you that much."

"I know. I just... Ed is so kind. I can't imagine him being involved in it, but what other conclusion can I draw? Why else would my dad have pushed me towards having him help me with the company?"

Mitchell never did anything by halves. It wouldn't surprise me if her cousin was groomed for the role.

"We'll find evidence either way."

"That's what I'm worried about."

I wished I didn't have to put all this pressure on her. I wished we could be a normal couple who talked about normal things instead of calmly discussing whether or not we'd have to kill her cousin at the dinner table.

"Do you want to back out of this, princess? Is it too much for you?"

She looked up at me, confusion in her eyes.

"No, that's not what I meant. I have to do this. If Ed is involved, then he has to face the consequences of his actions."

There was the girl I'd fallen in love with. Strong and resolute. I'd never told her this would be easy. I squeezed her hand before letting go. She gave me a half smile, then she stood up and started gathering up the plates. I helped her stack the dishwasher.

"You still want me naked in the bedroom?" she asked, putting a hand on my arm when I straightened.

My cock twitched at her words. I nodded once, not trusting my voice. I didn't want to turn into a feral animal at the thought of what I was going to do to her. She left me in the kitchen, going out into the hallway. I snagged my bag from the patio doors before following her.

Avery was stripping out of her clothes when I entered her bedroom. Thankfully, the flat had warmed up, but her skin still had goosebumps all over it. Under her clothes, she had a push-up bra on with little bows and matching underwear. My mouth watered at the sight of her.

"I've changed my mind. I want you to keep that on," I said as she was reaching around her back.

She dropped her arms immediately. Walking over to the bed, she sat down on the edge and waited. I dumped my bag on a chair in the corner and slipped off my trainers. I unzipped the bag and pulled out the harness and ropes I'd brought with me along with the cuffs to attach her limbs to it.

Her eyes went wide when I turned around and brought it over to the bed.

"Um, Aiden, what is that?"

I didn't answer her. I tugged her underwear down, slipping it off her legs. Then I took the first part of the harness and secured it around her neck, the second part around her waist and the last two loops around her thighs. She let me wrap the cuffs around her wrists and ankles, eyes on me the whole time.

"Aiden… please, what is this?"

I took each of her wrists and attached them to the loops on her thighs. I pressed her down on the bed.

"Aiden…"

Pressing her legs up, I attached the cuffs around her ankles to the collar around her neck by two lengths of rope. I pulled them tight so she was essentially completely immobile with her knees bent up to her chest and her pussy on display for me.

I stepped away and looked at my handiwork. Avery was completely at my mercy. It made my cock throb, seeing her trussed up. I walked over to her bedside tables and flicked the lamps on before turning out the main light. I preferred to have more intimate lighting for this.

"Tonight, princess, you will keep your mouth shut and take what I'm giving you. Do you understand?"

Her doe eyes met mine. I was sure she didn't know whether to be terrified or aroused.

"I understand," she whispered.

"Good."

I made sure to stand in her eye-line as I took my clothes off slowly, wanting to savour every moment she had to wait for me. Her eyes never left mine.

I left my boxers on and went over to one of her cupboards. I pulled out a scarf and brought it over to her.

"Open your mouth."

She did as I asked. I made her bite down on it whilst I secured it around the back of her head. I probably should've stopped this and let her out immediately, but I couldn't. I had to remind Avery exactly who she belonged to. Exactly who's cock she craved inside her every night.

"Are you ready, princess? There'll be no safe words or mercy tonight."

She didn't try to speak, just stared at me with fear in her eyes. And as fucked up as it was, her fear fed the darkness inside me.

I knelt on the bed and pressed her legs open further. Fuck. She looked so fucking sexy, it hurt. My cock throbbed, aching to be balls deep in her tight, wet pussy. Except I wasn't just going to take her pussy tonight. I'd already had her mouth, so that left only one other place. I'd savour every fucking moment.

I stroked my cock through my boxers.

"Mmm, do you want to see how fucking hard I am for you? Want to see what I'm going to fuck you with, princess?"

If she could've responded, I'm sure she would've told me to stop, but she didn't. Despite her fear, there was also desire in her expression. She craved my control. Craved what I gave her. She wanted to be tied up on the bed and fucked hard.

I pulled my boxers down, kicking them away before tugging her up onto my knees by the harness. I rubbed my cock over her pussy. I looked down at her sweet spot and felt how wet she was for me.

"You like that, don't you? So fucking wet even though you're scared of what I'm going to do. Scared of how hard I'm going to fuck you. You should be. You might not be able to walk after we're done this evening."

I thrust inside her up to the hilt without giving her any time to adjust, grunting at how tightly she gripped me. A muffled yelp sounded from behind the scarf.

"That's it, princess. Take my cock."

I held onto her hips and fucked her. There was no gentleness to my thrusts. I slammed into her over and over again, feeling her contract around me with every stroke. Fuck. She felt amazing.

"Do you want me to fuck you harder? I think you do. You want me to fuck you until you're crying because it feels so good."

Her muffled moans fed me. I gripped the harness at her thighs as an anchor, pulling her into me as I fucked her with deep, hard strokes. Our eyes locked. Hers told me she was enjoying it. They screamed at me to fuck her ruthlessly.

"You're mine, Avery. You hear me? Mine. You belong to me and only me. You come when I say you fucking come. And you'll only fucking come on my cock, my fingers and my tongue."

She nodded as best she could, moaning into the makeshift gag. This felt so fucking good. Having control of her made me feel right again. Things had become so messed up and I needed to find balance. This was the only way I knew how. The bedroom was the place I had full control. She'd granted it to me.

I slowed and pulled out of her, shifting off the bed. As sweet as her pussy felt, I wanted what I'd had on New Year's. I wanted anal and she was going to fucking give it to me. I'd been patient with her. My patience was shot to pieces. All of it went up in flames the moment she told me about her and James.

I tugged the lube out my bag and brought it back over to the bed. She stared at me when I flipped open the cap and spread it over my fingers.

"That's right, princess. I'm having you here tonight."

I pressed one finger inside her. The heat and tightness made my cock throb restlessly. Then she tried to talk, the noises she made muffled. She struggled against the bonds she was in.

"No? I told you. You're taking what I give you tonight. You want to disobey me?"

She didn't stop moving, but I'd tied her up too tight for her to escape. She grunted when I pressed another finger inside her.

"I want to see your face as I plunge inside you and you come all over my cock. I didn't get to see how you came apart last time, so yes, princess, you're going to let me fuck you here. It'll feel good when I'm in there, you know it will. You loved it. Don't fucking try to deny it."

Three fingers worked inside her. Her eyes bugged out and she moaned, going still before she rocked into my fingers.

"That's it, good girl."

I made sure to open her up as best I could before I slicked my cock up. It was still wet from her arousal, but that wouldn't be enough. I lined myself up and pressed against her entrance. Her face scrunched up as the head sunk in. I groaned. Fuck, so tight. Even though I'd only had her here once before, I fucking missed it. Missed the way she clenched around me. Missed the heat.

"Fuck, being inside you is torture of the best fucking kind, princess."

I didn't wait for her to give me any sort of response. I thrust a little deeper. Her face was still scrunched up. I knew it was hurting her. I just couldn't stop. I had to have her. Had to be balls deep. I couldn't fucking hold back my needs any longer. No matter how precious Avery was to me. No matter how much I loved her. I was still a fucking slave to my desires. My sick and twisted needs.

What kind of man tied his girlfriend up without asking her if it was okay and then made sure she couldn't talk or fight back?

I'd tried to prepare her beforehand but being in her drove me fucking crazy. She knew what being with me entailed. I'd fucking warned her enough times and she'd pushed to be with me anyway. She knew I'd need the restraints. Need to take things from her she wasn't ready to give.

I thrust into her again, making her take more. Her eyes opened. Tears welled in them, but even that wasn't enough to make me stop. I couldn't even say fucking sorry because I wasn't sorry at all.

"It'll feel better in a bit, I promise."

She gave me one sharp nod. The relief I felt was fucking palpable. Avery wasn't mad at me for what I was doing to her. She wasn't upset. I'd make her come to make up for all this shit I subjected her to. I'd give her the same level of pleasure she'd had before when she'd begged me not to stop.

I pulled back and started to build a steady rhythm, trying not to go too deep too soon. I was determined she'd enjoy it as much as I was. I gripped one side of the harness at her thighs, keeping her steady as I fucked her. And when Avery moaned, it was like fucking music to my ears even though it was muffled by the scarf.

"You want more, princess? You love this as much as last time?"

She nodded, wriggling against me despite the restraints holding her in place. Her hands flexed at her sides. My other hand went to her clit. I circled it with my thumb. She jerked, moaning again. Her body begged for more. So I gave her more. I pressed deeper and harder.

"I want you to come for me. It's so fucking hot seeing you take it. I'm almost balls fucking deep. I can't fucking believe how well you're doing. That's it, come for me, Avery. Come."

I was getting far too close to the edge. She felt so good and her tightness almost fucking killed me. I couldn't hold back for long. The pulsating need to coat her insides with my cum was almost fucking unbearable.

One final thrust and I bottomed out, fully seated inside her. She was stretched so obscenely on my cock and it was every-fucking-thing at that moment.

"Fuck, come for me, princess. You're so fucking amazing for taking it all."

I pulled back and thrust deep again. The need to come was killing me, but she had to let go first. I strummed her clit faster. Her hands jerked against the restraints, her head rolling to the side as she moaned. I fucked her until I couldn't take it any longer.

Avery clenched around me so hard I thought I was going to fucking pass out as she came. Her screams were muffled, but loud enough for me to hear how much she loved it. And her face, she looked so fucking beautiful in that moment.

I finally let go, my cock spurting inside her, unloading all I had to give. I shuddered above her, my whole body going into spasm as the pulses washed over me. Fuck. No one had ever made me completely lose all sense of fucking reality. But she did. She fucking did.

When I finally stopped panting so hard, I reached down and untied the scarf from her mouth. She coughed and took several gulping breaths of air. I leant down and captured her mouth in a soft kiss. Pulling away, I rested my forehead against hers.

"I love you," I whispered.

"I love you too."

And I knew all was right between us.

"Was it too much?"

She shook her head, giving me a lopsided smile.

I let her out of the harness. She stretched her legs and arms out before she gingerly got to her feet. I didn't let her take a step, scooping her up in my arms and carrying her into the bathroom across the hall. She went about her business and I cleaned myself up before I carried her back to bed and tucked us both under the covers. She took off her bra and threw it off the side.

"Aiden," she whispered as I wrapped myself around her back. "Are you still mad about the James thing?"

"Yes."

I decided being honest with her was better than pretending as if everything was okay.

"Is that why you needed the restraints tonight?"

"I suppose it had something to do with it."

She wrapped her hand around one of mine.

"I haven't told him I told you. I don't want this to turn into a huge thing between the three of us. I promise I'm not keeping anything else from you."

I clutched her tighter.

"I'm trying to be okay with all this, Avery. I'm not annoyed it happened, but I am pissed off with you keeping it from me. I'm especially fucked off with the way you decided to tell me."

I felt her tremble in my hold.

"I'm sorry. I'm so, so sorry."

I kissed her shoulder.

"Shh, I know you are."

"I want to make it up to you."

I almost sighed. She didn't need to do anything of the sort. This was my fucking shit to deal with and I would. I had to get over it, especially after all I'd done to her.

"No, you don't need to do that. We'll be fine. Just give me some time."

I kissed her shoulder again, my lips trailing up her neck. She arched against me, turning her face. I kissed her properly, nipping at her bottom lip. Even though I'd come twice that evening already, I wanted her again. I reached between her thighs and stroked her clit. I didn't think I'd ever be sated when it came to her.

My princess.

She was the fucking one for me.

The only one.

That girl had my heart and my soul in the palm of her hand.

And I wasn't going to mess it up this time.

There's a funny thing about good intentions.

Sometimes, they weren't enough.

Sometimes, the world was just determined to shit all over you.

And that's exactly what it did to Avery and me.

Chapter Eleven

Avery

I sat holding the pen over the dotted line. At the conference table in front of me, the five members of the board sat. All but Mrs Sophia Anderson were male. Their eyes were turned my way. I swallowed. I was going to be the owner of my father's company. Whilst the board took charge of most of the day to day work, I'd have the final say when it came to all the important decision making. A concept which terrified me.

I pressed pen to paper, signing my name on several documents.

It was official.

I owned my father's business.

"Congratulations, Miss Daniels," Mike Manning said.

He was another of my father's close friends who'd been elected to the board ten years ago. He was a stout man with an idiotic twiddly moustache.

We'd already spent the past hour discussing business with each other. Well, I'd sat listening because I didn't have much to add. I didn't want to seem like I was stepping on anyone's toes. Thankfully, they'd agreed to Ed's appointment. I was going to text him after the meeting to let him know.

Mike stood and collected up the papers I'd signed, giving me a nod. The meeting was over. It was merely a formality, the signing of the documents. I shook hands with each member, who left one by one. Mike stayed in the conference room.

"I do hope you don't mind me saying I think you'll do just fine, Miss Daniels."

I smiled at him.

"Please, call me Avery. And thank you."

He smiled back and nodded at me again. I walked out, intending to go back to my office. I was pulling my phone out of my pocket when I bumped into someone coming out of the lift.

"Oh, sorry," I said, looking up and stopping in my tracks.

Standing there with his dark hair slicked back, mud brown eyes appraising me with no small amount of disdain was Tristan Shaw. I fought back the urge to hurl an insult at him for merely being alive. I took a step back, needing to be away from him.

"Hello Avery."

His voice grated on my ears. He sounded like a stuck up posh twat. I took a deep breath.

"Hello Tristan. What brings you here?"

His lips curved up into a cruel smile.

"Why, I'm here to collect copies of the handover documents for my father."

I should've known Frazier would send him here just to taunt me. He knew exactly how much I hated his son. The two of them made me sick.

I waved at the door I'd just come out of.

"Mr Manning has them. It's nice to see you, but if you excuse me, I have a lot to get on with."

I didn't give him a chance to respond. I walked away and shoved open the door to the ladies. I planted both hands on the sink counter, staring at myself in the mirror. Tristan being here rattled me. I didn't want to go back out there.

The door to the bathroom opened. I straightened, looking over at it expecting to see another woman. Instead, the man I wanted to avoid strode towards me. I tried to back away, but he caught me and pressed me up against the counter.

"Running away from me, Avery?"

There was a deadly note to his voice. I trembled, unable to keep my limbs locked in place.

"What do you want?"

Tristan's cruel smile made the hairs on the back of my neck stick up.

"I want what's owed to me."

What's owed to him? What the fuck does that mean?

I must've looked confused because he continued.

"You were promised to me. I intend to make you suffer for telling your father you wouldn't have me."

I swallowed, my skin suddenly clammy. My pulse skittered as the fear took hold. I was alone with Tristan and he was fucking crazy. I wasn't promised to him. I owed him nothing.

"Get off me."

I put my hands up, shoving him away from me, but he didn't budge. He took both my hands and pinned them down on the counter behind me. I struggled in his grip. He'd wedged me against the counter, his body flush with mine and a knee in between my legs so I couldn't even kick him in the balls if I wanted to.

"Now, I expected you to fight back, but you'll soon learn that's useless. I'll take what I want from you whether you like it or not."

"Get the fuck off me, Tristan."

He leant down, running his nose up my neck. It made my skin crawl.

"Mmm, your fear smells so sweet."

"Stop it, let me go."

I struggled again, but it was completely useless. I wasn't strong enough to fight him off or get out of his grasp. Panic set in. Was Tristan going to rape me in the bathroom of my own office? The thought of it made my limbs lock up. Tears pricked at the corners of my eyes.

No, no, no, no, no. This can't be happening.

His lips trailed up my neck, replacing his nose. I swallowed, trying to breathe air into my lungs. My body prickled all over and not in a good way. I felt sick to my stomach, nausea coiling around me like a vice.

"Stop it, please. I don't want this."

"I don't care," he whispered against my skin.

I shuddered, feeling trapped and claustrophobic with him pressed up against me. And I could feel his semi pressing into my thigh. This was the complete opposite of what my boyfriend made me feel when he restrained me.

Aiden.

My heart shattered. I couldn't stand the thought of what this would do to him, but I knew for a fact, Tristan wouldn't survive long. His words rang in my ears.

"If anyone else tries to put their dick in you, I will put a bullet in their head."

And Aiden really would. He'd fuck Tristan up beyond recognition and then put him down like a dog just for putting hands on me. It should terrify me. The knowledge that my boyfriend was a killer should send me running for the hills. It didn't. I loved Aiden. Faults and all. I loved that man with every breath I took. The force of my emotions overwhelmed me.

"You don't want to do this. Please, just let me go."

Tristan ignored me. He shoved both my hands behind me and pinned them down with one hand. The other curled around my neck. He stared down at me, his intent clear on his face. He was going to hurt me.

"Oh, I think you'll find I do. I've waited a long time to have my hands on you. Your disappearing act did you no favours. Poor little Avery Daniels with her murdered parents and her sad pathetic cry for help."

"Fuck you," I hissed, feeling his fingers tighten around my throat.

He leant closer to me, his mouth brushing over my jaw.

"No, Avery. I'm going to fuck you," he whispered.

I snapped. I bucked against him wildly, trying to dislodge him. His grip on me tightened further, but I didn't let up. I screamed. His hand left my throat and clamped around my mouth, sealing away my voice.

149

"Shut the fuck up you little bitch."

I didn't stop struggling. I wasn't going to let him rape me. He wouldn't have an easy target here. The last thing I wanted was his dick anywhere near me. The thought of it made me feel sick all over again.

"Christ, you really are a fucking little feisty cunt, aren't you? I'm going to enjoy breaking you."

I screamed against his hand. He could call me all the names under the sun. I didn't give a fuck. All I wanted was to be away from him. I hated the feeling of his body pressed against mine. Hated everything about him. I was so focused on trying to get away from him, I barely heard the bathroom door open.

Tristan was ripped away from me and slammed up against the wall opposite the door. I gulped down oxygen into my lungs, feeling disorientated and confused. I gripped the counter, holding myself up.

When I looked over at the two men by the door, my heart did a backflip in my chest. I couldn't believe my eyes.

Aiden.

He had Tristan by the throat, his fingers digging in.

"I don't think Miss Daniels appreciates being manhandled, do you, Tristan?" Aiden said, his voice brimming with barely concealed rage.

Tristan glared at him.

"What the fuck are you doing here, Aiden?"

"Visiting our good friend, Chuck. Now, are you going to apologise to Miss Daniels for your behaviour?"

Tristan was silent for a moment before he nodded. Aiden let him go, taking a step back. He didn't look at me. I didn't know what the hell to make of what just happened. All I knew is I couldn't let on that we knew each other.

Tristan straightened his suit, trying to maintain his composure. He looked between us.

"Do you know your saviour here?"

He pointed at Aiden. I shook my head. He stepped around Aiden and walked over to me.

"I'm sure he can make those introductions himself. My apologies, Avery. I'll be on my way now."

I didn't say anything. The disdain dripping from his voice put this in the top ten least genuine apologies of all time. His eyes told me so. He hated me with every inch of his being. And if I was ever alone with him again, he'd punish me for this.

Aiden's reaction to the whole thing confused me. He hadn't ripped Tristan a new one nor had he even glanced at me. I couldn't see his face and it really bothered me. I thought he'd be so pissed off, he wouldn't be able to control his anger.

Tristan left the bathroom. I took a steadying breath. The tension in the air didn't dissipate. If anything, it ramped up a notch. What could I say? I'd been stupid enough to think Tristan wouldn't follow me into the bathroom. I blamed myself for this situation even though it wasn't strictly my fault. I didn't ask for it.

"Are you okay?" he asked finally.

"No."

He didn't turn around and I couldn't move.

"I'm not okay at all."

He paced over to the cubicles and opened one of the doors. He waited outside it with his hand on the door. I took a shaky step towards it and then another. I didn't trust myself or my legs. My movements were jerky as I stepped through the doorway. He walked in behind me, shut the door and locked it.

I turned around and looked up at him in the confined space. Aiden's grey eyes were dark with anger. And there was something else in his expression which chilled me to my very bones. Helplessness.

I let out a small sob before bundling myself up into his arms and crying into his chest. He rested his cheek against my hair, stroking my back.

"Shh, it's okay. I've got you," he whispered.

"How did you know?" I sobbed.

"I heard your scream when I was walking to Chuck's office. I know that scream anywhere."

I didn't know whether to feel comforted by that fact or not.

"Princess, I have to go or it will look suspicious. Okay?"

I pulled away from him.

"Okay," I sniffled.

He leant down and kissed my forehead, wiping under my eyes with his thumb. He unlocked the cubicle door and let himself out. I heard the bathroom door slam behind him.

Everything happened so suddenly, I barely had time to process any of it. I put the toilet lid down and sat, kicking the door shut. I pulled out some toilet paper and dabbed my eyes. I probably looked like a complete fucking mess.

The reality of what occurred crashed down on me. If Aiden hadn't come in when he did, Tristan would've raped me. I was sure of it. Raped me in my own fucking building.

He would've been cruel and made it hurt. It wouldn't hurt in the good way either. Not the way Aiden fucked me so brutally, it blurred the lines between pleasure and pain. The difference? I wanted Aiden and I most definitely did not want Tristan. The whole thing was completely batshit crazy on so many levels.

I couldn't stay hiding in a toilet cubicle all day. I stood, smoothing down my skirt and walked out. I went to the sinks and sorted out my messy face. My eyes were bloodshot, but there wasn't much I could do about that. Chucking the tissues in the bin, I washed my hands and left.

Thankfully, I didn't see anyone on the way to my office. I breathed a sigh of relief when I strode in and shut the door behind me. Except my office wasn't empty. Uncle Charlie was sitting on one of the chairs in front of my desk and Aiden was leant up against one of the bookshelves. I blinked rapidly, trying to compose myself all over again.

Uncle Charlie turned and smiled at me, although it didn't meet his eyes.

"There you are. How did the board meeting go?" he said.

I stared at him before realising he'd asked me a question. I shook myself and began walking around my desk, trying to ignore the fact that Aiden was right there.

"Fine. The paperwork is complete which means the company is officially mine. They agreed with Ed's appointment. Clara can speak to HR."

I sat down, facing my uncle. His eyes flicked over to Aiden for a moment.

"I'm pleased to hear it. I'd like to introduce you to someone." He waved at my boyfriend. "This is Aiden

Lockhart. He looks after the company security amongst other things."

I sent a cursory glance his way.

"Nice to meet you, Mr Lockhart."

"Miss Daniels," he replied.

I wondered why my uncle was introducing me to Aiden. My skin prickled. This felt wrong. Was he trying to test us? Did he know we already knew each other? I had too many questions.

"I heard there was an altercation between you and Tristan Shaw," my uncle said.

And there it was. My heart sank. I didn't really want to talk about what happened in the toilets. Why had Aiden mentioned it to my uncle?

"It was a simple misunderstanding."

Uncle Charlie pressed his fingers together.

"Even so, I worry about you, Avery. You're still young and people might take advantage of that fact."

What is his point?

"I think you should have someone with you for your own protection."

I stared at him. Was he seriously suggesting I should have a bodyguard? I didn't need babysitting.

"Is that what he's here for?" I asked before I could stop myself.

My uncle looked at Aiden again, frowning.

"No… Although, perhaps…"

I sat up straighter. Uncle Charlie was out of his mind. I wasn't going to let him put Aiden in charge of looking after me. That was a sure fire way to fuck everything up completely.

How could we keep our relationship a secret and how on earth could Aiden work from behind the scenes if he was stuck with me twenty-four seven?

"I don't need protection, Uncle Charlie. What happened with Tristan won't happen again."

Except I knew it would. He wasn't going to stop now he'd made his intentions clear. I'd have to deal with that outside of the office.

"What about the paparazzi camped outside the office and all the rumours circulating about your involvement in your parents' deaths?"

I rubbed my forehead. I had seen those and ignored them. It was just idiotic speculation and would die down when the next celebrity scandal broke. It was part and parcel of being in the public eye.

"What about them? I've been having Davis drive me to and from work each day. I'm not scared of a bunch of conspiracy theorists making up crap about me from behind their computer screens."

I didn't dare look at Aiden. What did he even think about all this? It's not like I could come out and ask him. I really wished he wasn't in the room right now. This conversation wasn't going the way I wanted it to.

"These things can escalate."

I rolled my eyes, folding my arms across my chest. My uncle was full of shit. He just wanted to keep tabs on me.

"What happened to Mum and Dad has nothing to do with me. If there's something you're not telling me then I'm all ears, otherwise, I don't need a bodyguard."

My uncle eyed Aiden again. I was getting nervous now. My skin was sticking to my blouse.

"I disagree."

I sighed, leaning forward and placing my hands on the desk.

"I appreciate your concern for my safety. I will think about it."

My uncle nodded slowly. I thought the conversation might be over, but he didn't move to get up. I waited, tapping my foot against the floor.

"Aiden has some proposed changes to our security systems. I thought he could speak to you about them."

I looked over at Aiden then. He seemed nonplussed by my uncle's announcement.

"To me? Why? Isn't that your department?"

"Don't you want to get to know the company better?"

Now I was sure my uncle was testing me. *Prick.* Fine, I would play his games. I smiled at him.

"Well yes, I do. Is now acceptable? I've got to speak to Ed, but it can wait."

Aiden shoved off the bookcase and walked over to my desk. He placed a tablet down on it and looked at my uncle.

"Are you staying?" he asked.

Uncle Charlie bounced his hands on the chair and stood up. His smile made my skin crawl.

"No, no, I have things to do. I'm sure Avery can approve these if she wishes."

He strolled out of the room without another word, leaving my office door open.

"What the fuck is going on?" I hissed at Aiden.

"Fuck knows," he whispered back.

If Aiden didn't know what was happening then this was really fucked up.

"Do you want to sit?" I said, louder.

I got up from the desk, walked over to my office door and shut it. I leant against it, staring at my boyfriend with wide eyes. He indicated with his head that I should come back over.

When I sat back down, he leant over the desk and started showing me the new security system he was thinking of having installed.

"Chuck asked me to look into the latest technology, which I've done. It's an expensive bit of kit, but it will make my job easier and give you and the company peace of mind."

I looked down at what he was showing me. I wasn't quite sure what exactly I was looking at, but I was sure he'd explain it to me. I scrolled down at the financials. Expensive, but if Aiden thought this would help, then I was all for it.

He went through the whole proposal with me. Neither of us mentioned the elephant in the room. There were cameras in here so we couldn't exactly talk about anything other than company business.

"You're very meticulous," I said, sitting back.

He raised an eyebrow at me, a small smile playing on his lips as if to say, 'did you really expect anything else from me?', to which I shrugged. Of course I didn't. Aiden could be very regimented in the way he dealt with things like work. I knew he'd have gone over every detail and left nothing out.

"There are other less expensive options, but Chuck usually insists on the best and leaves the details to me."

"Do I need to sign off on anything to get this approved?"

He took the tablet and scrolled through it before handing it to me. There was a box for my signature. I swiped over the screen, signing the necessary documentation digitally.

"Is that everything?" I asked.

He nodded, taking the tablet and standing.

"Thank you for your time, Miss Daniels."

I really fucking wished I could do more than just smile at him. Aiden and I had too much to discuss. I was itching for the day to be over. We'd decided to split our time between our respective places. During the week, it'd be my flat and his at the weekends. I hated being at mine, but until we got my uncle off our backs, it was necessary.

"I'm sure I will see you around," I replied.

He nodded at me once before turning and leaving. Barely thirty seconds after he was out the door, my phone buzzed.

AIDEN: I love you princess.

My heart flipped in my chest. Even though we'd been through a whole bunch of crap today, he still managed to make everything okay. And I loved him all the more for it. Aiden might be a little unhinged and did questionable things at times, but he gave me something no one else had. Freedom to be myself.

ME: Today sucks.

AIDEN: Tristan is a dead man walking.

ME: And here I thought you were old friends.

AIDEN: Ha fucking ha. I'll talk to you later.

I smiled, leaning back in my chair and remembering there was someone else I needed to speak to. I scrolled through my contacts and hit dial.

"Hi Ed, you got time to talk?"

Chapter Twelve

Aiden

What the fuck was Chuck's game? I couldn't work it out. I'd only mentioned there'd been some kind of altercation between Avery and Tristan because he'd questioned why I'd been late. I was too worked up about it not to say anything. That fucking worthless piece of shit was on thin ice. Son of a fucking bitch. I almost lost my mind when I found him pinning my fucking woman to the sinks.

Tristan Shaw was a dead man walking.

I was going to enjoy the moment the bullet pierced his skull, snuffing the life out of the sick motherfucking cunt.

First things first, I had to find out what the fuck his father had on Daniels Holdings. Rocking the boat was a bad idea, so I couldn't off Frazier's son quite yet. It would only arouse suspicion, especially after what happened today.

I'd got to her at the right time, but now I couldn't feign innocence and say I'd never met Avery. We'd been officially introduced and there was no fucking taking that shit back. I needed to find out what Chuck was playing at and fast. Whatever he suspected needed to be nipped in the bud.

I rubbed the back of my neck, slamming my hand down on the steering wheel as I sat in traffic. This whole thing frustrated me no end. Not having Avery right there with me. Not being able to protect her at all times drove me insane.

I'd been seriously perturbed about being called into the office in the first place, but now I was fucking glad Chuck insisted on me coming in person to go over the new security equipment. He'd tasked me with this at the beginning of the month, but it had taken me a while to do all the necessary research. Especially dealing with the fact that my girlfriend had to go back out into the real world.

My phone rang. I hit the button on the steering wheel to answer it.

"Did she approve the new plans?" Chuck asked without preamble.

Why was he ringing now?

"Yes. You didn't mention you wanted me to drop in and let you know."

"No, no. I didn't need you to. So… Aiden, I heard the police questioned you regarding an anonymous tip they had back when my niece was missing."

And there it was. He had been fucking testing us. He'd obviously found out from his informant on the force. Why it had taken so long, I had no idea, but this didn't sit well with me at all.

"Yes. It was bullshit though."

"So today really was your first introduction to Avery."

"Yes, why would you think otherwise?"

"I don't, but you can see how suspicious it looked when someone says they saw you with her."

The traffic started to move, which I was fucking glad about, but I wanted to get off the phone. This conversation was dangerous.

"My friend's wife looks a little like her. Mistaken identity. Did Ethan tell you about this?"

"Ethan? No, he's been reassigned to another case now Avery is back. Anyway, I have some more work for you. I'll send you the details."

He hung up without letting me respond. What the fuck? If he didn't get the information from Ethan, then who the hell else would know? He didn't have any other informants on the force. It made absolutely no sense.

Unless...

Who was the anonymous tip? My skin prickled. Had Chuck got someone to follow me around? He'd been acting suspiciously when he'd come over that time, asking questions about if I knew who'd killed Mitchell and Kathleen. I couldn't shake the feeling now I thought about it. There was only one person Chuck would get to fucking follow me.

John.

I needed a word and I knew exactly where I'd find him. I turned off at the next junction and made my way across the city. Thankfully there was less traffic. I parked up a couple of streets over and walked the rest of the way. Dusk had already fallen and it was close to the time she'd be on her way home, so if he was here, then now would be the best time to ambush him.

I found his car parked a little way down from Avery's house. Rapping on the window, John looked up at me, eyes wide. He was in his late forties, bald head with a shit ton of tattoos. John wasn't a man you messed with, but he wouldn't fuck with me either.

I opened the passenger door and got in.

"Aiden, what are you doing here?" he asked.

"Chuck had you follow me around for a while, did he not?"

John had the decency to look away, his green eyes darkening.

"He should know better than to keep shit from you," he muttered.

"Were you the anonymous tip?"

"Yes."

"Why didn't you press the police further about it when I provided them with a plausible explanation?"

He drummed his fingers on the steering wheel for a moment.

"I told them I must've been mistaken, but I wasn't. I know it was her. Just like I know you've been in and out of her place since she moved back in here."

"Does Chuck know?"

"No."

John had always been loyal to Chuck. I wasn't quite sure what to make of this. The fact that he'd cover anything up for me came as a surprise. I waited, wanting to know if he'd give me an explanation.

He sighed, looking over at me.

"I'm not going to tell him about you and Avery."

"You going to tell me why not or do I have to guess?"

He shook his head.

"Whatever is going on between you and Avery is none of my business. Just take care of her. I watched that girl grow up into the young woman she is today. She deserves better than the shit her family is involved in. I really don't care how you two know each other or why you're keeping it from Chuck."

I had no idea what to say. I stared ahead at the car parked in front of us.

"You've had a shit hand dealt to you, Aiden. I don't wish to add to that after what they did to you and your mother."

My heart tightened at the mention of her. I still hadn't told Avery who I suspected had murdered her. I wasn't sure I ever could.

"You know about that."

"I was young back then. The old man got me in with the Daniels. Bad business. Very bad business. Nick was furious with Mitchell. He didn't know about the late night visits until after everything went south."

This was news to me. I didn't know John had been in their employ for so long. Perhaps I could learn more if he was willing to share. I didn't want to push my luck. He was already doing me a huge favour by not telling Chuck about Avery and me.

"How much longer is Chuck planning on having you watch her?"

He shrugged.

"Beats me. I've had nothing to report to him. Why do you ask?"

"She prefers not to stay here is all, but neither of us wanted Chuck to get suspicious."

He gave me a nod and a knowing smile. Talking openly about my relationship with her wasn't easy for me. Especially not to someone who could turn us into Chuck at any time.

"I'll see what I can do. I'd rather not have to sit out here every evening, especially when I know nothing will happen to her with you around."

"Thanks… for everything."

My phone rang. I checked it. It was her.

"I have to take this. Just let me know when he decides to put you to better use."

John gave me a nod. I got out of the car and answered the phone.

"Princess, you on your way home?"

"Someone is following us," she said, her voice sounding panicked.

"What?"

"Davis thinks someone is following us. I don't know what to do. I'm scared."

I started walking towards my car. I needed to get to her as soon as possible.

"What does the car look like?"

"It's a Range Rover, tinted windows from what we can make out."

She rattled off the number plate for me. It could be anyone. I didn't have time to search for the plate. I walked faster, needing to get back to my car and on the road.

"You can't go back to yours and you certainly can't go to mine."

Where could she go? I wasn't about to send her off to one of her family members where I couldn't get to her. It hit me. There was somewhere, but it also meant an extremely awkward situation for the three of us. I didn't see another option.

"Tell Davis to take you to James'. Call him and tell him to wait outside the building for you, okay, princess?"

"Are you sure that's a good idea?"

"It's the only idea I have right now. I'll meet you there."

She was silent for a long moment.

"Okay. Please be quick. I don't feel safe without you."

Her words were like a fucking dropkick to the heart. Not being there to protect her, keep her safe, that was the absolute fucking worst. The fear in her voice. The need. All of it ruined me. I hated this fucking situation we were in. Despised us being apart. It had been so much easier when I knew she was safe in my flat and no one knew where she was. Except keeping her there wasn't fair on Avery.

"I know, princess. I'm getting in the car now, okay? I love you. Call James."

"I love you too."

She hung up. I reached the car, ripping open the door and getting in. I revved the engine as I pulled out. I had no idea how far she was from James' but I had to get there as soon as I possibly could.

Why the fuck would someone be following her? I knew there were some crazies out there, but this took the fucking piss. I didn't think it was the Shaws because Tristan and Frazier wouldn't be that stupid. Could it be the paparazzi?

I almost growled. This whole thing set me on edge. All I could think about was getting to her. Holding her. Keeping her safe. That was my fucking responsibility. I had to do everything in my power to make sure my girl wasn't in harm's way.

I drove like the fucking devil despite the traffic. I screeched into a car park nearby and set off at a jog, checking my phone. She hadn't messaged me. It concerned me. I didn't have time for this. I got into his street and eyed the road. There didn't seem to be anyone stopped near his building or any suspicious looking cars or people about.

I reached the building and pressed the number for James' flat. A moment later, the door buzzed. I ripped it open and slammed it shut behind me just in case someone tried to get in. I didn't wait for the lift. I jogged up the stairs and was knocking on his door two minutes later.

The door cracked open, James eyed me warily before closing it and taking it off the latch.

"Where is she?" I asked, barging into his flat.

I hadn't been here before, but I didn't care about that.

"Aiden?" Avery's voice filtered through from a room next to the hallway.

I strode towards the sound and found her in the living room. Her doe eyes filled with tears. She rushed over to me, burying herself in my chest. I stroked her hair and kissed the top of her head.

"Princess," I whispered.

The relief I felt at having her right there almost fucking killed me.

"Well hello to you too," James said as he walked in.

I ignored him, focusing on my girl. She trembled, her limbs shaking as she clutched me.

"What happened?" I asked.

When Avery didn't answer, James did instead.

"Well, she ran out of the car as soon as it stopped. The other car pulled up and some seriously scary looking blokes got out, but we were through the door before they had a chance to get anywhere near us. Davis was out of there like a shot."

"Did you get a good look at any of the men?"

"No, I was too busy trying to make sure Avery was safe."

I nodded. So it wasn't the paparazzi. It most definitely wasn't someone hired by the Shaws as that wasn't their style. Who the fuck could it be? Why the hell would someone send a bunch of guys after Avery?

"I think we need to stay here. Getting her out now is too much of a risk."

James eyed the two of us. Avery looked up at me finally. Her eyes were wide with fear.

"James only has one bedroom," she said.

"The sofa pulls out," he said with a shrug. "I mean obviously you two are always welcome to stay here."

I didn't really care where we slept, just that my girl was safe and in my arms. The tension in the air wasn't helping matters though. Neither of us had seen him since she'd admitted to me about them sleeping together before we met.

"Thanks."

I looked down at Avery. She wasn't trembling so hard any longer, but her doe eyes spoke volumes. Today had been taxing for her.

"Come on, princess."

She let me take her over to the sofa and sit her down. I squatted by her feet and slipped off her heels for her, setting them next to the sofa. I put a hand on her knee, rubbing it.

"How are you feeling?" I asked, my voice low.

"Like everything has gone to shit."

I looked up at James.

"Do you have something she can change into?"

He nodded and shuffled out of the room. Pressing her legs open, I knelt between them and tugged her towards me, cupping her face.

"We haven't talked about what he did."

"I don't want to."

"Avery…"

"He was going to rape me, Aiden. I could see it in his eyes. If you hadn't been there…"

Tears welled in her eyes. I stroked her cheek. I didn't want to think about what would've happened if I hadn't been there. If that sick fuck raped my girlfriend, he wouldn't have walked out of that building alive. Fuck the consequences. I would've killed him on the spot.

"I was there and he didn't."

"It was horrible. He was saying all sorts of crazy things like I owed him and he was going to punish me for telling my dad I wouldn't marry him. I was terrified he'd go through with it. He'd have made it hurt. I couldn't stand it."

If keeping Tristan alive for now wasn't so fucking important, I'd go around there right now and beat the shit out of him. I'd fuck him up so badly, he'd be unrecognisable. Tension rippled through me, rage flooding my veins. I wasn't into inflicting pain, but fuck if I didn't want to make it hurt before I snuffed his life out.

"I'll put him in the fucking ground for this."

"Put who in the ground?"

I looked up, finding James standing in the doorway with a bundle of clothes in his arms.

Well fuck.

Avery looked behind us, her eyes going wide.

"No one. It was just a figure of speech, wasn't it, Aiden?"

James came further into the room, eyebrow raised.

"And I'm the fucking pope. Who are you talking about?"

She looked at me. I gave her a nod.

"Tristan."

"What did that cunt do?"

At least he wasn't under any illusions about Tristan Shaw. I knew from Avery the three of them went to the same school.

"He pinned Avery to the sinks in the toilets earlier today," I said. "I stopped him before he could do anything to her, but only because I had a meeting with Chuck."

James dropped the clothes on the sofa. His expression turned dark.

"Seriously? Why didn't you tell me, Ave?"

She turned back to me, her eyes filling with tears again. For fuck's sake, she really was in a state today. I blamed the Shaws and whoever else was after her. I wrapped my arms around her and pulled her into my chest. She let out a pitiful sob. My heart cracked at the sound.

"Shh, it's okay, princess," I whispered.

Turning my head up towards James, I gave him a dark look.

"I'll talk to you about it later," I told him.

He gave me an apologetic look, shuffling on his feet.

"I'll just go see what I have in the kitchen for dinner," he said.

He retreated from the room.

"I'm not hungry," Avery sobbed into my chest.

I stroked her back.

"I know, but you need to eat. Here, James brought you something more comfortable to wear. Do you want me to help you change?"

She nodded against my chest. She pulled away, her face tear streaked. I unbuttoned her blouse, tugging it off her shoulders. I helped her out of her bra and put on the t-shirt James had left along with a jumper, both of which swamped her small frame. I unbuttoned her trousers and pulled them off her before helping her into jogging bottoms. I folded her clothes up and placed them on the side table next to the sofa.

"Do you feel a bit more comfortable now?" I asked.

She nodded. I picked up a blanket which was lying over the back of the sofa and wrapped it around her. I gave her the remote from the coffee table.

"Why don't you find something for us to watch whilst I go talk to James?"

"Okay," she sniffled.

I wiped her face with my coat sleeve and gave her a kiss on the forehead. She tipped her face up to me before I got up. I kissed her lips, careful to be soft and gentle with her. Avery didn't need rough right now. She needed me to look after her. I was fucking glad it was Friday because if she had to go to work tomorrow, I'd have lost my shit.

I pulled my coat off and went through into the hall. I hung it up behind the front door where James' coats were and found him in the kitchen. I leant against the doorframe, eying him warily.

170

"Is she okay?" he asked.

"Not really. I can cook if you want unless you don't have anything."

He sighed, running a hand through his hair.

"Well, I wasn't exactly expecting you guys to show up here. I've been meaning to go shopping."

I whipped out my phone, pulling up an app and searching through it for a nearby takeaway.

"Pizza okay?"

"Sure. I'm not fussy."

I ordered us two large pizzas along with sides and a bottle of coke, checking with him about toppings. I was well aware of what my girl preferred.

"It'll be here in half an hour," I said.

He turned to me and leant against the counter.

"What is going on, Aiden?"

"With those guys who were after her? I have no fucking idea. It's not Frazier. Not his style. Chuck is all but insisting on her having a bodyguard so it can't be him either. I can't think who else would have their eye on her."

"And with Tristan?"

I folded my arms across my chest.

"I think you know what he would've done if I hadn't been there."

James looked at the floor, his blue eyes dark with anger.

"In her own fucking building. No wonder she's traumatised."

That was one word for it. I should really get back to her, but me and him needed to have it out. If I was ever going to get over what happened between them, then James and I should come to an understanding.

"I'll take care of her."

I shifted, dropping my arms to my sides, trying not to let my emotions show. Being around him didn't do me any favours.

"Hasn't she been through enough already? I get why she needs to deal with the shit her family is involved in, but surely there's a better way."

A way that didn't involve getting our hands dirty is what he meant. We were in too deep for that now. No one was coming out of this unscathed. This was war. War is messy and takes no prisoners. So no, there wasn't a better way.

"This is how it has to be."

He didn't reply, eying me with no small amount of trepidation. Now or never. I took a breath.

"Avery told me what went on between you two before I met her."

His face paled and he looked away. She wouldn't have lied to me about it, but this just confirmed the truth.

"Look, I'm not mad. It is what it is, but I have a question for you," I continued.

"And that is?"

"Are you in love with her?"

I didn't really want to know the answer, but I had to ask. Boundaries needed to be established and the only way we could do that is by having the truth out in the open.

He fidgeted under my gaze and I knew.

"No... I mean yes... Fuck. It's not like how you think. I love her like she's my family, like my sister. That sounds really fucking wrong given what happened, but it's the only way I can describe it. I'm not in love with her romantically and even if I did feel that way at one point, it's in the past. We promised each other we'd never let it get in the way of our friendship."

He rubbed the back of his neck.

"You do realise you're like her entire world, right? The way she talks about you, there's a light that comes on in her eyes. She loves you, I mean like really loves you. I think she'd follow you to the ends of the earth if you asked her to. So whatever it is you think about me and her, just don't. There's nothing between us and there never will be. I mean, you should've seen her when she was getting ready to go on that date with you. I've never seen her fret so much about her appearance. I swear she was going to burst into tears at one point because she couldn't get her hair just right."

He looked up at me, giving me a shrug and a smile.

"All I want is for her to be happy. She's different with you. She's just Avery, almost as if she's left the Daniels part of her identity behind. I'm glad she finally admitted it to you though because secrets only hurt people. It wasn't my place to say anything."

Of all the things I expected he might tell me, that wasn't it. I believed her when she told me she loved me, but to have the person who knew her the best tell me just how deep her feelings ran. It caused my heart to pound in my ears. She cared for me that much. Fuck. I needed to do right by her. Now and always.

"We're good, right?" he continued. "I wouldn't really want to get on your bad side like Tristan or anything."

That made me snort.

"We're good."

And I meant it. I didn't need reassurances nothing was between them. All I wanted to know was the truth from him. I'd got that. So we were good. We had to be for Avery's sake. Not sure she would forgive me if I didn't try to get along with her friends. I knew how important James was to her. He'd been there her whole life. I couldn't get in the way of that. It might have made me fucking pissed off and jealous before, but things were different now. I was secure in the knowledge Avery was my girl. I trusted her.

"I should go be with her. I left her to pick something to watch."

James gave me a horrified look.

"You're letting her pick? Oh no. No, no, no. We need to fix this unless you want to get stuck watching cooking shows or a sappy love film."

I laughed, stepping back and going towards the living room with him following me. I'd let her watch whatever she wanted as long as it made her happy. I hated seeing her so distressed. It reminded me of when she'd been in the cell. I was never putting her back in that place again. In all honesty, I was thinking of getting rid of it completely. Reconverting it back into what it should've been, a part of the second bedroom which was currently my office.

I didn't need it any longer. It only held bad memories. I wanted to make new ones. With her. Only with her.

And I would. Avery was the world. I'd do everything in my power to keep her by my side.

Now.

And always.

Chapter Thirteen

Avery

*L*aying here curled up against Aiden's side on James'
sofa bed, I felt as though the world wouldn't stop
spinning out of control. I wished we were at home in
Aiden's bed. It's where I felt completely safe. Everywhere else
there were threats and people out to get me. Not that long ago
I had no idea how much darkness existed in the world. Now,
it's all I saw. Lurking in every corner of every room I stepped
into. Biding its time. Waiting to strike.

My hand around Aiden's waist tightened. He'd been so
good to me this evening. Making sure I had everything I could
want or need. He even stopped James complaining about
watching what he described as a 'puke inducing' romantic
comedy. I needed something to take my mind off the almost
rape and discovering a mystery person was after me.

"Can't sleep, princess?" Aiden whispered.

I shook my head, knowing he'd feel it against his skin
where I was resting on his shoulder. He shifted, his hand
coming up and stroking my cheek as he looked down at me.

"Do you need anything?"

"No. Thinking is bad but it's all I can seem to do."

I lifted my hand from his waist and traced the outline of Tezcatlipoca, the lord of the night. Aiden's tattoos still fascinated me. Such beautiful lines. Ben was so talented. I wanted a piece of his artwork on my skin. The A on my neck was only the start. I hadn't broached the subject of another tattoo with Aiden, but I was sure he'd be on board with it.

"Isn't Skye's baby due soon?" I asked.

If he was surprised by me changing the subject, he didn't show it.

"Yeah, two weeks, I think. Why do you ask?"

"I'd like to meet her and well… I want to ask Ben something."

"We'll go see them after the baby comes. What do you want to ask him?"

I should've known he'd be curious. I liked his best friend. When he'd come back to the flat with us after the tattoo session, he'd spent half the time ribbing Aiden. I loved watching them interact. It was clear as day how close they were. Brothers in arms.

I looked down at my fingers where they were still tracing the outline of his tattoo, not wanting to meet his eyes.

"I wanted to know if he could design something for me."

"You want another tattoo?"

I nodded. His fingers fell to my neck, tracing the line of the A behind my ear.

"What did you have in mind?"

I had an idea. Not just for one. I wanted a few. Perhaps discussing them all with Aiden would take my mind off the horrors of the day.

"A pair of wings on my wrist, a flock of birds across my shoulder and something else, but that's what I want to talk to Ben about. I want to see what he comes up with."

He took my hand, turning it upwards so the palm was facing him. His fingers brushed over my inner wrist, stirring my senses with his gentle touch.

"Birds for your name, right? An aviary on Avery."

I smiled. As much as I despised my parents for what they'd done, my name was something I couldn't change. I didn't want to. The more I thought about it, the more it made sense to me. The birds would represent my freedom. The freedom he'd given me.

"And wings for my angel."

I kissed his chest. He really was my angel. He might be dark and twisted, but I loved those parts of him as much as I loved the gentle, caring man he was inside. The sides of him only I got to see. Times like this when it was just me and him without any of the other bullshit going on.

He cupped my face again, tipping it up so he could kiss me. His lips were gentle, not in any way demanding like he usually was. I sighed into it, reaching up and curling my hand around his neck, drawing him closer. It was like a switch flipped. The innocent kiss turned into something else. Aiden's arm around me tightened, his hand falling from my waist to cup my behind, squeezing the flesh gently. His other hand moved from my face. He trailed his fingers down my sternum, sending sparks running up my back. Desire burnt in my veins.

I pulled away, suddenly struck by the fact we were in James' flat and fucking was not an option. The heady cocktail of lust in Aiden's grey eyes gave me heart palpitations.

177

"Not here," I whispered.

His expression cleared after a moment.

"I'm sorry, I didn't mean to... Fuck, not after what he almost did to you today."

He shifted on his side, wrapped both arms around me and held me close, kissing the top of my head.

"That's not... Aiden, that's not why. It's where we are not what he did. I'm not letting that affect anything between you and me."

He stared at me, frowning. I saw it the moment it dawned on him. His eyes widened and his arms around me tightened.

"Shit, no, you're right. I wish I'd taken you home now."

I smiled and shook my head. His grey eyes glinted in the moonlight streaming in through the gap in the curtains. He leant down, his breath hot against my ear.

"I can still make you come, princess. I just won't fuck you."

Heat flooded my core at his words. I squirmed in his grasp. I wish he'd taken me home too. Letting him do that here felt like we'd be crossing a line. I mean, I'd had sex with James in this flat for fuck's sake. I'd slept in the same bed as him on several occasions.

I was relatively sure James and Aiden had cleared the air in the kitchen because when they came back in, they were laughing and joking with each other like they were old friends. It still didn't make it right.

"You can't..."

Aiden didn't listen to me. His fingers found their way inside my underwear. I'd discarded the jogging bottoms James gave me before getting into bed. He stroked my clit, causing me to buck against him before two fingers thrust inside me.

"So wet for me," he whispered, his teeth grazing my earlobe. "I wish I could plunge my cock into your pussy right now. I want to hear you crying out my name as you clench around me."

I had to be quiet because of where we were. I couldn't help but find the whole thing incredibly dangerous and very, very wrong. Somehow that made it all the more appealing.

"Aiden," I whimpered as he found just the right spot with his fingers and pressed down.

"Mmm, that's right. Do you want my cock inside you instead of my fingers, princess?"

I could hardly breathe. His thumb brushed over my clit. The overload on my senses rendering it impossible for me to ask him to stop. I didn't want him to. The dark side of me wanted Aiden to take me right here on James' sofa. Wanted him to fuck me with brutal thrusts and treat me like I was his fuck toy. In the bedroom was the only place I wanted all of his control. Craved it. And in some fucked up way, after what happened today, having him take control was exactly what I needed.

"Please."

"Please what?"

His fingers grew more insistent, thrusting harder. I needed him inside me.

"Please fuck me."

"Are you sure?"

My body was pretty damn sure it didn't care about my logical reasons for not having sex in James' flat.

"Do you want me to beg? Please, Aiden, fuck me hard," I whispered. "I need it. I need you."

"I think I need you to keep begging, princess."

I whimpered, arching into his touch. His fingers worked me and his thumb picked up a relentless pace on my clit. It wasn't quite enough to make me come, but it had me spiralling out of control.

"I can't take it. I need your cock. Please, please, I want you to fuck me. I don't want to come on your fingers. They're not enough. I want to come on your cock."

The fact that I sounded so ridiculously wanton for the man who commanded my entire soul made me realise how far down the rabbit hole I'd fallen with Aiden. How I'd do anything he asked me to. Even have sex in my best friend's flat, on his sofa bed because I was so utterly enraptured by the man I loved. I'd already given up so much of myself and I was about to hand over the rest for his safe keeping.

"Please, I need it hard. Use me. My body is yours to command. Please, please, I need you."

His fingers left my pussy, causing me to whimper from the lack of contact.

"Get on your hands and knees, princess," he whispered.

I complied immediately. The warning bells went off in my head. If James came in, there would be no hiding what we were doing in this position.

Aiden peeled down my underwear and tugged it off. The next thing I knew, he'd stuffed it in my mouth as a makeshift gag. I could taste my own arousal on them.

"Don't make a fucking sound, you hear me?"

I nodded as I felt the thick head of his cock pressing against my entrance. He gripped both my hips and thrust inside me. I grunted around the gag, arching into him as he pressed deep.

"That's it," he said, his voice low and filled with heat. "You're a bad girl, Avery. Wanting me to fuck you on your best friend's sofa."

His thrusts were brutal, just like I'd asked for. And I loved every moment. The sound of his skin slapping against mine. The way he pushed my limits. Fucked me almost to the point of pain. He knew exactly how much to give me. It was never too much. He never hurt me. Aiden didn't do pain. Only pleasure.

I moaned, unable to stop myself. It was muffled by the gag. He knew how much noise I made during sex and that's why he'd stuffed my underwear in my mouth.

"Such a bad girl. After everything you've endured, you still want my cock. Still want me to use you. That's what makes me love you more, princess. You need what I give you."

My heart soared in my chest. We were perfect for each other. I gave him an outlet for his desire for control and he gave me freedom. This was more than just fucking. This was our own brand of making love to each other. As brutal and unforgiving as it was.

"You know what I want?"

I shook my head. Whatever it was, I'd do it.

"After I've made you come apart, I want you to clean your cum off my cock. Then I'm going to fuck your throat and feed you my fucking cum."

My insides clenched at his words. I knew how much he loved my mouth. How he got off on fucking me to the point of almost gagging. I trusted him not to go too far.

His fingers found my clit, stroking it and pressing down hard. I jerked and bucked. His pace increased, causing the familiar stirrings deep in my core. It didn't take much. I clenched around him, my body trembling and spasming out of control. I groaned, wanting desperately to cry out his name whilst I came apart completely.

His brutal thrusts slowed as I came down from my high and sagged in his hold. He ripped my underwear out of my mouth, pulling out of me and flipping me over onto my back. His grey eyes glittered as he towered above me.

"Come here and clean up your mess, then I might let you have these back."

He dangled my underwear between his thumb and forefinger. I wasn't sure I wanted it back given they were covered in spit and my arousal, but I couldn't exactly not wear any given where we were.

I got up onto my knees and took him in my mouth, using my tongue to caress his cock. He let out a low growl, which rumbled through his chest. His fingers tangled in my hair, anchoring me to him.

"Look at me whilst you suck my cock."

My eyes snapped up to his. The lust and heat in them almost made me tremble. Aiden exuded power and control. I revelled in it. I never thought I'd enjoy submission, but with Aiden, it was everything.

"That's it, princess. Show me how thankful you are I made you come on my cock just like you asked."

I did. I ran my tongue down his shaft, licking up my cum like he asked me to. When I took him in my mouth again, his fingers tightened in my hair, keeping me still. He fucked my mouth, thrusting his cock down my throat. I took it all, feeling him pulsate inside me. He was close. I gripped the base of his cock and squeezed. He grunted, fucking me harder. The first spurt coated my mouth, filling me with the evidence of his desire for me.

I swallowed every last drop he gave me when he pulled out. He stroked my jaw, a devious smile on his face as he handed me back my underwear.

"My dirty little princess," he whispered as he leant down and kissed me.

I fell asleep not long after that, tucked up in Aiden's arms. All my troubles melted away after his brutal fucking. Aiden always managed to make everything better. I shouldn't rely on him to fuck away my pain and bad memories, but I didn't care. Our connection wasn't just about sex even though we couldn't keep our hands off each other. It was two souls bound together. Two people who needed the right person to put their hearts back together. To heal from the pain and suffering.

I was that girl for Aiden and he was that man for me. And somewhere deep inside me, I knew I no longer wanted to be a Daniels. I wanted to bind myself to Aiden in name. In heart. In soul. He was it for me.

And I couldn't fucking tell him that for fear he would bolt. The fear he would tell me he wasn't ready for that kind of commitment to me even though I was his and he was mine. I wouldn't put that kind of pressure on him. I knew Aiden well

enough to know he needed time and space to decide these things for himself.

So I kept my mouth shut. Instead, I told him I loved him before I fell asleep and he whispered that he loved me too.

That had to be enough for me.

For now.

I was a little embarrassed the next day when James ambled in, yawning. He didn't say anything about our nocturnal activities so I had to assume he hadn't heard us. I stripped the sheets and stuffed them in the washing machine without being asked. I couldn't let him do it after what Aiden and I had done last night. I dressed in yesterday's clothes and we all sat down to a cup of tea. James and I had toast with ours, but Aiden didn't really do carbs first thing in the morning.

"You think it's safe to leave today?" James asked.

"We don't really have a choice. She'll be safer at mine," Aiden replied.

Aiden's building had higher security than most. He'd never let anyone get to me there.

"And I want a bath and change of clothes," I added.

"You can have whatever you want when we get back."

I felt less afraid in the morning light. Tristan hadn't managed to have his way with me and those men following me and Davis didn't get me. Those were positives. I was determined not to allow these things to get me down. Aiden

kept telling me I was strong. I just had to prove it to myself. I wasn't going to break again.

I hugged James and thanked him for letting us crash at his before we left. What he whispered in my ear made me smile all the way down the stairs.

"I was sceptical at first, but he's good for you. I'm glad you found your way back to each other."

I'd blushed, remembering what we'd done on his sofa. I really hoped James never found out about that because quite frankly, I don't think he'd ever look at his sofa in the same way again.

Aiden wrapped an arm around me and kept his eyes on the street. I felt tension radiating off him in waves. Being out in the open bothered him, but he'd always keep me safe. My incredibly dangerous tattooed protector. The only person I'd ever want for the rest of my life.

"Where did you park?" I asked.

"Not far, just over in the next street."

I nodded. Gert would always pick me up and park in the same carpark when we visited James considering I couldn't drive.

When we reached the car, Aiden unlocked it and left me there to go pay at the machine. I got in and settled myself in the seat, putting my bag in the footwell. I loved his Jag. The seats were plush and the interior beautiful. I was just about to lean against the door when it was ripped open. I looked up as two hands reached in and pulled me out.

It wasn't Aiden. A man in a black suit with a bald head and an earpiece held me. Another man stood next to him.

"What the fuck?" I said.

"Miss Daniels," said the bald-headed man. "It would be wise for you to come quietly."

He dragged me away towards a waiting Range Rover, its engine running. I dug my heels in.

"No, let me go."

I struggled in his grasp. The other man gripped my free arm and they both dragged me to the car. They were the same men from last night. I recognised the Range Rover.

"Get off me. What the hell is this?"

Neither of them replied. The bald man unceremoniously plonked me into the passenger seat and shoved me into the middle. He got in behind me whilst the other man walked around the car and slid into the other seat beside me. The doors slammed and the car set off.

"What the hell do you people want with me?"

I got nothing but hard stares. So I lunged at the other man, trying to get the passenger door open so I could get the hell out of this car. His arm slammed across my chest and pressed me back into my seat. I was winded momentarily. My heart raced. I was being kidnapped. And Aiden would fucking go mental when he found me not in the car.

"Seriously, what is going on?"

"You will find out soon enough," the bald man said.

"Tell me now. I'm not fucking joking. My boyfriend will come after you."

I no longer cared no one was supposed to know Aiden and I were together. I was done hiding our relationship in the shadows. This had officially pissed me right off.

"I didn't want to have to do this, Miss Daniels, but you need to calm down."

The next thing I knew, he jabbed a needle into my neck. I screeched, pain radiating from where he'd stuck the needle in. All too soon, I felt tired and my mind began to swirl.

"What did you do?"

"It's okay, Mis Daniels. Just go to sleep now."

I fought back against the need to sleep. My body started going slack as whatever he'd given me took effect. My head lolled on my chest.

"What... I don't want to... I can't..."

My very last thought before I fell away into oblivion was that Aiden would lose his shit when he found out someone had taken me. And my heart broke knowing he'd stop at nothing to get me back.

Chapter Fourteen

Aiden

The stupid machine closest to the car was busted, so I had to walk to the other end of the carpark to find a working one. I didn't want to leave Avery alone, but this wouldn't take too long.

As I walked back, I noticed the passenger door was hanging open. My senses tingled. I heard the revving of an engine. My eyes fell on a huge black Range Rover driving away from my car. I stared at the number plate. It registered with me immediately. That was the same fucking plate of the car Avery told me about last night.

My legs surged forward.

They'd gotten to her.

They'd fucking got her.

I didn't stop to check the Jag. Everything inside me screamed as I dashed after their car. Before I could even get near it, they got out onto the street. I ran out behind them, searching for the direction they'd gone in, but it was too late. I was too fucking late.

My knees almost buckled. Avery was gone. My fucking girl was gone. Some pricks had taken her. Just like someone had taken away my mother. Fuck. My heart pounded in my chest so hard I thought it might fucking burst out. I couldn't fall apart. I had to find her. I had to rescue her. Nothing would fucking stop me from getting my fucking girl.

I dashed back into the carpark and raced to the car. I found her bag in the footwell and cursed. So much for tracking her by her phone. She always left it in there rather than on her person. I slumped against the car, running my hands through my hair.

I needed to get home and on my computer. That was the only fucking way I'd find her. I slammed the passenger door shut and got in the driver's side. I got the fuck out of that carpark and on the road. I slammed my hands against the steering wheel as I drove.

"Fuck. Fuck. Fuck. Fuck."

I couldn't fucking believe it. The one moment I'd taken my eyes off her and they'd got to her. Whoever the fuck they were. If I didn't know any better, I'd have gone straight to Chuck's and demanded to know where the hell she was. Except Chuck was trying to keep Avery out of harm's way. He needed his niece alive and well to keep up appearances.

Frazier would be the next logical point of call, but he wouldn't send men after her. He'd have sent Tristan. So it couldn't be him either.

This left me with a big fat load of nothing. I connected my phone to the car via Bluetooth and dialled the only person I could think of to help me in this situation.

"Aiden," John said.

"Avery has been taken. I don't know by who or why, but she's gone."

"What?"

"Some fuckers in a Range Rover followed her last night, we stayed at her friend's place. I was taking her back to mine today, but they grabbed her."

"What do you need?"

Something to help me calm the fuck down before I lost all sense of rationality.

"I have the number plate so I can use that to find her. I'll need back up if I'm going to get her. I can't do it alone."

"I'll head over now. I take it you don't want me to inform Chuck just yet."

"Fuck no. If he gets wind of this, there will be hell to pay."

"I'll see you in forty."

He hung up. John was the only person I could ask. I wasn't about to involve Ben in this shit. Not when he had a baby on the way. I wasn't stupid enough to think I could go in all guns blazing when I found out where the fuck she was. I had no idea who I was dealing with. This made it a fucking nightmare. What sick fuck would take my girlfriend? I knew she was in danger from her own family and Frazier, but I hadn't counted on anyone else being after her.

I slammed my hand down on the steering wheel again and narrowly avoided some prick pulling out. The fucker hadn't been looking properly. I honked the horn and flipped him the finger. Some fucks didn't know how to drive properly. I was too fucking worked up to give anyone the benefit of the doubt. Someone had my fucking woman.

I took several deep breaths. I had to chill the fuck out. Keep my fucking wits about me and put my head back on straight. Thoughts of how scared she'd be filled me with uncontrollable rage. Avery was strong but being taken by men she didn't know to god knows where would be enough to make anyone afraid.

What the fuck did they want with her? If any of them harmed a single hair on her head, I'd fucking kill them. I'd burn the fucks to the ground. No one and nothing would keep me from Avery. Not like they'd taken away my mother. I wasn't losing another person who meant the fucking world to me. Never again. Never a-fucking-gain.

It took me twenty minutes to get back to mine. I rushed upstairs and into my office. When I sat down at my desk and booted up my laptop, it dawned on me. I was afraid for her. Afraid of what whoever had taken her would do to her. The crippling anxiety and helplessness almost paralysed me. I had to get her back. I had to make sure she was safe.

It didn't take me long to hack into the automatic number plate recognition system. I'd done it before and their security quite frankly sucked. I ran the number plate and waited. It would take a while for it to get a hit.

Getting up, I went into the kitchen and made myself a shake. It wouldn't do me any good to skip it. Not when I needed to keep my strength up and stay alert. If I had to fight my way into wherever they had Avery, then I'd need the fuel.

I downed it as the bell for the door went. *Thank fuck.* I discarded the glass in the sink and buzzed John in the front door. I paced the hallway, growing ever more agitated by the second. My body was coiled tight. I felt it in every muscle, the tension and anxiety within me.

How could I have left her alone and defenceless? I'd turned my back for a few minutes. A few fucking minutes is all it took. My heart felt as though it was in a vice, fracturing and cracking with each squeeze. I choked down air, trying to stem the tidal wave of crippling fear from drowning me completely.

They won't kill her. They're not going to kill her like they did my mother. I have to remember that. I have to.

As soon as the knock came on the door, I ripped it open and almost fucking slumped on the floor in front of John. I didn't care what I looked like right then. He shut the door behind him and put a hand on my shoulder, leading me away towards the living room. He made me sit down on the sofa without saying a word. John had been here before so he knew his way around.

"You need to breathe, Aiden," he said, his voice soft.

I drew in ragged breaths, putting my head in my hands and digging my palms into my eyes. This situation completely caught me off guard. I'd been too fucking complacent. I should've locked her in the damn car or taken her to the fucking machine with me.

"That's it. Just breathe. It's okay. She's going to be okay."

"They took her. Someone fucking took her," I said, hating the pitiful note to my voice.

"I'm going to check the ANPR and then we'll talk about what happened."

I nodded, not looking up at him. I hated anyone seeing me in such a fucking state. John wouldn't hold it against me. After yesterday, I was well aware he cared about Avery and her safety. It's why I called him and not anyone else. I didn't completely trust the man, but what choice did I have? I needed allies in this fucking war and if I could find one in John, all the fucking better.

He came back into the room a few minutes later. I looked up. His green eyes were dark and he shook his head. Nothing yet. He sat down next to me.

"Start at the beginning."

"Which beginning?"

He raised an eyebrow.

"Start with the phone call you got yesterday. I meant what I said, I don't want to know about how you and Avery got together. That's between you. I don't want to be lying to Chuck any more than I already am."

I couldn't fault him for that. Plausible deniability and all. So I explained the events leading up to when she got taken. The more I talked about it, the less the whole thing made sense. As if it made any sense to begin with. Was I missing something? A vital piece of information which would let me know who I was dealing with.

"Did her friend say how many men there were?" John asked.

"No, I don't think he was paying close enough attention."

"You need to ask him."

I sighed, pulling out my phone and dialling James' number. Not that I wanted him involved, but at this rate, anything to help us would be better than nothing.

"Hey, Aiden. You two get back okay?"

"How many men got out of the car last night?"

"Um… two I think, one of them was bald. Why? What's going on?"

If I lied and told him everything was okay, I doubt Avery would forgive me but how could I tell him I let her get taken? I mean I hadn't exactly allowed it to happen, but it was on my fucking watch.

"Do you remember any other details?"

"They were both wearing black suits and ties and they had earpieces. Aiden… what happened?"

I sighed, running my hand through my hair. Earpieces meant they weren't some low life scum. They were organised. This complicated things further.

"I don't want you to freak out, but they got to her."

James was silent for a long moment. I could hear his harsh breath down the phone.

"How?" he whispered.

"I turned my back for one minute to pay for parking and they ripped her out the car. I couldn't get to her in time."

"You're going to get her back, right? You have to get her back."

The fear in his voice cut me like a fucking knife. I had no choice but to get her back. Avery was the one person in this world I could not live without. I loved her with every inch of my soul. Except making that sort of promise was impossible. I had no idea where she was or who'd taken her.

"I'm going to try my damn fucking hardest. If you remember anything else, text me."

"You have to stop this shit with her family. You've painted a huge fucking target on her back by getting her involved. You know that, right? If you really love her, then you'll find her and keep her out of it. I don't care how you take down her family, just stop putting her in danger."

He didn't wait for me to respond. The phone went dead. I took it away from my ear and stared down at it. I couldn't even be pissed off with him for his outburst. James was right. I'd put her in danger. I'd put her in the line of fire and now I was paying for it.

James didn't know Avery quite like he thought he did. She was more than willing to do this. She'd laid down her cards. Ready to end this shit for good. I'd given her an out when we discussed her going back into the world. I'd told her she could sign the company over to her uncle and wash her hands of it if that's what she wanted. She didn't. Avery told me we were in this together. No matter what. She needed the shit with her family to end just as much as I did.

"You look like someone punched you in the gut," John said, pulling me out of my thoughts.

"Just got an earful for getting her into this situation is all."

"What did he say?"

I looked up at him.

"They are organised. Low-level idiots don't have earpieces. They're likely carrying. This won't be easy. That's if we even find out where the fuck she is."

John nodded. I stood up, slipping my phone back in my pocket and paced the room. I was still in yesterday's clothes and I was in desperate need of a shower. How could I think about my own fucking comfort when my girl was missing?

I walked over to my boxing bag and slammed my fist into it. The pain radiated up my knuckles, but I didn't care.

"Fuck."

"If you need to beat the shit out of that, then go ahead. I'll keep an eye on the search for you."

I stared at the bag. Taking out my frustration on it would calm me down. It would help me regain my senses. Keep a level head.

I gave him a sharp nod and started unbuttoning my shirt. John got up and left the room. Wrapping my hands up, I took out my anger on the boxing bag. I slammed my fists into it over and over again, grunting from the impact.

All my fears poured out of me. The fear she would be hurt. That someone might force her to do things against her will. That she might be raped and abused. And lastly, the crippling anxiety I felt at someone taking her life.

I couldn't stand it. I promised to protect her. To keep her safe no matter what.

Those promises were shattered in pieces on the floor. Would she be able to forgive me for letting her get taken? Would she still love me?

I hit the bag so hard, my hands felt like they'd been put through a fucking meat grinder. Shaking them out, I unwrapped them, finding bruised knuckles underneath it. Fucking myself up was not helping matters.

Since John hadn't come back in, I stalked into the bathroom and turned the shower on. I stripped out of the rest of my clothes and got under the steady stream of water.

I remembered the last time I'd had her in here with me. She'd let me pin her up against the wall, her tits squished up against it as I fucked her from behind. I'd left marks on her hips where I'd gripped her too hard. She hadn't seemed to mind one bit even though I apologised.

197

My princess.

My fucking goddess.

Gone.

I didn't want to break down, but the leash I had on my emotions snapped. I let out an anguished howl, feeling my insides ripping to shreds. This was almost as bad as when she'd left me of her own free will. That crushed me completely. Whereas this left me angry, frustrated and ready to kill the motherfuckers who thought they could get away with taking my girl.

I'd kill for Avery.

I'd snuff out their lives one by one, relishing in the sick, twisted justice of it all.

My girl needed me. Fucking needed me and I wasn't there for her. I needed her back. Desperately. This whole fucking thing was eating me alive. It'd only been a couple of hours and that was too fucking long. They say the first seventy-two hours after someone goes missing are the most crucial. I had no fucking time to waste.

I got out of the shower after cleaning up properly and got dressed before going into the office. John was sitting at the desk. His gaze flicked up to me.

"We've had a couple of hits, but then it just stops. I think we need to find CCTV footage of the area around the last hit," he said.

He got up off my desk chair and let me sit down. I got to work immediately. Hacking into the national CCTV network, I found the last ANPR hit and the cameras around it. They were still in London. Thank fuck.

"There," John said, pointing at a car on the screen.

I paused the footage, zooming in on the vehicle. The number plate was a little blurred but clear enough for me to know it was the right fucking Range Rover.

"Let's see where these fucks go."

We followed the footage as far as we could until we found the car turning into a carpark. More cars went in and out as we scanned through the footage, but the Range Rover didn't leave. And we couldn't see Avery or any of the fuckers who took her on the footage surrounding the carpark. Why the fuck would they have taken her in there? And where the fuck did she go after that?

"Do you want me to check it out?" John asked.

"No. Something is off about this."

I couldn't put my finger on it, but the whole fucking situation felt wrong to me. I checked around the carpark. It was close to Mayfair. That struck me as a little odd. Rich pricks owned property around there.

"Do any of Chuck's clients live around here?"

I looked up at John. His brow furrowed for a moment.

"A few, but none who'd pull shit like this."

"Names and addresses. We leave no stone unturned."

John wrote them down for me. He was right. None of them stuck out to me. Mostly older clients from Nicholas Daniels' generation. I had no fucking clue what to do with this bit of information. For fuck's sake, this was turning into a fucking nightmare.

"This doesn't make any sense. How much does she know?" John asked.

"Avery? She knew nothing until we met and even now, she doesn't know the full story. No one knows she's aware of it except me and her friend. Nothing about this adds up."

I stared hard at the list of names.

Fuck. No fucking way.

"John… Is he here?"

I pointed down at the name of the man who was connected to the one person who I could never get close to.

"You think he's back in the UK?"

"He can't be. All my fucking backdoor alerts would've gone off if he went through border control here. It can't fucking well be him, can it?"

"Why would it be? You said yourself, no one knows she knows. He has no reason to be here. He's left you alone this long."

What John said made logical sense. Except something fucking nagged at me. Telling me I shouldn't rule him out completely. What if it was him? What if he'd discovered my relationship with Avery and had taken her because of it?

Fuck.

The question remained. How the fuck would he have got into the country without crossing through passport control? He wasn't a fucking British citizen.

"I think we need to pay Robert Bassington a fucking visit."

"Are you sure that's wise?"

I shook my head. It would never be wise to go after any man with power in this business, but I had to find out if that sick piece of shit had arrived back here. And if he had my fucking girl.

"Aiden, you can't go battering down doors on a hunch. What if he tells Chuck you paid him a visit? He's already suspicious of everything to do with you and Avery."

I drummed my fingers on the desk. Doing nothing felt fucking wrong. Going around Robert Bassington's and beating the shit out of him was also wrong. Fuck.

And there was something else fucking nagging me. I looked up at the man next to me. His willingness to talk this through with me. To work out why Avery was gone and who had taken her. Those things didn't add up.

"Why are you helping me, John? Don't give me any bullshit. You must know how much I hate the Daniels and what they represent if you know what happened to my mother. I don't work for them out of fucking choice."

He leant against the desk and folded his arms over his chest.

"I've been involved with this business too long. Let's just say I'm not averse to seeing the empire crumble. It's not something you can do cleanly. More blood will be spilt. I'm okay with that. If it means I can walk away from this shit finally, then I'm in."

I stared at him for a long moment as if seeing the man for the first time. I couldn't honestly say I ever expected him to want to leave this life behind.

"How do I know if I can trust what you're saying is true?"

"You can't, but I know things about the Daniels you don't. Hit them where it hurts the most and the rest will fall."

"Hit them where exactly?"

I was curious about his take on all of this. Curious if he'd come to the same conclusions as me. If he knew how to win this fucking war.

"Their relationships with each other are built on mutual trust. They know too much about each other. Plant the seed of doubt. Play on the fear of exposure, they'll rip each other apart like a pack of wolves."

I really did see this man in a new light. Could he really be my ally in this sorry fucking mess?

"And you'll help me achieve this?"

I'd already started on this path by killing Mitchell, but John didn't know that. They were already out for each other's blood. Things within Mitchell's inner circle hadn't been the same since that day. I could tell from Chuck's erratic behaviour. He was under a fuck ton of pressure and all the shit which had gone down with Avery hadn't helped him in the slightest.

I was fucking glad of it.

"I want out. I'll help you if it means I can leave this godforsaken island behind and not worry about looking over my shoulder for the rest of my life."

I wasn't sure I trusted John, but then again, he had kept my relationship with Avery a secret.

"Okay. You have yourself a deal. Double cross me and you'll be leaving this fucking island in a body bag. Understood?"

He smiled.

"From you, I wouldn't expect anything less."

John had seen me rough a fair few people up. He knew what I was capable of.

"None of that matters if I can't get Avery back."

"Leave it to me."

He pulled out his phone and dialled. He whacked it on speakerphone so I heard it ringing.

"John," Chuck's deeply irritating voice sounded through the phone.

"Boss, we have a little problem."

"And what might that be?"

"Your niece has been taken."

"What? Are you fucking kidding me? I told you to watch her."

I could tell by Chuck's agitated tone this was news to him. I didn't know if I felt fucking relieved by that or not.

"You didn't tell me two hulking men who looked like professionals would pluck her off the street and hustle her into a Range Rover."

"God-fucking-damn it. Did you see the plate? Have you contacted Aiden to see if he can help track her down using it?"

John smiled at me.

"Yes and yes. You think I'd call you without all the information?"

"No. Tell me what he found."

"They took her to a carpark in Mayfair."

We both could hear something smash on the floor and Chuck cursing profusely.

"You think one of them took her."

"I don't think anything, boss."

"None of them would have the fucking balls to think they can pluck the head of the fucking company off the streets without consequences. They all know she's needed to keep their fucking dirty little secrets where they belong."

"Just giving you the facts."

"I wish Mitch was fucking here. He'd know how to deal with this shit. Fuck. That little fucking upstart is more fucking trouble than she's worth."

I refrained from saying Mitchell wouldn't have allowed his daughter to be harmed under any circumstances. I might hate the man and be glad I killed him, but he did one thing right. He took care of Avery.

"I don't think she asked to get kidnapped."

"No, you're right. When we get her back, you're going to be with her at all fucking times. I don't care what she says, she needs a fucking bodyguard."

John smirked.

"Yes, boss."

"I'll be in touch when I've tracked down my wayward niece."

Chuck hung up. I stared at John as he tucked his phone back in his pocket.

"Problem solved," he said.

"That's your plan?"

He shrugged, leaning back against the desk with his arms folded across his chest.

"No stone left unturned."

Having Chuck hassle his clients kept me off the radar. I could hardly fault John for using a resource I hadn't thought of. I wasn't sure if I was prepared to find out he was back here. If Robert Bassington squealed, what the hell would I do?

Storm in and demand he give me Avery back? Fuck. That was never going to end well.

I just had to fucking hope it wasn't him. Hope she never had to deal with that sick son of a bitch. He was the worst one of all.

"Now, let's check that footage again, see if we didn't miss something first time around."

Chapter Fifteen

Avery

1 opened my eyes, blinking slowly. My head felt like it was full of cotton wool. My body ached. Where the fuck was I?

The room was brightly lit. The harsh light burnt into my retinas. I forced myself to keep my eyes open and take in my surroundings. In front of me was a desk with an open laptop. The screen sat unblinking. I tried to move my limbs but found my arms secured behind me and my legs tied to the chair I was sat in.

What the actual fuck?

I struggled to remember what happened. My mind felt like I was trying to drag myself through a tar pit. Men were after me. We'd stayed at James' place. Then it hit me all at once. They got me and jabbed me with a fucking needle, rendering me unconscious for fuck knows how long. Who were these people?

"I see you're finally awake, Miss Daniels," came a disjointed, robotic voice from somewhere above me.

I glanced around, finding cameras in the corners of the room. Otherwise, it was bare except for me, the chair, the desk and the laptop. A bare concrete room, much like the one Aiden held me in when he'd taken me. Except the wall in front of me held what I assumed was a two-way mirror.

"No thanks to your men," I muttered.

"Yes, it was rather unfortunate Kurt had to drug you, but no matter, you're here now."

Even when Aiden chained me up in the cell, he'd never restrained me like this. Those restraints only came out during sex and I liked it then. I didn't like this at all. Not one bit.

"What do you want?"

"Straight down to business. Good."

"Yes, I'm most curious why you'd kidnap, drug me and tie me up in a room alone. Seems rather shady to me, don't you think?"

My mouth was running away with me. Possibly not the smartest move given where I was.

The disjointed voice chuckled, making my skin crawl.

"Oh, but aren't you a little firecracker? I see why he kept you."

My heart hammered against my chest.

Aiden.

How did this person know about me and Aiden?

"I'm not a possession."

"Why no darlin', you're not. Head of a global empire now."

The reminder left a sour taste in my mouth. A corrupted empire I wanted nothing to do with.

"Are you going to explain why you've decided to kidnap said head of a global empire?"

If I was going to fucking hell, then I'd go there with my sarcastic mouth in full force. I didn't care any longer. I should be terrified, but I was fed up. Fed up with being taken and used for other people's purposes. Done being a pawn in a game I didn't understand.

Aiden had already broken me down once. I knew how to survive this. My demons weren't going to haunt me any longer. I had everything to live for.

"Merely wanting a little conversation darlin'."

That term of endearment grated on me. He kept dropping the G. Whoever he was, he wasn't British.

"Couldn't we have chatted without the need to tie me up?"

"You like it when he ties you up, don't you? I always knew he'd have a taste for kink."

This man talked about Aiden as if he knew him. It bugged me. What concerned me further was his knowledge of our sex life.

"What do you want?"

"Don't want to talk about your Dom and Sub relationship?"

That wasn't what we shared with each other. I didn't need to put labels on our relationship. We were just Aiden and Avery. Two people who loved each other in their own way.

"It's none of your fucking business."

"Touchy subject."

I gritted my teeth.

"How do you know about us?" I ground out.

He chuckled again. This man was getting on my nerves. Asking me intimate questions like he was an old friend.

"I like to keep an eye on your family's operation."

"And that means spying on their sex lives, does it? I think you're the one with the weird kinks here."

He laughed. A full belly laugh which sounded wrong in that disjointed robotic voice.

"Oh darlin', you really are a hoot. I don't care what sick fantasies they like to act out. Our mutual acquaintance is different. I have my reasons for keeping him under surveillance."

My skin prickled. Something about this had all my senses tingling. I should know who this is. I should be able to work it out. Who would want to keep an eye on Aiden if not Chuck and Frazier? Who else would care? He had no one except Tina and Ben.

And you. Don't forget, he has you.

He'd have me again when I got out of here. I'd had enough of all this shit.

I wanted to shed my identity as a Daniels.

I wanted to be his weapon.

I wanted to be his.

Completely.

"I don't want to talk about him. Tell me why you brought me here."

"All in good time darlin'. You see, I want to talk about you and Aiden."

I shivered hearing him refer to Aiden directly. I wasn't exactly in a position to argue. Tied to a chair in a room with a man I didn't know behind a two-way mirror. So I waited instead.

"No more objections? I'm disappointed. I like you talking back. Does he?"

"No, he doesn't."

We got into arguments when I did. Aiden made me so crazy sometimes, I couldn't hold back. And he'd fuck me into submission afterwards, that was my punishment. I almost scoffed. Some fucking punishment when I adored his brutality in the bedroom.

"He likes to be in control. I imagine you caused him no end of trouble."

I clamped my mouth shut. If he wanted me to talk back to him, then I wasn't giving him the satisfaction.

"I can see the allure you hold. A pretty little young thing like you. A siren. You called out to him with your song, wound him around your little finger by giving him exactly what he needed. You think he has all the power? You're wrong. It's you who controls him. He's a slave to his desire for you."

He snorted.

"I imagine he's tearing his hair out now, knowing you're gone."

This man was certifiable. Me having the control? What a fucking joke. He had no idea what it was like when Aiden got into one of his moods. He was the most unreasonable and stubborn man I'd ever met.

"I'm sure he is," I said as calmly as I could.

I didn't let him see how his words cut me. My heart was in pieces at my feet knowing what this must be doing to Aiden. I had no concept of time any longer. Not since they drugged me. Who knew how long it had been since they'd taken me.

"You don't seem too concerned about that darlin'. Is he keeping you against your will still?"

"No, but you already knew that."

He chuckled.

"Smart girl."

I flashed him an entirely fake smile, which only afforded me another laugh. Perhaps if I answered his questions, he'd let me go. He did say he just wanted a conversation with me.

"I didn't expect him to fall for the daughter of the man he hated."

I stiffened. Neither of us expected this, but I stopped questioning it. What was the point when it defied explanation? Love wasn't rational or reasonable. It was all consuming and took no prisoners. I could no more stop loving Aiden than he could stop loving me. Where we came from didn't matter.

"How much do you know about Aiden and me?"

"I wouldn't worry your pretty little head about it darlin'."

Except I was worried. Did he know Aiden murdered my parents? He seemed to know Aiden had taken me against my will. I could only assume he did know, but as to why he wouldn't have turned Aiden in, that was a question I knew he wouldn't answer.

"Are we done talking about my relationship yet?"

"What did he tell you about his mother?"

"Why?"

"Humour me darlin'."

I wanted to tell him to stop calling me that. It was really pissing me off.

"He told me enough to know what my family did to her was despicable."

"Did he tell you who killed her?"

I shook my head. I hadn't asked either. For all I knew, it could've been my father, but he was obsessed with her

212

according to Aiden. Would his obsession have driven him to murder? I wasn't quite sure it had. I might not have really known who my father truly was, but that didn't add up in my head. It would make sense Aiden killing the man who murdered his mother, except I knew it wasn't my dad.

"Pity. It wouldn't matter anyway, he's wrong in his assumption."

Wait, what?

"Wrong?"

"Yes. He clearly didn't tell you he was there the day she died."

My already battered and bruised heart broke further. Had Aiden seen it? What really happened that day?

"How do you know?"

"Next time we meet, I'll tell you who took her life. In fact, I will tell you everything you've ever wanted to know about the man you love. It will be under very different circumstances. This meeting was an unfortunate necessity."

I didn't think this was a necessity at all. It'd left me with more questions than answers. Like who the fuck was this and why did he have a vested interest in Aiden and me? Why did he care so much?

"I want you to do something for me, Avery. Ask Aiden who killed his mother. Ask him to tell you the truth about the day she died from his perspective."

"Is that all you want me to do?"

He chuckled. I hated that laugh. To be honest, I hated everything about this situation. Being tied up and questioned wasn't my idea of fun.

"We still have much more to discuss."

Oh wonderful. Just what I wanted. More time with this robot voice and his weird obsession with my boyfriend.

"Aiden has only told you so much. I want you to know what truly went on behind closed doors."

The laptop screen in front of me turned on. A picture showed up with a play button on it. Did he have remote control of it? He must do. What the hell did he want to show me? I hoped it wasn't anything like those videos Aiden showed me because I wasn't sure I could stomach seeing men abuse women again.

When the video played, my worst fears were confirmed. Bile rose up in my throat. Why the fuck would he show me this?

A naked woman was bent across a desk, her arms shackled to each end, stretched to her limits. Her legs were spread wide. Her eyes were grey and her brown hair splayed out across her back. Mitchell stood behind her with a crop in his hand whilst Kathleen sat in a seat opposite the desk. The two of them were fully dressed. There were various whips and floggers on the desk along with vibrators and plugs.

"What have I told you about speaking back to me, slave?" he said.

"I'm sorry, sir. I'm sorry," the shackled woman said.

He lashed out with the crop, striking her across her back. She howled in pain.

"Sorry is never good enough."

He struck her again and again. Her back and behind were painted in red marks.

"Please, please, sir. It hurts," she screamed.

"We're only just getting started."

He dropped the crop and picked up another whip. This one was a long length of plaited leather with a solid handle. He stepped back a few paces and lashed out with it. The strike across her back was a long red line. She screamed again.

The lashes came quick and fast, each one stark against her skin until her back was covered in marks. Tears streamed down her face and the howls echoed around the room.

The whole time, Kathleen sat watching, her expression impassive, almost as if the entire thing didn't affect her in the slightest.

"Have you learnt your lesson, slave?" Mitchell said.

"Yes," the woman sobbed. "Yes, sir. I won't disobey you again."

"Good girl."

He stroked her back, running his fingers down the lash marks. She hissed but didn't object to his touch. His other hand worked his belt open. His fly came next.

I turned my head to the side and promptly threw up. It coated my arm and the floor, but I didn't care. I could hear the sounds of the video still playing but I couldn't look. I could not watch my father having sex with Aiden's mother. I knew it was her from the moment I saw her eyes.

"Turn it off," I groaned. "Please, turn it off."

The sounds promptly stopped. My gut twisted. I didn't look up again. All of this was wrong. Why did he show me that? Why did he force me to confront the reality of who my parents were? I already knew enough from what Aiden had told me. This was just adding salt to the wound.

"Too much for you?" the robotic voice rattled around my brain.

"If you think anyone wants to watch their father whipping and having sex with their boyfriend's mother whilst their own mother watches the two of them then you've got some seriously fucked up twisted view of the world."

"I never said you'd enjoy what I had to show you."

"Why show it to me? What does this achieve? I already knew he was obsessed with her."

The smell of my own sick assaulted my nose. It made it difficult not to hurl all over again. I didn't recognise the room they'd been in, so it couldn't have been the penthouse. Was this where the girls were kept? That didn't make sense since Aiden told me he'd lived with her. I supposed they could've taken his mother there. It would be the only logical reason why footage existed.

"You need to understand the world you live in now."

"A sick as fuck world where men rape and abuse unwilling women. I already fucking knew that thanks. I didn't need to see my own father abuse someone."

"He doesn't know this footage exists."

If Aiden did, he would fucking lose his shit. I doubted he wanted to see the extent of what my father had done to his mother up close. I hadn't wanted to see any of it.

"Good. He doesn't need to see it. He's already been through enough."

"He's going to go through a lot more before this is all over."

I couldn't tell if it was a promise or a threat. Why did he feel the need to hide his voice? Why did it matter if I knew his identity? I was desperately curious at this point no matter how much I hated being tied up to this chair and made to talk about and see things I didn't want to.

"Well, Avery, it seems you've made a mess. Perhaps you've had enough for now. Our little chat will resume later."

I'd defy anyone not to vomit after being confronted with a video like that. I'd hated the videos Aiden showed me, but this was far worse.

The door to the room opened and in stepped the bald man who'd ripped me out of Aiden's car. He squatted down behind me and untied my wrists from the chair. The blood rushed back to my hands, causing my fingers to tingle. He unbound my ankles next before hoisting me up to my feet and dragging me out. The hallway we walked down had a plush carpet and fancy decorative red wallpaper with black swirls which looked a little garish to me.

The bald-headed man, who I assumed was called Kurt, shoved me through a doorway.

"There is a bathroom for you to clean up in over there," he told me. "Do not try to escape, Miss Daniels. There is nowhere for you to run."

He shut the door behind him without waiting for me to respond. I looked around. It was an overly ornate bedroom. A four poster bed with red drapes dominated the space. There was an antique oak ottoman at the foot of it with matching bedside tables. Laid out on the bed was a clean set of clothes for me. A long, plain t-shirt and a pair of leggings. I supposed it would have to do considering I'd thrown up over my shirt.

I walked over to the door Kurt had indicated and went through into the bathroom. I stripped off my shirt and washed the sick out of it as best I could. I cleaned the splatters off my trousers and stripped those off too. I rifled through the bathroom cabinet and found some toothpaste. I used my finger to rub it over my teeth and washed out my mouth from the tap to get rid of the taste of sick. Drinking some water helped clear my head a little.

I took my wet clothes back out into the bedroom and draped them over the ottoman to dry. I put on the t-shirt and leggings before sitting on the bed.

I wasn't sure what to do. It wasn't like I had a phone with me and Kurt told me not to try and escape. It hadn't crossed my mind until he said it. How would I even get away anyway? I was pretty sure he'd locked me in here.

My mind raced with possibilities. Who was this guy? Why did he know so much about Aiden and me? How come he knew who'd really killed Aiden's mother? What the hell was really going on here?

The door opened and Kurt walked in with a tray. He placed it next to me on the bed, turned and left without a word. I looked down at it. A platter of cheeses and meats with bread and a bowl of fruit along with a glass of juice. My stomach growled. I hadn't realised how hungry I was. It occurred to me this might be poisoned, but I was relatively sure they weren't going to harm me.

I wolfed down all the food and finished off the juice. Then I sat back against the headboard and waited. The ache in my chest grew. I missed Aiden. He'd be looking for me. There was no doubt about that. I knew he had ways and means of tracking me down. His resourcefulness knew no bounds. I just had to make sure I stayed alive and whole for him through this. That broken girl I'd been weeks ago no longer existed. The one who'd suffered hallucinations and nightmares brought on by seeing her parents die in front of her eyes. She wasn't the sort of girl I wanted to be any longer.

Aiden might have broken me, but he'd put me back together again. He'd made me whole. Showing me my inner strength and teaching me to be the woman I was always meant to become. Opening my eyes to a whole new world of pleasure and introducing me to the darkness he lived in. Most girls wouldn't have put up with the shit he'd put me through. Most girls wouldn't have bothered looking inside at the man behind the walls he'd put up or tried to understand why he was damaged and broken. I wasn't most girls. I'd gone toe to toe with him and come out the other side.

I didn't need Aiden to complete me, but I was a better version of myself because he was in my life. I could withstand this current situation. I could get through it. Aiden was waiting for me and he'd make it better. If I could handle dealing with Frazier Shaw and my uncle, I could handle this.

It was that determination that had me standing up when the door opened again after what seemed like hours. I met Kurt's gaze head-on.

"Come, Miss Daniels."

I strode out of the bedroom with him and back down the corridor to the concrete room. I sat down in the chair.

"You don't need to tie me up," I said. "I won't do anything."

He eyed me for a moment, putting his hand to his ear. He nodded and left the room, shutting the door behind him.

"Are you ready to carry on our little talk?" the robotic voice said.

"Yes."

"Good. Now, that was only a taster of the footage I wanted to show you."

My skin prickled, sweat beading at the back of my neck, but I didn't show my fear. I steeled myself. Whatever he had to show me couldn't be worse than what I'd already seen.

Except it was.

It was so much worse than I ever imagined.

I didn't know how much more I could take after being subjected to video after video of men raping, beating and abusing women. There were men I knew and men I didn't. All of it sickened me, but I managed to keep my meal in my stomach this time.

The screen finally went blank. I looked down at my hands, my breathing laboured as I tried not to think too hard about the sickening videos he'd shown me.

"Do you see now why Aiden wants to destroy your family?" the robotic voice asked me.

"Yes," I whispered.

My hands shook in my lap. I couldn't help my reaction. My chest ached. I wanted to curl up in a ball and cry. Cry for those women. I wanted to scream and rage at the cruelty. I wanted to do so many things, but I didn't. I sat there staring at my lap, trying not to let my emotions cripple me.

"You know darlin', I was good friends with your granddaddy when he was alive. Sad way to go."

Why the hell was he bringing up my granddad? It had hit my dad pretty hard when Nick died. Lung cancer wasn't pretty. He fought it, but he'd smoked all his life, cigarettes, cigars, you name it.

"Were you? Is that how come you know so much about their shady operations?"

I looked up. If he knew my granddad, it might mean he was of the same generation or at least of a similar age. Did that bring me any closer to working out who he might be?

"Why yes."

"Next you're going to tell me, you partook in the girls as well."

That awful laugh came again.

"Why, of course, darlin'. We all did."

I shivered. So he was a sick fuck just like the rest of them. I wasn't sure why I was even surprised. He had shown me all those sick videos after all. I had no idea why they'd even keep that type of evidence. It was incriminating. Maybe that was why. If any of them stepped out of line, they could be ruined by those videos.

The real question was, why did this man have them? Who was he?

"Good for you, just as despicable as the rest of them."

"Perhaps I am."

"Normal people don't go around kidnapping women nor show them rape videos."

"You're right. I'm not a nice man darlin'."

That bloody word again. I wanted to see his face so I could tell him to shut the fuck up and stop calling me his 'darling'. I was no one's fucking darling.

221

"Glad you realise that."

"Neither is your Aiden."

He was wrong. Aiden was nice to me when he wanted to be. He was trying anyway. I didn't want him to change. I saw the good inside him.

"At least he doesn't hide behind mirrors and robotic voices. He doesn't apologise for who he is and I don't expect him to be anything else."

"Your loyalty to him is charming."

It wasn't loyalty, it was love. I would do anything for him because I loved him. Stay by his side as long as he wanted me there. As long as he kept caring for me the way he did. As long as he kept loving me.

"You don't know anything about me and Aiden. What we share is between us and none of your business."

There was silence for a long moment.

"Well darlin', I think we've come to the end of our little tête-à-tête. Don't forget what I asked you to do."

"Ask Aiden who murdered his mother."

"That's right. Until we meet again, Miss Daniels."

The door to the room opened and Kurt appeared again. I stood up and followed him out. We walked down the corridor until we came to a large lobby. Sitting next to the front door were my heels. Kurt had a bag with him, which he handed to me. I looked inside and found my soiled clothes.

I slipped on my shoes whilst he opened the front door. We walked out together into a waiting car. It wasn't the Range Rover, but a BMW. He opened the door for me and I got in the passenger seat.

"Safe trip, Miss Daniels," he said before he shut the door.

The doors were locked and the car pulled away from the curb. The driver didn't speak to me. I looked back at the house we'd left by. I recognised this part of London. My father had often taken me here to visit some of his friends. Mayfair. An affluent and expensive part of the city. This raised my suspicions further about who'd taken me. And why had he allowed me to see where I was?

I made sure to note what street we were in so I could tell Aiden.

"Where are we going?" I asked.

"I've been told to return you home, Miss Daniels," the driver responded.

Home. It could mean my home or Aiden's. I didn't dare enquire which one it would be. After twenty minutes, I had my answer anyway. We pulled up outside Aiden's block of flats.

"Enjoy the rest of your day, Miss Daniels."

I nodded at him and got out of the car. I didn't have my key with me so I'd have to ring the buzzer. I watched the BMW pull away before I went to the door. Pressing down on the button labelled 'A. Lockhart', I waited.

After two minutes, there was no answer and I wondered if he was even in. Was he out searching for me? Had he already discovered where I'd been held? I was about to buzz again when the front door was ripped open and I found myself squashed up against a solid chest.

"Princess," he breathed.

And I dissolved into tears, unable to help the small sob emitting from my lips.

Chapter Sixteen

Aiden

When I'd seen it was her at the door, I'd grabbed my keys, wrenched open my front door and bolted down the stairs, not even bothering to wait for the lift. I heard John call after me. Nothing would stop me from getting to Avery.

When I reached her, my whole world stood still as I dragged her against my chest and held her tightly.

"Princess."

Her pitiful sob broke my fucking heart. It'd been twenty-four hours and now she was back. John and I spent the entire time trying to work out who would've taken her. Chuck had shaken down doors, but even he couldn't find out where she was. No one was talking. All his clients who lived in the area denied all knowledge. One of them was lying. One of them knew the truth.

"What day is it?" she asked.

"Sunday."

She shook her head against my chest.

"They knocked me out for an entire day."

"They did what?"

Did the fucks drug her?

"Can we go upstairs? I'm exhausted, Aiden."

I pulled away and took her hand, unlocking the door and leading her inside. We rode up in the lift together. She leant against me with her eyes closed. I had no idea what the fuck she'd been through or why she was back now. Why had they let her go?

When I unlocked the front door, she let go of my hand and went straight into the bedroom, ignoring John standing in the hallway.

"Is she okay?" he asked.

"I don't think so."

"Did they hurt her?"

"I haven't had a chance to talk to her properly. She seems shaken up."

I rubbed the back of my neck. I wanted to demand answers from her. The look in her eyes outside stopped me. World-weary and downtrodden. She needed time, not the inquisition.

"Do you need me to stay? I need to let Chuck know she's back."

Avery came out of the bedroom. She'd changed out of what she'd been wearing into a robe, her bare legs on show.

"Hello John."

"Miss Daniels."

She grimaced, putting a hand up.

"Please just call me Avery. I don't think I can stomach hearing another person refer to me as Miss Daniels right now."

John said he'd seen Avery grow up, but I didn't know how well the two of them knew each other.

"If that's what you wish."

She leant against the doorframe.

"I take it if you're here then you know…"

He nodded, giving her a half smile.

"Aiden can fill you in. I'll be back tomorrow morning to take you to work. Your uncle insists on you having protection."

She looked at the floor.

"So he knows I was taken."

"I'm afraid so. He did make some noise amongst his clients, so perhaps that's why you've been returned."

She sighed.

"I know why I was returned, but if you'll excuse me, I really need a shower."

She shuffled past the both of us and walked into the bathroom, shutting the door and locking it. Locking me out. What the fuck happened to her?

"I'll be making tracks then."

I gave him a nod, my eyes still on the bathroom door. I wanted to fucking break it down, but if Avery wanted space, I'd give it to her.

"Let me know what Chuck says." My eyes flicked to his. "After I find out what happened to her, we need to plan our next move."

"Of course."

He walked to the front door and opened it. He paused, turning back to me.

"I'll keep her safe, Aiden."

"I know you will."

He nodded and left. I stared at the bathroom door, listening to the sounds of the shower. All I wanted was for her to be okay. She was safely home, but that didn't mean she'd had an easy ride. I sat up against the wall outside the door, waiting for her to come out. There wasn't much else I could do with myself.

Having her back soothed my aching chest. Knowing she was here where I could protect her calmed me. My princess. My girl. She was home. Those twenty-four hours had felt like a lifetime. A lifetime of pure fucking hell. I couldn't deal with it.

Staring down at my still bruised knuckles, the evidence of my despair, the feeling of helplessness threatened to overcome me all over again. I'd been powerless to stop them taking her and powerless when it came to finding her again. What good was I if I couldn't protect the one person who mattered more to me than my own fucking life?

I dragged my hands through my hair. These dark thoughts weren't fucking helping anyone. Especially not when it'd dragged up memories of what happened to my mother. How I couldn't stop them hurting her. How they'd taken her away from me. All of it killed me.

Avery would never blame me for what happened. That girl was the brightest fucking star in the sky. She always understood. Always cared. Always did everything in her power to make me fucking happy.

The door to the bathroom opened. She stared down at me, her damp hair falling around her face. Falling to her knees, she crawled in between my legs and lay her head against my chest, her hand over my heart. I didn't care that she was getting my t-shirt wet. She was right there. Her solid form against mine. I wrapped an arm around her, trailing my fingers down her bare arm.

"I love you," she whispered. "I love you more than I can ever express in words."

I looked down at her. Tears welled in her doe eyes. The sight of it crushed me.

"I don't want to be a part of them any longer. I can't. Not after what I saw."

I stroked her wet hair, my heart fracturing with each word.

"What did you see, princess?"

"I don't want to talk about it right now."

She reached up, pulling me down so she could kiss me. It was tentative, almost sweet. The profound relief I felt slammed into me like a sack of bricks. I had her in my arms. She shifted, her hand sliding under my t-shirt and brushing across my stomach. The other curled around my neck, anchoring me to her. I could feel the wetness on her cheeks as tears ran down her face.

"Aiden, please make love to me," she whispered against my lips.

"Princess…"

"Please, please don't say no."

How the fuck could I when she was practically vibrating with sadness, crying in my mouth and asking me to take her pain away? What the hell had she seen?

I let her pull my t-shirt off me, her hands running over my bare chest sending sparks down my skin. I held her face and kissed her cheeks, her nose, her eyes, tasting the saltiness of her tears on my lips.

"I love you, Avery," I told her.

She choked out a sob, a fresh set of tears spilling down her face.

"Shh, shh, don't cry."

"Aiden, it was horrible. What he showed me was awful. I can't. I can't do this anymore. Please."

I captured her mouth again, swallowing her words. I couldn't stand to hear how upset she was, to know what she'd been through caused her so much fucking misery. My hands went to her towel, tugging it from her body. I trailed my fingers down her bare spine. She arched into me, her hands gripping my shoulders.

My mouth left hers. I trailed kisses down her jaw and neck. Across her collarbone, down her chest until I met her breasts. Taking a nipple in my mouth, I sucked and nipped it lightly knowing she needed a gentle touch rather than a rough one. She asked me to make love to her.

She mewled softly, clutching me tighter. Fuck. That noise. Everything about this girl gave me fucking heart palpitations and made my dick hard. I pulled her into my lap, grinding her against my thoroughly confined and aching cock.

"Aiden," she moaned.

She fucking knew what that did to me. My hand on her hip fell between her legs, stroking her pussy. Wet already. It was as if being close to each other was the spark, igniting the flame which constantly burnt between us.

"Please, Aiden, I need you."

I shifted her back slightly so I could reach my jeans. Her doe eyes held mine as I fumbled with the button and the zip. Finally freeing myself, I shoved my jeans and boxers down my thighs and pulled her back towards me. I held my cock as she sunk down on me slowly, inch by inch. She let out an agonising cross between a sob and a moan. It broke my fucking heart.

She wrapped her arms around my neck and buried her face in it as she rose and fell on my cock. I didn't know what else to do but hold her, kiss her and let her take what she needed from me.

"I love you," I whispered against her skin. "I'm here. I've got you. I'm never letting you go. I love you. I love you so much."

She cried into my shoulder, gut-wrenching sobs echoing around the hallway, but not once did she stop in her rhythm. I didn't know if this was fucking helping her or not. I didn't know what else she needed. That feeling of helplessness struck me again. I pressed my face into her hair.

"Avery, please, please don't cry."

"I can't... I can't stop."

"Princess."

"They all need to die, Aiden. All of them. They're monsters."

Her words chilled me to the bone. I never expected her to want people dead. She knew I would take their lives, but to have her actually express wanting it to happen was a new one on me.

"Is that what you need from me? To end them."

"Yes."

I kissed her hair. It would be better on my conscience than hers. I was already a killer. More bodies wouldn't make a difference to me. The pricks deserved it anyway after what they'd done.

"Okay, princess. We'll end them. I'll make sure they can't hurt anyone else. Okay?"

She nodded, pulling away from my shoulder. I wiped her tears from her face with my thumb. She took my hand and looked down at my bruised knuckles, her brow furrowing.

"What did you do?"

"I didn't hurt anyone. I took out my frustration on the bag."

She kissed each knuckle one by one before grabbing my other hand and kissing those knuckles too. Caring for me even though she was suffering herself. That was Avery all over. My girl. Such a fucking selfless soul.

"You're the one who needs taking care of, not me."

She smiled. The world fucking stopped along with my heart.

"We take care of each other."

She was right, as usual. Avery soothed my broken soul and I gave her all of me in return. I'd never let her go. Never again would I ruin things between us or ask her to do something she wasn't comfortable with.

She rocked her hips back and forth against mine. Her heat and the tightness of her causing me to groan. Fuck. Winding her hands into my hair, she kissed me again. This time it wasn't tentative or sweet. It was desperate and all-consuming. Her tongue melded with mine, her movements increasing as she rose and fell on me again. Fuck. I gripped one of her hips, whilst my other hand drove between her legs, fingers finding her clit.

She rode me harder as I stroked her. Her body vibrated with need. I felt her climax building inside her, the heat of her pussy reaching fucking boiling point. I grunted from the effort of holding back my own. This was about what she needed, not me.

She pulled away from me, burying her face in my neck as she shook. Her fingers dug into my shoulder. I could feel each clench and pulse as she came apart.

"Aiden. Oh fuck, Aiden."

Hearing my name on her lips was my complete undoing. I grunted, holding onto her hip and pressing deep inside her as I came too.

We stayed locked in each other's arms for a long moment after I'd collapsed against the wall, taking her with me.

Her lips pressed a kiss to my jaw.

"Are you okay?" I asked.

"No, but I feel a little better now."

I stroked her hair, kissing the top of her head.

"Why don't you dry your hair and get dressed. I'll make you some tea and you can tell me in your own time what happened."

She kissed my jaw again.

"Okay."

She shifted off me, grabbing the towel from the floor and going back in the bathroom. I used my discarded t-shirt to clean up before standing and pulling my boxers and jeans back up. I dumped my t-shirt in the wash basket in the bedroom before going through into the kitchen. Flipping the kettle on, I pulled out two mugs and put tea bags in them.

When I was done, I took the mugs through into the living room, set them down on the coffee table and sat on the sofa. A few minutes later, she walked in with her hair tied up in a loose bun dressed in pyjamas. There were little birds printed all over the bottoms. She sat down on the sofa next to me, curling her legs up underneath her.

I picked up a mug and handed it to her. She took a sip, smiling a little over the rim of the mug. I leant over and kissed her forehead.

"You're so good to me," she whispered.

I wasn't all the time, but when she really needed me, I put my shit aside and tried to be the man she deserved.

"I love you."

It was that simple. Love drove me to keep her safe and happy. Love was changing me. She was the reason for my existence in this fucked up world.

"I don't know who took me. All he wanted was a conversation and he showed me things I really didn't want to see."

"A conversation?"

She nodded.

"He hid his voice, it was some kind of robotic thing instead which was weird. He seemed very interested in our relationship. He knew things… intimate details. He talked about you like he knew you. It scared me. He said he'd been keeping you under surveillance."

I picked up my own mug and gulped down half of it to try and settle my fucking nerves. What the actual fuck?

"Then he started talking about your mother, asking me if you'd told me who killed her. He said you were there the night she died. He told me to ask you who you think it was and what happened. And then... and then he showed me something, I don't know if I can repeat what it was."

My suspicions about who it was burnt in my lungs. I put the mug down, afraid I'd throw it at the wall. It was him. It had to be. Fuck. This was the worst fucking thing that could've happened.

"Tell me."

She looked away.

"He showed me a video of my father... I... Aiden, I can't. It's too much."

I reached out, cupping her face and stroking her cheek with my thumb. I had to know. I had to fucking know what she saw.

"Tell me."

"It... it was my parents and your mother," she whispered. "He... he whipped her and then he was going to... to... and I couldn't look. I threw up over myself and the floor and made him turn it off."

My stomach dropped along with my hand. He'd made her sit through that. She started talking about what else he'd made her watch, but I was only half listening. There was video evidence of what Mitchell had done to her. How could I have never known this? I'd found his journal, which went into depth about how he'd used her, but a video. Fuck.

"Then he let me go, he said we'd meet again but the next time he'd tell me everything. I don't understand, Aiden. None of it makes any sense. I don't know why he'd show me all that stuff when he's involved in it. He was awful. He kept calling me darling, but he didn't pronounce it like that. He kept dropping the g, it was like darlin'."

"Take it darlin'."

"Don't lie darlin'."

Her words snapped me back to the present. I looked at her. The dread in my chest worsened. The knowledge of who had taken an interest in her burnt through me. I'd known he would never leave me alone. Hell, I'd fucking known he was probably keeping an eye on me just as I was him. And now he was threatening everything. He'd proven to me just how fucking untouchable he was by taking her. The girl he knew I loved.

"Because he could. That's what he does."

Her eyes widened.

"You… you know who it is."

I took a breath. I could no longer ignore my suspicions. It was the only logical explanation.

"Yes." I rubbed the back of my neck. "I told you one day he'd come after me and perhaps you."

She put her mug down on the coffee table and shuffled closer to me, wrapping a hand around my neck whilst the other cupped my cheek.

"Your… sperm donor?"

If this wasn't such a serious conversation, I would've smiled at the term she'd used. It was apt. I'd never call him, my father. He hadn't earnt that right. He was no one's fucking father. A monster in a fucking shiny suit with slicked-back hair and soulless eyes.

"Yes… Rick Morgan."

"Why have I heard that name before?"

"Because he's the CEO of The Harris Corporation in the US."

"My family does business with them regularly."

"Yes, they do and I can't do a fucking thing about him. He's dangerous. Far more so than Chuck and Frazier. You want to know why he knows so much about me? About us? Well, there you go. He has his fingers in too many pies."

Her expression was pensive, her body tense.

"He doesn't have any kids with his wife."

"No. Technically I'm his only offspring. I doubt she knows about my existence. He repeatedly raped my mother and knocked her up. That isn't the type of thing a man like him wants to be made public."

She was silent, looking at me with heart-rending sorrow. She didn't pity me or feel sorry for me. She just felt empathy. I was the spawn of a monster. Just like her in so many ways.

"I don't want you to worry about him, princess." I stroked her hair. "He won't harm you."

"How do you know?"

I sighed.

"Because I'm his son, Avery. Even if he's a psychopathic cunt, that still means something to him. After my mother died, Tina took care of me. He gave her the money to raise me, not your family."

"What happened that night?"

I looked away. Talking about the night she died was too fucking much for me. Not after the revelation he was back and he'd taken Avery. And my mind was a mess regarding it.

237

I didn't know what to think. I was no longer sure I knew who really killed her.

"I can't, princess. Not now."

She caught my face again and kissed me before leaning her forehead against mine.

"It's okay. I understand. You don't have to."

"I don't deserve you."

She smiled, putting her hand on my heart.

"All I could think about whilst I was gone is how much I wanted to be back in your arms. How much I need you. How much I love you. I don't want to be a Daniels any more, Aiden. I'm done with my family. After what he made me watch. All those men. I can't be a part of it. I don't want that associated with me."

"What are you saying?"

There were so many emotions flittering across her expression, I couldn't keep up. I understood why she didn't want that associated with her name, but what was she trying to tell me?

"You love me, right?"

"Yes, more than anything."

"And you want me yours forever."

"You know that."

She took my hand with her free one, slipping her fingers through mine and rubbing one of my bruised knuckles with her thumb.

"If I could, I'd tattoo your name across my heart. A permanent mark. And I'd tattoo the word soulmate below it because that's what you are even if I don't believe in bullshit like that."

Her doe eyes held so much. The love she felt for me poured out of them into mine.

"I vow to love you until the day I fade from this world, Aiden," she whispered.

The way she'd worded it felt like she was trying to communicate something significant to me.

"Vow?"

"I want to make many vows to you, but for now, I just vow to love you."

She wants… Wait, hold on… Avery… she wants to…

Avery wanted something I wasn't sure I could give her.

She wanted to marry me.

She wanted to be my wife.

That's what she was trying to tell me.

And I couldn't fucking speak any longer.

So instead of indicating I'd read between the lines and knew what the fuck she was talking about, I took the fucking coward's way out. I cupped her face with my free hand and kissed her. I did it because I couldn't deal with what she was trying to tell me. I couldn't go there right now. That was the biggest fucking commitment you could make to another person.

I wasn't ready.

Not now.

Not when everything was so fucked up in our lives. We had no idea if we had a future or if everything would crash and burn.

So I kissed Avery.

The girl I loved.

The conversation about commitment would just have to wait until I knew for sure I could give her everything she deserved.

Chapter Seventeen

Avery

1'd been looking forward to my first official day as the owner of Daniels Holdings before the weekend, but after I'd been kidnapped and returned, nothing felt the same.

John was sat on the sofas by the coffee table, fiddling with a tablet whilst keeping an eye on the door. I didn't much mind having him in here. My uncle had left not long ago after he'd seen for himself I was back safely. He'd been pleased I'd accepted I needed protection.

Ed was starting today. After I'd spoken to him on Friday, he was eager to get stuck in. I wasn't sure what he'd been doing before, but he'd dropped his other job at the drop of a hat. I was glad I didn't have to wait to have him start. Having someone I didn't hate would make me feel less alone here. He'd be up later when he'd gone through some paperwork with HR.

I sat back in my chair and stared at my computer screen. There were too many emails I had to deal with and I just couldn't think straight. Last night had been weird. The whole weekend had been a bit of a nightmare, but it was what I said to Aiden which bothered me the most. He hadn't said anything. Did he think I wanted more from our relationship? Was he freaking out?

I sighed. I had no idea.

"That's a big sigh. Everything okay?"

I looked up, finding John giving me a smile. He'd put his tablet down.

"Yeah, I'm just tired."

Liar. You're worried about you and Aiden, Rick and everything else in between.

"You had a tough weekend."

That was stating the obvious. No one wanted to get knocked out by whatever drugs they'd given me for an entire day. Then be shown a bunch of horrifying videos which proved just how sick their family was.

I rubbed my forehead. I'd explained to John what happened on the way to work like Aiden asked me to. I hadn't asked him if he knew Rick or had met him. I was curious about the man but not enough to pry just yet. Didn't think Aiden would want me to considering he told me not to worry about Rick.

"You can say that again. Are you sure you're okay with this whole protection gig? I can get my uncle to pick someone else."

"I don't mind sitting in the office all day if it means you're safe. Better than some of the things Chuck gets me to do."

"Speaking of my uncle, he keeps hinting at the company throwing me some kind of joint congratulations on the new job and birthday party. Has he actually arranged something?"

John smiled at me again.

"My lips are sealed."

"That means he has. Wonderful. Just what I wanted. No doubt he's invited all our clients."

Clients of both sides of the business. I didn't want to see any of those men. Not after I'd witnessed their sick fetishes and abuse of women.

"I can send you the memo which went out if you want."

"So you do know about it."

"He's put me in charge of security for the event."

I put my head on the desk, groaning. I didn't want a stupid birthday party thrown for me. Turning twenty one didn't mean much to me. I hadn't even spoken to Aiden about it.

"Is it really that bad?"

"You have been to a company event before, right? Boring small talk and being the centre of attention does not fill me with enthusiasm."

I heard a chuckle from his direction. Glad he found it funny. Becoming the face of Daniels Holdings was not my idea of fun or a good time. It had been hell, especially with the controversy surrounding my parents' deaths. We'd had countless requests for interviews, magazines wanting a tell-all. I'd told our media department to tell them all politely to fuck off. No interviews. No exclusives. Nothing. I was not a fucking circus performer.

There was a commotion outside my door and it was flung open, the slam against the wall ringing in my ears.

"Sir, excuse me, sir, you can't go in there," I heard my new secretary, Saskia, saying as I raised my head off the desk.

Frazier Shaw walked in, completely ignoring Saskia who had a deer in headlights look on her face. What the fuck did he want?

"Sir, you have to make an appointment with Miss Daniels."

I put my hand up.

"It's okay, Saskia. Mr Shaw is the firm's solicitor."

She stopped in her tracks and looked at me with a confused expression. I'd talk to her about it later. She'd only started this morning and Clara was still showing her the ropes.

"Can you make tea for Mr Shaw, Mr Williams and myself, please?"

She straightened, clearing her expression.

"Yes, of course, Miss Daniels."

She walked out of the room, shutting the door behind her. John had got up from the sofa, eying Frazier with a neutral expression.

"You need a better secretary," Frazier said as he walked over to my desk and sat down in one of the chairs in front of it.

"It's her first day and she is right. You do need to start making appointments. I have a very busy schedule today."

He gave me a smile.

"Of course, my apologies."

Except he looked anything but sorry. I hated this man. I clenched my fists under the desk, trying to remain calm. I was not expecting him to turn up today. As far as I was aware, there was no trouble with the paperwork from Friday. He had no real reason to be here.

"What can I do for you?"

His eyes flicked over to John, who was still standing, watching both of us carefully.

"I would prefer this conversation to be between the two of us. I'm sure John won't mind stepping out for a moment."

I didn't want to be alone with Frazier, but I couldn't exactly say no. I nodded at him before turning to John.

"We won't be long."

"As you wish, Miss Daniels."

I hoped he'd tell Aiden about this development because I couldn't exactly text him right now. He wouldn't be happy, but what else could I do? John nodded at me and walked out, shutting the door behind him. I turned back to Frazier.

"When is Ed starting?" he asked.

"Today."

"Good. Good."

He looked around my room for a moment before settling his dark eyes back on me. The skin on the back of my neck prickled.

"Before your father passed, we spoke a lot about you. Whilst I'm aware you and my son have your differences, I do believe it would be in your best interests to reconsider joining our families together. It was your father's wish."

I bit the side of my cheek, digging my nails into my palms. His eyes told me he knew very well Tristan had tried to assault me on Friday. Nausea coiled in my stomach. Why the fuck did it keep coming back to this? First my father, then Aiden and now Frazier. All wanting me to get shackled to a man who lacked any sort of morals or boundaries.

"As I told my father, if I am ever to get married, it would be on my terms and my choice." I sat back in my chair. "I do wonder why you are so concerned about me not having a husband. I don't recall my personal life being anyone's business but my own."

His eyes narrowed. What the hell did he expect me to say? I wasn't backing down on this point. The only person I'd ever consider getting married to was Aiden. The thought of him and what I'd said last night came rushing back. There was no doubt in my mind. He was definitely freaked out by it and I really hadn't meant to insinuate I wanted him to ask me to marry him. It was far too soon. We had so much to do before we were in the clear and could publicly acknowledge we were in a relationship.

As much as I wanted to take his last name so I could shed my Daniels identity, I would never pressurise him. I knew how hard it was for him to be in a relationship in the first place. How much he'd had to overcome since the day we met. My complicated man was healing his old wounds in the way he knew how. I couldn't add to that on top of all the other things we were up against.

I couldn't help but be suspicious of what Frazier was fishing for. Why the hell did he want me to marry Tristan? It wasn't like either of them could take the company from me if that happened. Was it to do with the company or something else?

"I merely worry for you. A woman at the head of such a large company. And now I see John is protecting you."

Is he for real? Sexist pig. Not sure why I'm even surprised. He makes me sick.

"Ask Uncle Charlie about that, he's the one insisting on me having a bodyguard."

"And so he should. The person who murdered your parents is still out there."

If he didn't keep stating the fucking obvious, I was going to lose my shit. As if I didn't know that.

"Well yes, but that doesn't mean they are after me as well."

"They could be. I'm trying to look out for you, Avery. You'd be the perfect wife for Tristan. He needs a woman who won't let him walk all over her."

I tried not to throw up in my mouth. What he needed was to be put down for what he'd tried to do to me, but we don't get everything we want in life. I don't know when my shift in mindset happened, but I no longer saw things as black and white. All of them should go to prison. That was the law. Except that wasn't enough justice for me. They needed to pay for what they'd done. And they needed to pay with their lives.

"You know Tristan and I don't get along."

He scoffed, raising his eyebrows.

"Do you think that's how marriage works?"

"You know, I thought the whole point of it was for two people who loved each other to make the ultimate commitment."

He laughed, throwing back his head.

"You really are innocent of this world. In this business, marriage is never about love. It's about who gives you the most power, advantage, money or social status."

It didn't come as a surprise he thought this way about it.

"Tell me, Frazier, what does Tristan bring to the table?"

He steepled his hands together, dark eyes appraising me.

"All of those things and more."

I fought back the urge to roll my eyes. My inheritance might be tied up in a trust until I was twenty-five, but I was one of the richest women in the world. So they definitely couldn't bring money to the table nor power. Frazier was talking a whole bunch of shit as usual. Did he really think I was that stupid and naïve?

"You'd do well to seriously consider it. There are many threats in this world and we wouldn't want you to end up like your parents."

A chill ran down my spine at his words.

Well, that's not creepy or threatening at all.

"Is this all you came to speak to me about? A phone call would've sufficed."

Did I care that I sounded borderline rude?

Not one bit.

Frazier could get fucked. We had to do something about him. I was tired of being threatened by everyone around me. It was like a never-fucking-ending cycle. Something had to give. I'd speak to Aiden about it later.

I'd only been back in the world for a few weeks and I'd been threatened by Frazier, had Tristan attempt to rape me, had Chuck all over my movements like I was some kind of criminal and I'd been kidnapped. My track record was not looking good.

Frazier stood up, staring down at me with unnerving intensity.

"Just think about it, Avery."

He turned his heel and began to walk away just as Saskia opened the office door after knocking. She looked startled when he stormed out without looking at her.

"Is he not staying?" she asked.

"No."

She came into the room and put down one of the mugs she was holding on a coaster for me.

"Mr Daniels is waiting for you."

As much as I wanted to get stuck in with Ed, I really needed a minute to compose myself after having Frazier in here.

"Take him that tea and give me five minutes. Send John back in too."

She nodded at me and shuffled out of the room. I grabbed the mug and took a gulp of scolding hot tea, not caring how much my mouth burnt afterwards. My nerves were frayed. I rubbed my throat and looked up at the ceiling. I needed to work out what the fuck Frazier wanted from me. What did he have to gain by me marrying Tristan?

"You look like you could do with another few days off," John said as he came into the room.

"You can say that again."

I lowered my head. He had a mug of tea in his hand and a concerned expression on his face.

"Dare I ask what he wanted?"

"Apparently everyone and his son wants me to marry Tristan. I don't know why he's so insistent. It's not like he has anything to gain from it, at least not that I can think of off the top of my head."

John dug his phone out of his pocket and fiddled with it. I knew he was texting Aiden.

"I'll keep an eye on it."

He gave me a nod and walked back over to my sofas, settling himself down again. I didn't strictly need him here, but after what happened with Tristan, I didn't trust anyone. If he could get to me in my own building, I wasn't safe.

I sipped at my tea again, grimacing at the pain from having burnt my mouth. My nerves were still unsettled despite the tea. Could this day get any worse?

"Morning little cousin," Ed said as he breezed into the office with the biggest grin on his face.

I popped my mug back on the desk, standing up and coming around it.

"Ed, welcome to the company."

I went to shake his hand, but instead, Ed enveloped me in a bear hug. I patted his back awkwardly. Even though I thought my cousin was a good guy, there was still the sneaking suspicion in the back of my mind that he had everything to do with the other side of the business. I stepped back when he released me.

"I'm looking forward to working with you."

"I'm glad to hear it. Let's get you set up in the office next door."

I started walking towards the door with him.

"You will be getting a brand new office, but it's been renovated alongside mine."

I pointed down the corridor to where my dad's old office was.

"Good stuff," he replied, rubbing his hands together. "Say, I saw Frazier storming out of your office a few minutes ago. Anything to be concerned about?"

"What? No. It was a personal call rather than a business one. As I said on Friday, everything went smoothly."

He gave me a strange look, but before I could question it, we were in his office and his expression cleared.

"This looks great. So, where do we start?"

I smiled at him.

"Someone from IT will be up soon. I thought we could go over the discussions I had with the board on Friday together."

He sat down at his desk, grinning from ear to ear. I didn't quite know what to make of his flitting from one mood to another so quickly. My palms started sweating a little. I wiped them on the back of my trousers as I sat down in the chair in front of his desk.

"Before that, can I ask why John is here?"

Most of my family knew John, so it wasn't surprising he'd asked.

"Uncle Charlie thinks I need someone protecting me."

I didn't dare tell him what happened over the weekend.

"Any particular reason?"

I shrugged.

"He's been overprotective since I came back. I can't blame him really after what happened to Mum and Dad."

Ed raised an eyebrow.

"No, I suppose I understand." He folded his arms across his chest. "Say, little cousin, are you seeing anyone?"

I froze. Why was he asking me that? It seemed like an odd question given what we'd just been discussing.

"Um, no... why?"

He waved a hand at me.

"You've got this kind of glow about you."

What the actual fuck is he talking about?

"I do?"

"Yeah, you just seem happier. I mean obviously things have been tough on you, but before your parents died, you were really closed off. You just seem different now."

I had absolutely no idea how to respond to that. Being with Aiden had changed me, but I didn't think it was that noticeable. And why would I seem happier when my whole life had gone to shit? My parents were dead. I was head of a company I wanted nothing to do with. I'd been kidnapped, held captive and found out my family were a bunch of sick bastards.

"Well, thanks... I think. Still not seeing anyone."

"Are you sure? What about that friend of yours? You know, the one you grew up with. It's high time you got snapped up. You're being called the most eligible heiress."

I chose to ignore his latter comment. I'd seen that shit on the internet. I was more concerned as to why he was asking me if I was seeing my best friend.

"What, James?" I frowned. "Um no, that would be weird."

"Doesn't he have an older brother?"

My eyebrows shot up. Where the hell was Ed going with this? Was he fishing for information? I wanted to put my head in my hands. This was suspicious as fuck, especially after I'd had Frazier in here. Was that what this was about?

"And now we're changing the subject."

I hadn't come in here to talk about my love life.

"Don't tell me you have a crush on him?"

I really couldn't believe my ears.

"As if I would date my best friend's older brother. I'm not that desperate."

He winced.

"Ouch."

"Oh god, look, there's nothing wrong with him, but just no. This conversation is officially over. Can we get on with some work?"

He clapped his hands together.

"Of course, sorry, I was merely curious."

Curious my fucking arse. I'm one hundred per cent sure he was fishing for information.

I really needed to have a word with Aiden about this shit. We had to do something about Frazier for starters, but this stuff with Ed made me uncomfortable. What the hell was his agenda? Who was pulling his strings? Was it Troy? Chuck? Why was everyone so fucking interested in who I was seeing and who I was or was not getting married to?

Everything was getting messier by the fucking day. There were too many players on the board. Too many people pulling me this way and that. Everyone wanted something different from me. I had no idea what to do or think about any of it.

I was being pulled deeper and deeper into the web of lies and secrets. All of it confused the fuck out of me. I had to get out in front of this. Had to find a way to stop it all from coming crashing down in front of my face.

The only way I was going to do that is if Aiden and I actually came up with a solid plan to deal with each threat. It had to start with Frazier. He was my most pressing concern. I had to know why the hell he wanted me to marry Tristan so badly.

When I got back this evening, Aiden and I were going to talk. Not about what I'd said last night, but about what our next move was.

It couldn't come soon enough as far as I was concerned.

Chapter Eighteen

Aiden

*A*very looked dejected when she walked in the front door. John hadn't come up with her so I assumed he dropped her off outside the building. I was still feeling a little weird after yesterday when she basically told me she wanted to get married without actually saying it at all. I was in two minds about whether I'd misinterpreted her or not. It didn't mean I was ready to talk about it. I loved this girl to death, but conversations about our future weren't easy when we didn't even know what the future would look like yet. Not when all the shit with her family was still up in the air.

"Long day, princess?"

She looked up at me as I walked over to her. She hung up her coat. I wrapped my arms around her and pulled her into my chest. My inner fucking turmoil which had plagued me since she'd been taken could do one. Right now, my girl needed me.

"Yes."

"Want to talk about it? I have dinner ready for you."

"Yes."

I pulled away slightly so I could look down at her. Her cautious expression concerned me as did her monosyllabic answers.

"What's wrong?"

"I'm tired. Today was really weird. The shit with Frazier and then Ed was asking me about my love life. I don't know what to think any longer."

John told me Frazier had turned up. I watched the footage from her office. He really was a fucking thorn in our sides. I realised I had originally wanted Avery to get engaged to Tristan, but that had been one of the most idiotic ideas I'd ever had. Especially given how I felt about her. I couldn't stomach the thought of that psycho near her again. I'd only just about held back from snapping his neck on Friday.

Nothing about this weekend had done either of us any good. I was still worked up about Rick taking her. It still killed me how helpless I'd felt. How out of control I'd been of the situation. I hated feeling this way. Hated how it brought back memories of a time I'd been so consumed by violent rage because they'd taken my mother's life. I couldn't allow myself to fall back into that black hole again. Not when I had to be the man Avery needed me to be.

"Ed asked you about your love life?"

"I denied being involved with anyone, but he was like what about James and after I said no, he thought I had a thing for Dante. Why would I entertain the idea of dating my best friend's older brother? We practically grew up together. Do I seem like the type of girl who's spent her whole life with some secret crush? Like what the hell? I don't even know. I was too embarrassed to tell John about it. And now talking about it to you…"

She buried her face back in my chest, but not before I saw her cheeks going red. I held back a smile. Fuck. Sometimes she was so fucking cute, it killed me. Even though she was talking about other guys, it didn't matter. I knew she was mine. The shit with James was over. We'd put it behind us.

"No, you don't seem like that type of girl at all."

Her cousin asking about who she was with should be an innocuous question. Except when it came to her family, nothing was innocent. There was always a hidden agenda. We just had to work out what Ed's was.

"I don't know whether to thank you for saying that or want the ground to swallow me up."

"Princess…"

"I just had a really weird day, okay? I'm so fucking done."

I held her, rocking her from side to side until she looked up at me.

"Aiden, we need to do something about Frazier."

I nodded, pulling away and taking her hand. She slipped her shoes off and we went into the kitchen. I made her sit down at the table whilst I dished up enchiladas. I thought she might want her favourite after dealing with Mr Shaw earlier.

"This smells amazing," she sighed, digging in.

I smiled. Avery always appreciated the simple pleasures I gave her like a homecooked meal and running her a bath after a long day. A part of me felt guilty for taking the easy way out yesterday. Not that this made up for it. I was just trying to make her happy. She was on the front line dealing with her family and Frazier every day.

"I feel like there's something I'm missing," she said after a few minutes. "Something important about why Frazier wants me to marry Tristan. They can't take the company from me. The paperwork is signed. It's mine by rights."

"Maybe it has nothing to do with the company."

"Then what could it be?"

There were only a few things men like Frazier desired more than anything. Money and power. It was a question of which one he wanted more. Did he think he could use Avery as a puppet or did he want her fortune?

"What does he have to gain from it? In your opinion."

Her brow furrowed as she stuffed a forkful of food in her mouth.

"He could want to manipulate me, but why would he tell me Tristan needs a girl who will stand up to him if he wanted that? I don't know, maybe he wants the money. It's wrapped up in a trust until I'm twenty-five."

She shook her head, putting her fork down.

"Neither of those options make sense."

And yet one of them had to be right. I knew her money was wrapped up in a trust. It wasn't like I wanted it and neither did she.

"Have you seen the paperwork?"

"For what? My trust fund… No. My dad took care of all that."

"Maybe you should look at it."

She picked up her fork again.

"Yeah… maybe. I feel weird about going to the penthouse though. The police released it back to my uncle when they concluded their investigations, but it's legally mine."

I didn't blame her. I didn't want to go back there either. Not to the place we'd first met. Where I'd killed her parents and started us on this fucked up path we seemed to be on together. One that was fast approaching a messy conclusion if we didn't deal with Frazier.

"Is that the only place he'd have kept it?"

"Yes, in his office. I guess I don't have much choice."

I reached over the table and took her free hand, rubbing my thumb down the back of it.

"Do you want me to come with you?"

She shook her head, giving me a sad smile.

"No, that's too dangerous considering everything. I'll be okay."

I hoped she would. Avery was stronger than she realised. She'd been through so much and she was still standing. Still proving to me day in day out how she took everything in her stride and kept giving no matter what. The most selfless girl I'd ever met.

"There's something else... Uncle Charlie is throwing me a congratulations on owning the company slash birthday party."

"He's what?"

This was the first I'd heard of it.

"Yeah, I know... John sent me the memo. Charlie hasn't officially told me yet, but he keeps dropping hints like it's some kind of stupid surprise thing. I didn't ask him to do it. I may have cornered Clara and found out all the details."

It would create more publicity for the company and perhaps put a positive spin on everything when all they'd had was bad press recently. There were still rumours circulating about Avery being involved in her parents' deaths. She was tired of hearing about it. She'd told me just last week before all the shit with Tristan and Rick had gone down. She'd barely been back in the world for a few weeks and it was already wearing her down.

"He's no doubt doing it to show the world the company is moving in a positive direction after everything."

"I hadn't thought of it like that. You're probably right. Still, I feel like I'll be up on display like some show pony, trotted out to say 'look how progressive we are, a woman is at the helm' — it makes me sick to think of it like that. Especially after dealing with Frazier the chauvinistic pig earlier. He obviously thinks I'm incapable of running the company because I'm female. I'm not saying I'm qualified, but it has nothing to do with my gender."

I tried not to smile. She could be so fucking cute when she was ranting. The little furrow between her eyebrows and the way she looked like a little kitten getting frustrated by the big bad world.

"I seriously don't know what his problem is. He was all like oh you'd be the perfect woman for my son. Like what is that? We hate each other. You know what, I'm done with talking about this. It's just pissing me off. I've been linked to three different men today and I'm done."

I felt bad for smiling, but I couldn't help it.

"You know who you are perfect for?"

She looked up at me, her eyes narrowing.

"Who?"

"Me."

She sat there for a moment, biting her lip. Was she trying to hide a smile? She got up and walked around the table before she slipped into my lap and wrapped her arms around my neck. We hadn't finished eating but having her close to me was a welcome distraction.

"Are you trying to be smart?"

I caught the back of her neck and pulled her closer, trailing kisses along her jaw. She shivered.

"No." I reached her ear, nibbling the lobe slightly. "I love you. No one else makes me happy. Only you."

"Aiden…"

"I want to worship every inch of you. I love everything about you. You're so fucking beautiful, smart, strong… you're my everything, princess."

Even if I couldn't talk about what she'd said last night, I could still tell her how much she meant to me. I could still reassure her I was in this with her. Even with our future up in the air, I was hers for as long as she wanted me.

"Frazier can go fuck himself along with anyone else who's bothering you," I continued. "Just remember you come home to me every night. I take care of you. I give you what you need. And what you need right now is to forget about everything else but you and me."

I gripped both her hips, tugging her into me until her chest was right up against mine.

"I'll take it away for you. Do you want that?"

"Yes," she whispered, her hand curling into the hair at the back of my neck. "Please."

"How would you like it? Do you want to sit on my cock or do you want me to bend you over the table?"

"I want you to fuck me hard."

I smiled. The table then.

"Finish your dinner first. I want to take my time with you."

I let her go. She had a shy smile on her face when she got off me. I could never get enough of her and she knew it. It wasn't just about the sex even though we had a lot of it. It never had been. She was right when she said we were soulmates last night. As fucking cheesy and cliché as it sounded.

She was mine

And I was hers.

"Do you know what you want for your birthday?" I asked as we lay in bed together later.

"I thought you'd never ask."

I looked down at her. She was smiling at me.

"Did you think I'd forgotten?"

I hadn't. I knew she was turning twenty-one. It was something I'd put in my phone calendar. I'd been trying to work out what to get her but hadn't come up with any solid ideas.

"No…"

I ruffled her hair. She batted my hand away, scowling. I knew she hated it when I did that.

"You did. I'm not completely useless at this relationship business, princess. Now, other than this birthday party you don't want to attend, is there anything else you want to do?"

She looked at her hands, tracing lines along my tattoos.

"Well, it would be nice if we went away together, but that's not going to happen with everything else that's going on. So no... but I do know what I want."

I wish I could take her away from all of this, but it was our responsibility to finish what we'd started. To end the fucking shit her family had been involved in for so long. Perhaps it would finally put to rest all my demons. All my memories. I couldn't think of those now. Couldn't allow myself to get wrapped up in that violence again.

"And that is?"

"You know how we talked about tattoos? I want to get them for my birthday."

"The birds and the wings?"

She nodded, her fingers still brushing across my chest.

"And something else. Out of all of yours, these ones here, they're my favourites and... I want one of my own. On my arm."

I blinked. She wanted an Aztec god tattooed on her. She'd studied mine when she thought I was sleeping. I'd felt her fingers on my chest, tracing the outlines over and over again. What I hadn't realised is how much she wanted it done to her.

"Are you sure?"

"Yes. I've researched them and I identify most with Xochiquetzal, the goddess of fertility, beauty and female sexual power."

I held back a smile. She was certainly beautiful and well, sex with her was fucking amazing. She had that way about her. If she wanted another tattoo, who was I to stand in her way? The fact she wanted something to match mine made my heart fucking soar.

"I'm sure Ben will be more than happy to do them for you."

She stopped stroking my chest and looked up at me.

"Do you think it will look good on me?"

"Princess... you'll look even sexier with tattoos. You know I think you're perfect the way you are, but if you want to get more ink for your birthday, then we'll get you more ink."

She kissed my chest.

"In fact, I'll text Ben now."

I leant over and grabbed my phone off the bedside table.

ME: How's Skye & bump? I need a favour.

BEN: They're good. For you? Anything within reason ;)

ME: Avery's birthday is soon & she wants a new tattoo... or two.

BEN: I'm in. Text me the details & I'll start designing.

ME: I owe you.

"He's happy to do it. Here, you can tell him what you want."

I handed her the phone. She smiled at me and rolled over onto her back, spending the next few minutes typing out a long message to him. She gave me the phone when she was done.

"I hope he'll have time to do it before the birth, but if not, then we'll just have to wait. Is that okay for you?" I asked.

"Yes, I'm just happy it's happening. It feels right. This is the one thing I can control unlike everything else in my life. It's all such a fucking mess."

I rolled onto my side and stroked her bare stomach with my fingers.

"I know. I wish things could be different."

"If they were, we might not have met each other. I don't know about you, but I can't imagine my life without you."

I leant down and kissed her, savouring the way she tasted. Fuck. She made me so fucking happy. How could I not want this girl? I needed her. We still had so much to discover about each other, but the things I did know made me love her all the more.

We'd been arguing less recently. There hadn't been a blow-up between us since she told me about James and her. I'd been trying not to let my control slip again. She didn't need it on top of everything else. Another reason why I didn't want to talk about the marriage thing. I didn't want to end up in yet another fight with her over it.

It was too soon, wasn't it?

We'd known each other such a short time and yet we'd been through so much together. It felt like longer. With Avery, it felt like forever.

"I love you, princess," I whispered against her lips, shifting over her fully.

I tucked my fingers into her underwear and pulled them off, discarding them over the side of the bed so she was naked beneath me. I might have fucked her over the table earlier after we'd finished dinner and dumped everything in the dishwasher, but I couldn't get enough of her. The way her skin felt against mine. The noises she made when I hit just the right spot. The way she cried out my name over and over again when she came.

Most of all, I couldn't get enough of the way she loved me. How open she was. How she gave herself over to me again and again. I looked up at the painting she'd given me for

Christmas. I wanted more of her paintings on the walls. I wanted to make a home and a life with this girl so fucking bad. I loved her so much.

I spread her legs, running my fingers down her inner thighs. She arched up against me, moaning into my mouth. Her hands wrapped around my back, nails digging into my skin. I cupped her breast, rolling her nipple between my thumb and forefinger. Her fucking perfect set of tits.

"Aiden, please," she whimpered into my mouth. "Please, please."

"Patience."

"Please fuck me. I want your cock in me."

Fuck. The need in her voice did things to me.

"If I fuck you right now, you need to do something for me."

"Anything."

I tugged off my boxers, kicking them away as I settled between her legs, rubbing my cock up and down her pussy. She whimpered, arching into me.

"I want you to paint more. I want to fill our bare walls with your art."

Before she could respond, I thrust into her. She cried out, nails digging further into my skin.

"Our walls?" she asked when she caught her breath, her doe eyes wide.

"Yes, this is our home, princess. I'm going to convert the cell and my office back into the second bedroom, but if you want to find somewhere that's ours, we can do that too."

She shook her head.

"No. This is our home. I'll paint for you. You know I'll do anything for you."

"I know."

I set a steady pace, feeling her heat surround me. This was fucking heaven. Having Avery with me. Knowing she wanted to spend the rest of her life with me. Wanted to make a home with me. It really was everything and more.

Maybe…

Just maybe…

I wanted to marry Avery too.

Chapter Nineteen

Avery

Sat in a coffee shop next to James with John seated a few tables down watching the door, I stared off into the distance. It'd been exactly a week since my conversation with Rick Morgan. I'd spent time reading up about him at work. I felt awful for doing it and not telling Aiden, but I had to know who he was. I had to understand. Rick's hair was the exact same shade as Aiden's and his features far too similar. Perhaps it was because I knew Aiden so intimately, but it was clear as day to me. That was the man who gave life to the one I loved so much.

"You're very quiet," James said. "What gives?"

Too bloody much. It wasn't like I could tell him about Rick. No one else knew except me, Aiden and John. It seemed my father's old driver and bodyguard had become an ally of sorts. He fed information to Aiden about Chuck and kept an eye on me during the day.

It was Sunday. Aiden had things to do so he'd asked John to come with me. James and I hadn't really talked much since I'd turned up at his flat the night before Rick had taken me.

He knew about my kidnapping, I just hadn't told him we knew exactly who'd done it.

"Stuff."

"Ave…"

I sighed, shifting slightly so I could look at him head-on. His blue eyes twinkled in the late afternoon sun. I might not be able to talk about Rick, but there was something else bothering me. Something else I could probably only voice to James. Gert was due to join us soon so it had to be now.

"Aiden is acting weird."

"Weird how?"

It was my own bloody fault. I shouldn't have said anything to him, but I had.

"He keeps looking at me like I'm made of glass. Like any minute things could all fall apart and he's scared of that happening. I don't know. Things aren't right between us."

Again. My fault. Entirely my fault. I should've known better.

"Did anything happen between you that might have brought this on?"

I stared down at my cup of tea.

"I may have said something which I think had a completely undesired effect."

"Now you're just being cryptic."

I sighed, fiddling with the cup and continuing to avoid eye contact.

"I may have told him in not so many words that I wanted to get married."

James almost spat out the tea he was in the middle of drinking.

"You did what? Are you fucking mental? Avery, guys don't want to hear that shit from women they've only been with for a few months."

I knew I'd been an idiot and now I'd scared the shit out of Aiden. He hadn't really said anything about it. He'd barely acknowledged my words, but I'd seen the terrified rabbit expression flitter across his face when I'd told him I wanted to make several vows to him.

"You think I don't know that."

"What the fuck brought this on?"

I looked up at him. He was giving me one of those 'I need to knock some sense into you' looks.

"I can't stand people calling me, Miss Daniels."

"So what, you want to get married to Aiden so you can stop being called Daniels? Do you know how fucking batshit crazy that sounds?"

I picked up my cup and gulped half of it down.

"That's not why and you know it. Fuck, I'm such a mess right now. Everything has just gone to shit completely. I'm ruining my relationship by pressurising Aiden into thinking he has to make some kind of big commitment to me. I don't know who the fuck to trust in my family any longer. Frazier keeps turning up at the office and bothering me about Tristan. I don't fucking know any more."

James rubbed my arm.

"Hey, hey, it's okay. Christ, Ave, you really know how to complicate things."

I put my cup down and dropped my head into my hands.

"I wish I could take it back. He didn't even acknowledge what I said. I mean it's not like I outright told him I wanted to get married or anything, but fuck."

He tugged me towards him and wrapped his arms around me, stroking my back.

"I think you need to talk to him."

"And say what exactly? Hey, Aiden, I'm sorry I made out like I wanted us to get married and I didn't mean it."

"Who's getting married?" came Gert's voice. "Wait, are you and Aiden tying the knot? Oh my god, this is so exciting."

I wrenched out of James' arms, finding my other best friend planting herself in the chair opposite me with the hugest grin on her face.

"No one is getting married," James said. "It's way, way too soon so don't even go there, Gertie."

"But they're perfect for each other. Who cares if they've only been together for a short time? When you know, you know."

I groaned, banging my head on the table and keeping it there. This was just getting out of hand now. All I'd wanted to do was confide in James because I had no one else to tell.

"I am not getting married to Aiden. I said something stupid to him and now things are weird between us, that's all."

"What? Spill all."

I didn't want to repeat what I'd said. The whole thing was just plain embarrassing. Telling Aiden all that shit about wanting to tattoo his name on my heart and that he was my soulmate. No bloody wonder he was being weird. It wasn't like I expected him to ask me to marry him or even want to go down that road with me.

We did talk the next day, but it wasn't about this. I was happy he wanted me to feel like his flat was our home. And I'd been surprised by him telling me he was going to demolish the office and the cell to make a second bedroom. That didn't mean he was okay about the marriage thing. It didn't mean he wasn't freaked out by it. Why else would he have completely ignored what I said?

I lifted my head off the table. James's eyes were sympathetic and Gert's curious.

"Aiden keeps telling me he doesn't deserve me. I was trying to reassure him and it came out wrong."

"What exactly did you say?"

"I told him I vowed to love him until I died basically and he questioned why I'd said vow, so I said, 'I want to make many vows to you, but for now, I just vow to love you.' Now, things are really fucked up, okay?"

"Way to lay it on thick, Ave," James said.

I punched him in the arm. He just had to make me feel worse about it.

"Lay off her, James," Gert said. "Babe, it's okay. I'm sure he didn't think you were saying you wanted to get married."

I shook my head.

"Oh no, he did. You should've seen the look he gave me." I put my head in my hands again. "Why am I so bad at this?"

"Well, I hate to break it to you, but this is your first proper relationship," James said. "I mean you have moved pretty quickly. You do basically live together full time and have done since you met."

"Stop scaring the poor girl," Gert said. "Honestly, it'll be okay. You just need to talk to him and make it clear you weren't saying you wanted to tie him down."

"You have met Aiden, right? He is kind of a scary dude."

I peeked through my fingers at the two of them. James had a raised eyebrow and Gert was looking at him like he was stirring up trouble, which admittedly, he probably was. Aiden was a little intimidating at times, but I still talked to him about the difficult subjects. This was new territory for me. He'd been the one who broached the subject of us having a real relationship together. Now I'd just made a complete hash of trying to tell him I wanted him for life.

"If he loves Avery, then he'll listen and forgive her for the misunderstanding."

"I never said he didn't love her. You haven't seen him pissed off."

"And you have?"

"Well not exactly, no. I can imagine it though."

"Then shut up and stop being unhelpful."

"Hey, I resent that accusation."

Gert stuck her tongue out at him.

"What the fuck do you even know anyway, Mr 'I don't commit to girls because they're too much work'?"

"Hey!"

"Okay, that's enough you two," I said, dropping my hands. "I will speak to Aiden. I have no other choice."

It wasn't just that he was acting weird, we hadn't had sex since Monday. It had been fucking amazing, but it didn't make up for the fact we'd stopped sleeping together daily. He'd been working late dealing with the new security acquisitions for the company and spent a lot of time talking things over with John.

I had to fix this shit between us. I had to make it right.

"Anyway, I thought you had news," I continued.

Gert's ears went red. My senses prickled immediately. What on earth did she have to be shy about?

"Well…"

"You've met someone, haven't you?" James butted in.

Gert folded her arms over her chest and scowled.

"Way to ruin the surprise."

"I knew it. Come on, tell us all."

She was trying to hold back a smile and failing miserably because both of us could see that grin forming.

"Okay, okay… her name is Tilly, she's doing a fine arts degree, she's got pink hair and she's just so funny, smart and cute as hell."

Gert had been with a lot of different people unlike me. When we were twelve, she'd expressed an interest in both sexes and had come out as bi by the time we were fourteen.

"Fine arts? Really, Gertie? You know what happened last time you went out with someone doing an arts degree."

"That was different."

"Don't bring her up," I said.

Her ex, Manuela, was a fucking bitch who'd broken Gert's heart. I honestly could've strangled the girl. She'd lied about them being exclusive. Gert found her in bed with two other girls. It'd taken a month of Gert sobbing into my shoulder and eating ice cream for dinner every night before she got over it. James had been less than impressed with Gert's choice in partners ever since.

"What? She doesn't have a stellar reputation for picking the right girl… or guy for that matter. Don't forget what Rodrigo did to her."

Rodrigo was an exchange student who Gert had lost her 'guy virginity' to. She liked to think she'd lost her virginity twice, once to a guy and once to a girl. He'd basically wooed her into bed then told her the next day he was dumping her because she wasn't that hot compared to Lucy Danvers, the most annoying stuck up girl in our class.

James was right. Gert really didn't have the best track record when it came to dating. Probably why I'd been so reluctant to get involved with anyone after seeing what those breakups had done to her. The George thing hadn't helped either. I should never have slept with him.

"Can we not bring up all my failed relationships?" Gert said, folding her arms over her chest. "I really like Tilly and she likes me, okay? She's not Manny or Rodrigo. She's a nice girl and I want you two to be on board with this."

"I'm sure she's great," I said. "Do you have a picture of her?"

She nodded, grinning before she pulled out her phone. Her wallpaper was her and a pink haired girl with their arms wrapped around each other. She was kind of cute in a hippy sort of way.

"She's pretty, isn't she, James?"

"Yes, very nice, Gertie. You've done well," he responded.

I could tell he was just saying that to make Gert happy and he wasn't at all impressed with her new girlfriend. I could hardly blame him. He'd had to mop up Gert's tears alongside me. He hated seeing her upset just as much as I did.

I gave him a sharp look. All I got back was a shrug.

"I'm going to get a drink. You guys want anything?" Gert said, standing up.

I shook my head and James waved her away. When she was out of earshot, I turned to him.

"Are you trying to upset her?"

"What? No. It's just you know what she's like, runs headlong into these things without really knowing anything about them and then it ends badly. I don't want her to get hurt again."

I raised an eyebrow.

"Are you sure it's just that?"

"Do you think I'm jealous because both of you are seeing someone? Don't make me laugh."

"James…"

He sighed, rolling his eyes.

"I'm fine, Ave. Honestly, I don't have time for girls right now. Not with Dad and Dante on my case. There's something weird going on with them."

James started working for his dad when we left school in the corporate offices of Bensons. He worked in distribution, which he somewhat enjoyed, but it didn't mean he liked working for his dad.

"Weird how?"

"I overheard them talking about preparations and a girl, but I don't know what the fuck it's about. Dante was like, it's still over a year away and Dad said they can never be too careful. I didn't stick around, you know they'd only have got mad if they found out I was eavesdropping."

That seemed odd. James didn't really get along with Dante any longer. Shit with their family was weird. They'd lived away from their father for a while because of the abuse, but then something changed. James said Dante just flipped a switch and started being a dick to everyone. Things had just gone downhill from there.

I still got along fine with him whenever I saw him, which these days wasn't often. I saw him as my big brother in so many ways. I'd spent so much time with the Bensons when I was younger. I didn't care much for James' sisters, Jen and Fi. The twins stuck their noses up at me, but Dante was different. He was five years older than James and me and looked out for us when we'd been at school until he graduated. That was when he'd taken James, Jen and Fi away from Zach. They'd lived with him until they were old enough to move out themselves.

"I'm sure it's nothing, James. You shouldn't get involved either, that won't end well."

"You're right. I should just forget about it. Hey, what did UCL say when you told them you weren't coming back?"

"They were fine about it, especially after my parents dying and me needing to officially withdraw so I could take over the company. I'm not upset about not completing my degree. You know it's not what I wanted to do."

Gert arrived back with her latte.

"What are we talking about now?" she asked.

"Just about what UCL said when Avery ditched her course," James replied.

"I did not ditch my course. Don't be a dick, James," I said.

Gert grinned, rolling her eyes.

278

"She never really wanted to do architecture anyway."

"She didn't want to run a global company either."

And now we were back to arguing again. How did we ever get along when all we did was wind each other up and talk shit?

"And Avery would prefer you not to talk about her like she isn't here."

They both looked at me with sheepish expressions.

"Sorry, babe," Gert said.

"It's fine. What's done is done. I'm not really running it by myself anyway. Ed's started now so things are getting a little easier for me."

"Can I just say your cousin is one damn fine male specimen."

She winked at me, licking her lips.

"Seriously, Gert? Keep your fucking tongue in your mouth," James said. "You really have no shame."

"What? Ed has always been Avery's hot older cousin."

"Who is out of bounds and way out of your league," I said.

"I'm allowed to look, aren't I?"

I rolled my eyes. Gert would never go after my cousin. I was pretty sure Ed had a girlfriend anyway. I'd seen him with a blonde girl at some of our family events, although I'd never been introduced to her. Besides, I would never allow my best friend to get involved with my family. Not with what I knew about them.

"At least she hasn't said she has a crush on Dante."

"Oh Christ, Ave, that's just gross," James retorted.

"Okay, come on, even you have to admit he's attractive. He has girls fawning all over him at those galas your dad hosts."

He scowled.

"I don't have to admit anything of the sort."

I turned to Gert.

"Dante is hot, right?"

"Sorry, James, Ave is right. Your brother could melt the panties off most ladies," Gert said, grinning.

James' scowl deepened.

"You two make me sick."

"Aww, jealous?"

"Fuck off."

I shook my head. He knew we were just winding him up. Sure, his brother was pretty attractive with his dark hair and blue eyes which matched James' but to me, Dante was family.

"Is he seeing anyone?" I asked.

"You have Aiden."

"Okay first off, I don't fancy your brother. That would feel a little incestuous. I was asking after him you div."

James eyed me for a moment before sitting back and shrugging.

"How would I know? He doesn't confide in me."

"I'll take that as a no. Come to think of it, I don't think I've ever seen Dante with a woman."

"Oh, trust me, he had a revolving door of women when I lived with him, but I think he's grown out of it now."

James gave me a significant look. We couldn't talk too much about Dante and James' family in front of Gert. She didn't know about the abuse.

"Tell us more about Tilly, Gert. Are we going to meet her soon?" I said, turning to my other friend.

She grinned and launched into full freaking out over a girl mode. An hour later, both James and I were exhausted listening to it. We all said our goodbyes and they promised they'd come to the stupid birthday party the company was throwing for me.

I walked out of the coffee shop with John next to me. He hadn't bought the car today so the two of us trotted down the steps of the nearest tube station. Thankfully, the tube wasn't particularly full and we both got a seat.

"Did you have a nice time with your friends?" John asked.

"Weren't you listening?"

He smiled at me.

"The question still stands."

"Yes, I did. I haven't seen them much since everything happened."

"No, I suppose it's difficult now everything has changed for you."

I turned to him fully, deciding maybe he could help me. I'd known him most of my life. He'd been employed by my family for a long time, doing various jobs for them. I hadn't seen him much in the past few years because he stopped working directly for my dad.

"John, can I ask you something?"

"Hmm?"

"You heard what I said to them about Aiden."

His expression grew wary.

"Yes."

I hung my head a little.

"I don't know what to do. I'm scared I've messed it all up."

"You know this is a matter between the two of you."

I fiddled with the pocket of my jacket.

"I know."

He let out a long sigh.

"Avery, sometimes we say things we wish we hadn't when emotions are running high. That doesn't mean you've ruined anything. My only advice is to talk to him and tell him how you feel."

"Yeah, like that's easy to do with Aiden."

He chuckled, patting my arm lightly.

"You've managed just fine so far with him. For as long as I've known Aiden, he's been closed off. You came along and changed that. Do you think he would've been open to letting me help him if you hadn't taught him it's okay to let other people in?"

I shook my head. Aiden was different now from when we first met. He would never have told me anything about his parents or openly admitted his feelings.

"Well, there you go."

I fiddled with my jacket pocket again.

"Rick called me a siren and said I have Aiden wrapped around my little finger. He said I'm the one with all the control in our relationship."

John raised an eyebrow.

"Did you tell Aiden he said that?"

"No. I didn't believe Rick and I didn't trust Aiden not to get mad about it."

"He probably would've knowing Aiden."

He leant in closer to me.

"Women always have all the power, Avery. All you have to do is tell him the truth."

"What if he gets angry with me?"

He leant back again and gave me a look.

"Are you telling me he hasn't been angry with you before?"

"Well no, he's lost his shit with me on numerous occasions."

"And you're still with him."

I shook my head, smiling.

"Okay, yes, I get it. You're right. I need to grow a pair."

He laughed.

"I wouldn't quite put it like that. You're a woman after all."

I nudged my shoulder into his. I'd always liked John. My mum thought he had something going on with Esme, my nanny until she left when I was sixteen to go live with some guy she'd met on the internet. John had stopped working for my dad after that too. It'd always felt like too much of a coincidence for there not to have been some kind of affair going on between the two of them.

"I'll talk to him. I don't want things staying the way they are now."

He nodded at me, giving me a tentative smile.

We rode the rest of the way back to Aiden's flat in silence. He came in with me. Aiden was in his office, but he came out when he heard the door. He dropped a kiss on my forehead.

"How are James and Gert?"

"They're fine. Gert has a new girlfriend, so we mostly talked about that."

He raised an eyebrow. I'd forgotten to tell him Gert was bi.

"She likes girls and boys."

"I see," was all he said.

He looked over at John and I knew our little bit of small talk was over. Sighing heavily, I walked away into the bedroom, leaving the two of them alone.

I flicked the light on and stood at the end of the bed, staring up at the picture hanging above it. The one I'd painted of us. The representation of my submission to him.

Were Rick and John right? Did I really hold all the power? Could I fix the growing divide between Aiden and me?

There was only one way I could find out.

I walked over to the window and stared out at the dark city and its twinkling lights.

Aiden and I needed to talk.

And I wasn't going to let him continue to pretend like nothing happened.

Chapter Twenty

Aiden

1 leant up against the wall in the hallway, waiting for John to say something. His expression was a little wary.

"I don't want you to take this the wrong way," he said.

"The wrong way?"

He nodded, his face growing solemn.

"I'm worried about her."

My chest tightened. Things had been off between Avery and me since Rick turned up and she hinted at marriage. I was going to do something about it. I didn't know what yet so I'd left it alone. Maybe that had been a bad idea.

"Why?"

"I shouldn't be interfering."

"John…"

He couldn't back out now he'd started. What happened whilst she was out with her friends?

He put his hands up.

"All I'm going to say is you need to talk to her."

"That doesn't help me. Talk to her about what?"

Sarah Bailey

He shifted on his feet. I didn't know why he decided to talk to me about this if it was making him this uncomfortable.

"The day Rick returned her, something happened, didn't it?"

I stiffened, not wanting to acknowledge it either way. He nodded slowly.

"Your lack of response is telling."

I shoved off the wall and paced away, running my hand through my hair. This shouldn't have come as a surprise to me. It was my fault. I'd shut down and I knew it.

"Did she tell you?"

"She told her friends and then she spoke to me on the way home."

And now everyone fucking knew about our problems. This was a fucking mess. I shouldn't have been such a fucking wuss. It wasn't just that which was bothering me. I was worked up over Rick taking her. I was so fucking scared he'd do it again, just like he threatened. The helpless feeling wouldn't go away. It tore at my insides and dug into my skin. I had to protect my girl. I had to.

"What did you say?"

"I told her to talk to you as did her friends. I imagine she's waiting for you." He paused, giving me a significant look. "Let her talk."

"Are you giving me relationship advice now?"

He grinned.

"No, just life advice. Women are complicated. Let her talk and don't get pissed off. That's all I'm saying."

I wasn't angry with her. I completely understood her desire for a future between us. It wasn't as if I hadn't told her in the past I wanted to be with her forever. That was the honest fucking truth. I couldn't imagine life without her now. Avery made me happy. And now I'd made her unhappy by not dealing with the situation.

"You going to let me talk to her then?"

"I'll see you two tomorrow morning."

He gave me one final nod before slipping out the front door. I stared after him, knowing as soon as I stepped in the bedroom, I had to deal with everything. Rick had well and truly fucking stuck his oar in and given me a fucking headache to sort out. I wished he'd never got his hands on her. Wished we'd never had that fucking conversation. I couldn't stand it.

Stop being such a fucking coward.

I took a step towards the room. My phone rang. I dug it out of my pocket. It was Ben.

"Hey shithead."

"Aiden, Skye is in labour," Ben replied, sounding a little frantic.

Wait, what?

"She is?"

"Mate, I really need you here. I'm freaking the fuck out right now. Skye's parents are on their way, but she's screaming at me. Shit, I'm sorry, I know you're not good with this stuff."

"Hey, it's fine. Where are you?"

He told me which hospital they were at and to make sure to bring Avery along. Although Skye was screaming at him at that moment, she still wanted to meet my girlfriend.

Well shit.

Time was of the essence. Walking into the bedroom, I found Avery staring out the window. She didn't turn around

287

at my approach. I stopped a few feet away, not wanting to encroach on her space too much. My palms twitched, wanting to wrap themselves around her waist and feel her skin on mine. I fucking missed her.

"Princess."

"We need to talk."

"I know."

She shifted on her feet, wrapping her arms around herself. She was in a plain blue t-shirt and black skinny jeans which hugged her arse and made my mouth water. Fuck. She was so beautiful. So fucking perfect. And she was upset with me. How the fuck had I allowed it to get this far?

"Skye has gone into labour and Ben wants us there."

She turned around, staring at me with wide eyes.

"Oh, oh shit. Well, let's go then."

I felt like shit for having to postpone our conversation, but my best friend needed me. I mean I had no fucking idea how I would be any use in this situation. I wasn't good with babies nor screaming women. My messy relationship with Avery was evidence of that.

We both went back out into the hall, putting shoes and coats on. We didn't talk as we rode down in the lift and got in the car. After I pulled out of the underground carpark, I reached over and took her hand, running my thumb down the back of it. I just needed to touch her. My beautiful girl who made my heart fucking sing.

"Is it far?" she asked.

"Shouldn't take longer than twenty minutes, depends on traffic."

"He must be freaking out if he wants you with him."

I glanced at her. She was smiling to herself.

"I'm just doing this for him. There is no fucking way I'm going in that delivery room. I'd rather not see my best friend's wife pushing a kid out."

She giggled, squeezing my hand.

"How long have they been together?"

"Eight years. They got married when Ben and I left the army and before you ask, yes, I was his best man."

Talking about Ben was easy. Talking about us? Not so much.

"Did you tell embarrassing stories in your speech?"

I smiled. It had been the perfect summer's day for them. That was despite me telling all their guests how our unit had left a naked, passed out Ben outside our staff sergeant's quarters after he'd got drunk and sobbed to us about how much he loved Skye.

"Yes and he roped me and the boys into helping him propose to her. She came to base one weekend and he got us to wear these t-shirts under our uniforms which spelt out 'Will you marry me?'. So we all line up and she's like, 'Ben, what are they doing?' and when we all started to take our uniform shirts off, she was about to go off on him, but he was down on one knee. The fucking fool was crying like a baby trying to get his words out."

"Seriously? What did she do?"

"She said and I quote 'You little fucker'."

Avery snorted, letting go of my hand to put hers over her mouth.

"She dragged him off the floor, slapped him around the head and told him to take her back to his quarters so she could give him her answer without us all staring at the two of them."

"That's not exactly the most romantic way to propose."

I wasn't sure talking about proposals and marriage was the best idea considering we still needed to have a conversation about that topic ourselves.

"What do you think is romantic then?"

I looked over at her as we'd stopped at a red light. She squirmed a little in her seat.

"I don't know. Just not something in front of other people."

That was hardly a surprise. She didn't like being the centre of attention. Except when she was the centre of mine. Then she liked it a lot. It reminded me we hadn't had sex for days. She was always asleep when I came to bed and even yesterday, she'd spent all day painting in the living room. She passed out on the sofa when we were watching TV so I tucked her up in bed even though I wanted to kiss her awake and make love to her slowly.

I had to remedy this situation between us. We needed to reconnect and that started with a conversation about what she'd said last weekend.

I pulled up in the hospital carpark and we got out. I called Ben, who said he'd meet us outside the maternity unit. When we got up there, he was pacing outside the double doors.

"Thank fuck you're here," he said when he spied us.

I gave him a pat on the back when I reached him.

"How are you holding up?"

"Badly… Hey Avery."

She gave him a quick hug, smiling.

"Are Skye and the baby okay?" she asked.

"Well, Skye is screaming bloody murder every time she gets a contraction, but the midwife reassured me everything is fine."

He pressed the button on the doors and spoke to the receptionist who let us in. He pointed over to an open door.

"That's the waiting room, Grant's in there. I should get back."

I nodded, taking Avery's hand and leading her towards the room. Ben ran a hand through his hair before he turned away and walked a little way down the corridor to where we could hear a woman screaming. I felt sorry for him.

Skye's dad, Grant was sitting in a chair by the window with his phone in his hand. He looked up when we walked in.

"Hello Aiden."

"Hello Grant... This is my girlfriend, Avery. This is Skye's dad," I replied by way of introduction.

He stood up and took Avery's hand, shaking it.

"It's very nice to meet you."

She smiled at him, extracting her hand and curling it around my arm.

"Ben didn't mention you had a girlfriend."

He waved a hand between the two of us.

"It's kind of new."

We all sat down. Grant went back to his phone whilst I put an arm around Avery. She leant into me.

"So we're just going to hang out here until the baby comes?" she whispered.

"Yes… I know it's not what you expected to be doing this evening."

She rested her head on my shoulder.

"It's okay. This is more important."

She looked downtrodden and resigned. I felt like shit. I wanted to sort this crap out between us but now we couldn't because Grant was in here. I wasn't going to talk about our problems with an audience.

"Do you want me to get you a drink or a magazine?"

She shook her head.

"I just want to sit here with you if that's okay."

"Of course it is, princess."

She curled a hand around my waist and closed her eyes.

Hours passed without a word from Ben. I fiddled with my phone when Avery fell asleep on me. I didn't want to disturb her. Grant got coffee for both of us but didn't say much else to me. He'd always been the stoic type.

Finally, Skye's mum, Deb, came in around two in the morning to let us know Skye delivered a healthy 7lb 9oz baby boy. Grant went with her to the delivery room leaving me alone with my sleeping girlfriend. I told Deb to send Ben to get us when Skye was ready to have us in there.

Avery looked so peaceful curled up on the chair with her head in my lap. I stroked her hair back from her face.

"Princess, wake up."

I shook her gently. She shifted, turning her face up towards me and blinked.

"What time is it?"

"Like two."

She sat up, rubbing her eyes.

"Why'd you wake me up?"

"The baby is here. We'll go see them in a bit, but I thought we should talk first."

She eyed me for a moment before standing up, stretching and walking towards the window. She stood looking out at the city beyond. She didn't say anything for a long moment and when she did, she didn't turn to look at me.

"Aiden… I feel like this is all my fault."

It wasn't. I opened my mouth to speak, but then closed it again. John told me earlier to let her talk.

"What I said… I didn't mean anything by it. I mean I did, but not in the way you're thinking."

She sighed.

"Fuck. Why is this so hard?" she muttered.

I wanted to reach out to her, tell her it was okay. If she didn't mean she wanted to get married, then what had she been trying to tell me?

"You keep telling me you don't deserve me. It's frustrating. I can't seem to convince you that's simply not the case. It's not about who deserves who. I want you. I need you… I fucking love you and that's not going to change. You can hurt me a thousand times over and I'll still be here. I'll still love you."

I sucked in a breath. That's what all this was about?

"I won't deny I want a future with you and I hope it will include marriage one day, but I don't want it to cause this distance between us. This isn't moving forward, it's taking a hundred steps back."

Fuck. I'd been such a fucking idiot thinking she wanted to get married right now.

"I'm lonely, Aiden. I miss you. I miss us."

Each word sucker punched me in the gut. I got up and went to her, unable to stay away any longer. I turned her around and wrapped my arms around her. Burying my face in her shoulder, I breathed in her familiar scent of coconut. Fuck. I loved this girl so much. And I'd missed us too.

She exhaled slowly and wrapped her hands around my back, holding me close.

"So you don't want to elope?"

"I hope that's a joke."

I smiled, tightening my hold on her.

"I'm sorry, princess. I meant to talk to you…"

"But you got freaked out by the prospect. It's okay. Honestly, my head is all over the place right now and everything that happened with… him. It all just got too much for me. People keep calling me, Miss Daniels. I hate everything associated with my family, including my name. It's the one thing which still ties me to them and their sick legacy. It's like having it dangled in front of my face on a daily basis."

I had no idea she felt that way about it. Why hadn't she just told me? I would've understood. Hell, that's why I was fucking glad my mother gave me her last name rather than his.

I pulled away, staring down at her. There were still things I should say to her, but I found I couldn't. I couldn't tell her how terrified I was about Rick taking her away again. How enraged it made me feel that he had the audacity to stick his fucking nose into my life when he'd left me alone all this fucking time.

"When this is all over... We'll talk about the future. We need to make sure we have one first."

"You're right, we do."

She shifted up on her tiptoes and kissed me, her hands curling around my neck. Fuck. I'd missed the simple act of having her kiss me. Having her pour out her feelings in this way. I felt the connection between us deep within my chest. Her heart and soul bound to mine.

There was a whistle behind us. I pulled away from her, finding Ben in the doorway looking a little worse for wear. I gave him the middle finger and he just grinned at me.

"Deb and Grant are going home, but if you want to meet him, you can," he said, shrugging.

Avery took my hand, her face eager, so I nodded. We followed Ben out of the waiting room and down the hall.

"Can I start calling you Uncle Aiden?" she whispered to me.

I rolled my eyes.

"Please don't."

"Spoilsport. It's the only time you'll ever be an uncle since neither of us has siblings."

Ben was family to me even though we weren't blood-related.

"I'm not good with kids."

"You have me. I'll teach you."

And this was now getting officially out of hand. I looked down at her face and the mischievous glint in her eye told me she was messing with me.

Ben opened the door to their room and we all walked in. Skye was sat up in bed with a bundle in her arms. She looked tired but happy.

"Aiden, come meet your nephew."

I eyed Avery who was grinning from ear to ear. I tugged her over to the bed and we both stared down at their son. I wasn't sure what to say because to me, babies were these tiny humans with squishy faces who looked like they could break any moment. Plus, they were usually kind of ugly.

"Do you want to hold him?"

"Um…"

She smiled at me and indicated her head towards Avery.

"Oh… shit, okay, Skye, this is Avery."

"It's nice to meet you," Skye said. "You're welcome to hold him since Aiden looks like he'd rather be thrown off a cliff."

"I know that look all too well," Avery replied. "But yes, if that's okay."

Skye nodded and passed her son over to my girlfriend. She held him like she was a natural, cradling him to her chest with one arm. She stroked his little face and he reached up, grabbing her finger in his tiny hand.

"What's his name?"

Skye looked up at me with a glint in her eye.

"Joshua Aiden Andrews."

I glanced back at Ben who shrugged as he came around and sat in the chair by Skye's bed.

"Don't look at me, it was Skye's idea."

"Hello Joshua," Avery whispered, rocking him in her arm whilst he held her finger. "I'm Avery. Maybe one day you can call me Auntie Avery and this here, is your Uncle Aiden. Your mummy named you after him."

Fuck. Seeing her like that with a baby gave me a really weird feeling in my chest. Her eyes twinkled and she looked so fucking happy. It made me wish we lived normal lives where this sort of thing didn't seem like a pipe dream. Unless we could sort out the shit with her family, we'd never be free.

"Are you sure you don't want to hold him?"

I didn't know how. He looked so small and fragile. Avery gave me the softest smile and turned to me.

"Here, you just need to support his head properly," she told me as she held him out to me.

I carefully put my hand under his head and took him from her, holding him close to my chest. Such a tiny human. He had blue eyes and a little tuft of dark hair on his head.

"You got him?"

"Yeah… I think I do," I replied.

I stepped back, letting Avery speak to Skye as I stared down at the little human in my arms. My nephew. The weird feeling remained. I wanted to protect him. I carried him over to where Ben was sitting.

"Never thought I'd see the day you held a kid," he said, grinning.

"You're the one who decided to knock your old lady up."

I almost didn't want to put him down.

"You sure you're not getting broody?"

297

"Don't make me rip you a new one in front of your newborn son."

He chuckled, shaking his head. This little bundle in my arms needed to grow up without all the bullshit and violence Ben and I had witnessed in our lives.

"You sure Bob and Val will be okay with you naming him after me?" I asked.

"They're just happy they're having a grandchild. I sent them a text, but they're probably asleep. Avery still ready to get her ink done?"

I looked at the two girls who were deep in conversation.

"She doesn't mind waiting."

He shook his head.

"You two can come to the house and I'll do them there. I've already made a head start on designing and I want to do it in time for her birthday."

"You really don't have to."

"I never thought I'd see the day you found a girl who makes you this happy, so don't be an idiot. I'm happy to do it. Skye gets it. We're all family here."

Ben was the only person I kept in contact with from the army. We'd done a lot for each other over the years. Loyalty, friendship and trust ran deep with us.

"I appreciate it."

We left not long after that. Avery needed sleep if she was going to work tomorrow. I wanted to keep her at home and make love to her now we'd cleared the air, but it could wait until the evening. It was almost four by the time we got in bed. Her alarm would go off in a couple of hours.

"I like Skye," she said, curling up against my side.

"I thought you might."

She yawned, closing her eyes and wrapping her hand around my waist.

"Are you sure I'm not allowed to call you, Uncle Aiden?"

I shook my head, stroking her hair.

"Only when speaking to my nephew."

She nodded, yawning again.

"Night princess."

Her breathing became steady and even. She'd dropped off to sleep. I watched her for the longest time. I wanted all this bullshit to be over. I wanted a normal life with her more than I'd ever wanted anything else.

I decided right then and there, I'd stop at nothing to make sure we could have that. To make sure we had a future we could look forward to. Nothing and no one would stand in my way.

I wish I'd known then our future would never turn out the way we'd planned it.

I wish I'd known what was about to befall us.

Then I might have been able to stop the descent into complete and utter chaos.

One thing was for sure.

No one was coming out unscathed.

Chapter Twenty One

Avery

ncle Charlie paced in front of my desk, his brow furrowed. He'd come in here to officially tell me about the company party he was throwing for me, but I'd ambushed him instead.

"Why would you want to go to the penthouse?"

"I didn't get to go to their funeral. I want to say goodbye."

That was a complete lie, but I wasn't about to tell him I wanted to find the paperwork for my trust fund. Going back to that place felt so wrong. I had no choice. I couldn't ask Frazier for copies of it or he'd get suspicious and demand to know why. Keeping him in the dark about what I suspected he wanted was for the best all round.

"And whose fault was that?"

His tone chilled me to the bone. Why would he get so worked up about me going there?

"Look, it's mine, isn't it? Dad left it to me. Unless you want me to get a locksmith to break in and change the locks, then just hand over the key."

He stopped, eying me with no small amount of distaste.

"You don't need to go there to say goodbye. Go to their graves, you know where they are."

I sighed, rubbing my forehead.

"Why are you against me going?"

"You ran off for three months after they died. Do you think it's wise to go back to where they were killed?"

If I didn't know any better, I'd say my uncle was worried about my mental state. Sadly, I did. He didn't care about me. All he cared about was keeping me at the helm of the company so their dirty dealings didn't come to light.

They would one day when Aiden and I were ready. When we'd amassed enough evidence to destroy them for good. I'd known asking my boyfriend to execute them all had been a knee jerk reaction to what Rick had shown me. All I really wanted was for them to be stopped so they couldn't hurt anyone else.

One of the biggest problems we faced was knowing where exactly they kept the girls. My uncle didn't keep records nor could Aiden find a paper trail leading to them. He'd told me my father had handled it all until he took over Daniels Holdings, but he had no idea who they'd given the role to after that.

Neither of us could stand the thought of those women being handed around Charlie's associates like they were slaves ordered to do their master's bidding.

"Didn't know you cared that much."

"You're my niece, of course I care about you."

He had a funny way of showing it.

He sighed, sitting down in the chair opposite my desk.

"Is it really that important to you?"

I nodded. My dad's office held the key to working all of this crap out. I was sure of that much. It was a wonder it hadn't occurred to us earlier. Aiden had never checked the room when he was there, too busy getting me out quietly. I really had messed up all his plans. Turned his life completely upside down.

"I know we haven't really seen eye to eye since they died. I'm sorry for that. We're family and family should be there for each other. Instead, I've been treating you like an inconvenience when none of this is really your fault."

He rubbed his face with his hand.

"Them being gone has been tough on all of us. It's not like when Nick died. We still had each other to rely on. You're still young and this is a lot to put on your shoulders."

My uncle apologising to me was about the weirdest thing to happen since my parents were murdered in front of me and a lot of weird and fucked up stuff had happened since. Was this genuine or not?

"I'm sorry too."

He gave me a tentative smile.

"Frazier has been visiting with increased frequency. He was in twice last week. Do you want to tell me why?"

I sighed, leaning back in my chair.

"He wants me to get engaged to Tristan."

I didn't see the point in holding back the truth. In all honesty, I was curious what my uncle thought about it. Did he agree? Did he also want me marrying into the Shaws?

His expression darkened significantly.

"And what do you think about that?"

"I don't like Tristan nor do I want to be his wife."

He fiddled with the arm of the chair for a long moment. His expression was still dark.

"Mitch wanted the two of you to be together."

"I know. We argued over it. He conceded and said it was ultimately my choice. Now, I don't feel like I have a choice at all."

He leant forward in his seat.

"There is always a choice, Avery. Always."

I looked away, trying to work out why he'd say something like that to me.

"Is there? Do you think I should?"

"Honestly? No. Frazier was Mitch's friend, not mine. His son is a prick."

My eyes met his. He looked entirely serious. I had no idea he felt that way.

"Is that why you insisted I have a bodyguard?"

"Partially. Look, I know we never spoke of what happened when you were young. I know it was wrong and I apologise for that. Contrary to what you might think of me, I don't want you to be subjected to an abusive relationship you can't escape from. That is all you would get if you married Tristan."

I bit the inside of my cheek. I hadn't misheard him. He'd just apologised to me again and this time for what he'd tried to do to me when I was a kid. Who was this man in front of me? He didn't sound like my uncle at all.

"Thank you for saying that."

"It's the truth. Don't marry Tristan. No matter how many times Frazier insists you should. Don't trust either of them."

"Don't you trust them?"

He shook his head.

"No. There are very few people I trust in this world. The Shaws do not count amongst that number."

I stored away that titbit of information to mull over with Aiden later. Perhaps we could use his distrust to our advantage. I didn't know how, but Aiden might.

"I'll take your advice into consideration."

He stood up.

"I'll get you the keys for your parent's penthouse. I suppose it's the least I can do."

I nodded as he left the room before pulling out my phone.

ME: Getting the keys.

AIDEN: Have any trouble?

ME: A little. I'll tell you later x

When my uncle came back, he handed the keys over and sat back down.

"Now, we still need to discuss this event."

I sighed, settling in for a long discussion about the birthday event I didn't want thrown for me.

I stepped out of the lift into the hallway, taking a deep breath. John had driven me here, but I asked him to wait in the car. This was something I had to do by myself. Being back here made my heart thump in my chest and a cold sweat beaded at the back of my neck.

I couldn't pick my feet up from the floor. Looking around the hallway, I noticed nothing had changed. There was a vase of dead flowers sitting on the side table. I remembered they'd been blooming with lilies the last time I was here. Above it hung a family portrait my dad had commissioned when I was younger. I stood between them. My dad's hand was on my shoulder and my mum looked happy.

The sight of it made my heart ache. It reminded me of the portrait I'd started of him which was still in my studio, untouched. I had to do something about it, but I still wasn't sure what.

The two people who were my world had turned out to be monsters of the worst kind. Hiding behind masks and the illusion of civility. Their true depravity might not ever come to light. I could end this all now. Show the world the truth. It didn't feel right to do it like that. There were still things we didn't know. Still pieces of crucial evidence we needed. That meant I couldn't stand around in the hallway.

I walked towards the first open doorway. My pulse skittered. My fists clenched. I came to a standstill just beyond the threshold, trying to keep the terror at bay.

Right here is where it happened. There was still a faint stain on the hardwood floor in the dining area from where they'd bled out from their gunshot wounds.

The memory of that day hit me. The full force of it causing me to drop to my knees, my hands planted on the floor to steady myself.

I gasped for air, fighting back the tears springing to my eyes. They fell down anyway, streaking across my cheeks.

Dead.

Dead.

Dead.

Coming here was a mistake. No matter how much I hated my parents, watching them die was one of the worst moments of my life. The gunshots rang in my ears. Even though I knew now he'd used a silencer, the shots weren't exactly quiet. The movies and TV shows got that so wrong.

I needed to get out of this room, but I couldn't move. I was glued to the floor, watching the scene happen over and over again in my mind. I saw myself hiding behind the kitchen counter. How Aiden had walked over to me and told me he wasn't going to kill me. How terrified and confused I'd been.

Knowing they deserved this didn't make it any better. Knowing how I'd come to fall in love with Aiden wasn't a consolation either. He'd still done this. How could I ever forget his cold, remorseless expression when he took my parents' lives?

I felt awful. I'd justified everything he'd done. I'd made it okay when it really wasn't.

"Who are you?"

"Your worst nightmare."

Except Aiden hadn't turned out to be my worst nightmare at all. He'd been exactly what I never knew I needed.

I sat up, raking my hands through my hair and dashing away my tears from my cheeks. I couldn't allow myself to break all over again.

You're stronger than this. You know you are.

This was something I had to face. I couldn't hide behind my love for the man who killed them. I had to accept the harsh realities in this life. Aiden was a killer. He'd done something unthinkable. He felt no remorse for it. And I still loved him.

The only remorse he felt was that I ever saw him do it. That I was there that night and had to witness my own parents dying. Aiden still had compassion and empathy even if sometimes his form of justice wasn't right or legal.

Remember his face when you left him that day. When he thought he was losing you forever. It broke something inside you, didn't it?

All those awful memories we shared bound us together. No matter how sick and twisted this entire thing was, I still had him and he had me. I wasn't falling apart completely. I was still here. My heart still hammered against my chest and oxygen filled my lungs. I'd faced the memory of that day.

Getting to my feet, I knew I had other things to do. I hadn't come here to rehash the past. I'd come to find out what conditions my father had put into my trust fund. I wasn't sure why I felt so strongly about it, but I did. There was a reason Frazier kept pushing me towards Tristan.

I turned and walked out of the kitchen. I passed the bedroom I'd grown up in. There was no point me going in there. It would only make this harder. Those memories weren't worth reliving.

Reaching my dad's office, I paused outside the closed door. The dark wood was so familiar. The number of times I'd run in and out of here as a kid, pestering him for one thing or another. The closed door meant he was busy and didn't want to be disturbed. Except he wasn't alive any longer.

I grabbed the handle, turned it and pushed open the door. The faint smell of whisky and cigars hit me immediately as I stepped in. The sight of his desk with his chair tucked neatly behind crippled me. Wave after wave of nostalgia and sorrow hit me. Crushing me under its weight.

Sacrifice

"Daddy!"

I ran into the room as fast as my little legs could carry me. He was sitting at his desk, but he pushed his chair back and opened his arms. I launched myself into his lap, savouring the bear hug he gave me.

"Morning Angel, did you sleep well?"

"Yes, Mummy said we're having pancakes this morning."

"She did? Well, aren't we in for a treat?"

I nodded. He ruffled my hair.

"You're getting so big now. Soon you'll be as tall as Mummy."

I grinned, wriggling in his grasp.

"Will I be as beautiful as Mummy?"

"Between you and me, I think you'll be the most beautiful girl in the whole wide world."

He looked over my shoulder, smiling.

"Careful, Mitch, you'll have her thinking she can take on the world if you start talking like that," my mum's voice came from behind us.

I turned around, sitting in my dad's lap properly.

"She will. My little girl is going to do great things. Just no boys, you hear me?"

"Boys are gross."

He ruffled my hair.

"You'll change your mind about that one day."

I shook my head.

"No way. Boys are stupid."

"Even James?"

I put my finger on my chin.

"James is okay."

"I thought you didn't like any boys."

"James is my friend."

Mum came further into the room.

"If you don't come and get dressed, then you won't get to see James later."

I shot out of my dad's lap, running towards my mum.

"No, please. I want to see James."

She took my hand.

"Come along then, pancakes will be ready soon."

"Will Dante be at James' when we go?"

She smiled at me as we walked out of my dad's office together.

"I'm sure he will."

"He owes me a new Lego set."

She raised an eyebrow.

"Does he now?"

"Yes. He promised to get me one for my birthday."

"Well, I'm sure he will if you're a good girl."

I heard my dad chuckling as we walked out the door.

I took a shaky step forward, trying to remind myself that was the past. I couldn't get lost in it. At that moment, all I wanted was my best friend. He'd understand why this hurt me so much. Dredging up memories I wanted to forget. What he didn't know was what happened that night in the kitchen. He didn't know I'd watched them die.

I could do this without James. I could do this without Aiden. I had to stand on my own two feet.

I approached the first filing cabinet and pulled open a drawer. It would take time to go through the contents of these. I had no idea where he'd have put the paperwork.

The office was littered with paper by the time I found the folder. My dad had always been one for keeping hard copies rather than relying on computers. I'd found some useful documents other than my trust fund paperwork. I piled up everything I needed into the bag I'd brought with me and carefully put everything else back in its place. I didn't want to stay here any longer than I had to, so I'd read it back at Aiden's.

I shut the office door behind me and walked back down the hallway into the lift. I looked at the portrait of my family one last time before the doors closed. This place could burn to the ground for all I cared. At least I would never have to relive those memories again.

When I reached the car, John got out and opened the passenger door for me.

"Did you get what you needed?"

"Yes, I think so."

I strapped myself in and turned to look out the window. I didn't really want to make small talk. The lingering fear I felt at being back there still threatened to break me. I wasn't going to let it. Those memories couldn't hurt me now.

John thankfully left me to my own thoughts. He dropped me off outside Aiden's flat, waiting until I got through the door before he drove away. I trudged through the front door a few minutes later. I popped the bag of documents on the kitchen counter before taking off my coat and kicking off my shoes. I hung the coat up on the rack before I walked down the hallway. I came to a standstill when I noticed the cell door was open.

What the fuck?

I approached it cautiously, peering around the doorway. Two women were huddled together in the corner. They were barely clothed and had bruises all over their bodies. They both looked at me, fear in their expressions.

Why were these women here? And where the hell was my boyfriend?

"Aiden, why are there two women in our flat?" I called out.

I stepped away from the door, looking down the hall towards the living room.

"Aiden?"

I heard a masculine grunt coming from the bathroom. So that's where he was. I had questions for that man. Bringing home bruised and battered women without telling me. What the hell had he done today?

I pulled my phone out of my pocket and checked it. There were no messages. He really hadn't stopped to tell me. I slipped it back in my pocket before striding towards the bathroom. I shoved the door open.

"You better have a damn good explanation as to why—"

I stopped in my tracks. He was sitting bare-chested on the side of the bath. The first aid kit was on top of the sink counter. He had a black eye, split lip and a gash down the side of his forehead. He had bruised knuckles and another gash across his chest along with rapidly colouring bruises.

Oh my god.

"Aiden, what the hell happened?"

Chapter Twenty Two

Aiden

*T*oday had been a fucking mess from start to finish. I'd lost the plot entirely. Everything ached, especially my head. It had all gone to shit and now, I sorely regretted every moment.

Avery stared at me with wide eyes. I knew I was in for one hell of a conversation when she got back, but now I really didn't feel like explaining myself. I was in pain and needed to sort out all this blood.

She approached me, taking the antiseptic wipe out of my hand and squatting down.

"Let me do that."

I wanted to protest but decided against it. I normally fixed myself up. The look in her eyes told me she wouldn't take no for an answer.

I winced as she cleaned the gash on my forehead. She plucked the first aid kit off the counter and dug through it. I'd already looked over the cuts. They weren't deep enough that they'd need stitches. Besides, it's not like I would let her take me to hospital if they were.

"That one," I said, pointing at the bandages and tape.

She picked them up and bandaged up my head. Then she cleaned the gash on my chest and taped that up too. Getting a face cloth, she wiped away the rest of the blood and carefully cleaned up my split lip. She packed the first aid kit back up and popped it on the counter.

"Why did I have to come home to find you beaten up with two half-naked women in the cell?"

I sighed, looking away from her. I really did owe her an explanation.

"I got into a fight."

"With who?"

"One of Rick's friends... Well, technically it was his security guard who did all this, but he looked worse than me. I left him unconscious."

She put a hand on my thigh.

"Why did you go see Rick's friend?"

In all honesty, it hadn't been my intention to go see Robert Bassington at all. It was only after Chuck rang to speak to me about this party for Avery, I found myself frustrated. He'd told me who was meant to attend. It reminded me of Robert and how he'd helped Rick abduct Avery. I wanted to send them both a message. If they went near my girlfriend again, I would have their heads.

Dealing with the fact that Avery had to go to her parent's penthouse today without me and knowing she'd probably relive that night killed me. I'd bottled up all my feelings regarding that and Rick taking her. And now, they'd reared their ugly head making it impossible for me not to completely lose control.

I really had lost it. Spectacularly. I'd been so angry when I'd got there. So fucking pissed off at the world for making me feel like I couldn't protect Avery. Making me feel helpless. It was seriously fucked up and I knew it was a mistake.

"I was pretty sure he helped Rick take you. When I got there, my suspicions were confirmed. He practically laughed in my face when I accused him. He tried to have me escorted out, but you can see how that turned out. I beat the shit out of him and discovered he had two of your uncle's girls at his house. So I took them."

Her expression darkened.

"Are you insane? What if Charlie finds out about this?"

"He won't."

"How do you know?"

"He thinks Chuck sent me."

"Aiden…"

I cupped her face. She didn't believe me. I'd spun him a story. Chuck would be none the wiser. Besides, Robert wouldn't want to admit to me beating the crap out of him to anyone. He'd rather save face than show any sign of weakness. And if he did talk, he'd end up in the gutter where he belonged.

I knew I was trying to justify it all to her even though I'd messed everything up and I didn't know what to do about it now.

"Princess, I know it was impulsive. He won't say anything. I promise we're safe."

"How are we safe, Aiden? We have two women in our flat. Charlie will look for them when he finds out they're missing.

315

He'll know who had them last. What the hell are we going to do?"

I hadn't really thought that far ahead. I had to take them away from Robert. I couldn't leave them there to be abused any further. They hadn't wanted to come with me at first. When I assured them, I would keep them safe, they left with me willingly. I had to do right by them because I could never do right by her.

Tina held me back. She was lying on the floor, her arms wrapped around her stomach, groaning in agony.

"Let me go," I shouted.

"Aiden, you need to calm down. Your mother needs medical help."

"Tina, please."

Tears ran down my cheeks. I was only seven and most of our lives had been plagued with this. Some weeks the men didn't come, but others, like this, they hurt her worse than ever.

She held my shoulders and squatted down to my level, looking into my eyes.

"Sweetie, your mum is hurting right now. I know it's painful to see, but you have to let me help her, okay? Can you do that for me?"

I just wanted to hold her. She always called me her angel. Didn't angels look after their charges? Didn't they save them? But how could I do anything? I was a kid who couldn't fight back with his fists. Who couldn't protect his own mother from horrible men and women.

My shoulders slumped and I looked at the floor.

"Okay, Tina."

She bundled me up in her arms, kissing the top of my head.

"Be a good boy and get the first aid kit from the bathroom."

Tina pulled away, standing up and patting my head. I gave Mummy one last look. Her wracking sobs killed me inside. Turning away, I walked out of the room, determined to help her in any way I could.

Little did I know in two short weeks, she'd be dead and my world would crumble before my eyes.

"We're going to keep them away from him, that's what we're going to do."

"And where do you suggest we keep them? They can't stay here with us."

I knew that. They'd be better off far away from London where it'd be harder for Chuck to find them. I thought she'd be happy I'd rescued them.

"We'll take them to one of my places outside the city. They can stay there until this is resolved."

She sighed, pulling away from me. She stood up and paced the room. I'd done something stupid all because I'd kept everything inside rather than admitting to how much her abduction had affected me. I'd allowed my control to slip. Now we had to deal with the consequences.

"Why did you put them in the cell? They look terrified."

"I don't know."

"You know you've put us in a dangerous situation, right? We're already in enough shit as it is."

"Did you expect me to leave them there?"

"No. I would've taken them too. Charlie is going to question Rick's friend. He's going to ask who took the girls away. What do you think he'll say when he finds out it was you?"

She rubbed her face. She was right. I should never have gone to Robert's. I was just so fucked off with everything. I was fed up with feeling so fucking helpless. So I'd done something about it instead. As idiotic and selfish as that sounds.

"I'll sort it."

"How?"

"It's not for you to worry about."

She threw her hands up.

"What has gotten into you? You've been acting all weird since Rick took me."

I ran a hand through my hair. Having Rick take her drove me fucking crazy. I just hadn't realised she'd noticed. I opened my mouth to speak, but she cut me off.

"Do not tell me it's nothing, Aiden."

"I wasn't going to."

I knew better than to tell her nothing was wrong when that clearly wasn't the case. I looked away, staring down at the bathroom mat on the floor.

"Do you know how fucking terrified I was for you? How helpless it all made me feel. I'm meant to protect you, princess. I couldn't even do that. You were almost assaulted by Tristan and then Rick took you away. It fucking killed me. I couldn't deal with it. Any of it."

I dared look up at her. Her expression softened. She walked over and knelt before me, taking my hands in hers.

Admitting this to her was fucking hard. Telling her how it chewed me up inside. How much it destroyed me that she was taken on my watch.

"Aiden…"

"I fucking hated it. I lost all my fucking control and did something stupid as shit and I know that. Okay? I know I messed up. All I want is for you to be safe. I dragged you into all of this. I made it dangerous for you. I did this."

"You're not to blame for what happened to me."

"I am. Do you know James had a go at me over this whole thing? He told me I shouldn't have made you get involved and that you had a target on your back because of me."

She shifted closer, letting go of one of my hands and reaching up to hold my face instead. Her touch soothed my racing heart a little. The way she was looking at me without any judgement, just compassion, made my chest constrict.

"He shouldn't have. You couldn't have stopped Rick taking me. He was determined to speak to me. You need to stop beating yourself up about this. And you need to talk to me instead of bottling it up. If you're struggling with something, then tell me. That's what I'm here for, to listen and help you deal with it."

Fuck. My princess. Her words tore at me.

"I know how much you struggle to let anyone in, but we're partners, Aiden. We're in this relationship together. You're there for me when I need you so let me do the same for you. Don't think I don't know how you put aside everything to help me after Rick took me. I was a mess, but you gave me what I needed. You made it okay. Please, tell me what you need."

I let go of her hand and crushed her to my chest, burying my face in her hair. No matter how much it pained me to show any weakness in front of anyone, Avery was different. She mattered most to me in this world. She was the one.

"I just need you," I whispered. "Just you. The rest of the bullshit doesn't matter."

She wrapped her arms around my back, not complaining about how tightly I held her.

"I love you so much, princess. I'm sorry I put us in danger again. I'm so sorry."

"Shh, it's okay. We'll fix it. It'll be fine."

She pulled away, looking up at me.

"You tell my uncle it was Rick's friend who helped take me. That's why you went around his and beat him up. He'll be happy about that, trust me. He apologised to me today and told me never to marry Tristan or trust the Shaws. If he finds out who helped kidnap me, he'll be livid. Perhaps enough that he might not notice the girls are gone. That will give us time to get them away from here."

Chuck had apologised to Avery?

"He did what?"

"He said sorry for what he did when I was a kid. It doesn't change how I feel about him."

I was glad he'd apologised. Still didn't negate what he'd done. He'd hurt other girls and that was unforgivable.

"Do you really think he'd be that pissed?"

"I don't know, but I don't have any better ideas. Do you?"

I shook my head.

"We just need to keep him away from Rick's friend long enough for us to work out what our next move is. He's got a

320

lot on his plate with this birthday event, so we can use that to our advantage."

I stared at her. I wasn't quite sure why I was surprised by her resourcefulness. She'd full on taken charge of the situation. It didn't bother me. In fact, it was quite the opposite. Seeing her so assertive and in control was hot. Here I'd been all fucked up and unable to think straight and she'd handled it for me.

Maybe she was right. Maybe I did need to let her in properly. I did want her for life. I could start here, by making sure I learnt how to rely on her just as she'd always relied on me.

"What?" she said after a few minutes went by.

"Just you."

Her brow furrowed.

"What about me?"

I smiled.

"You're telling me what to do."

She flushed, looking away.

"Well… I'm just trying to help."

"Princess, you've more than helped. You've worked out a plan. And you're right, we are in this together. You and me."

She shifted on her knees, staring up at me with wide eyes.

"So… you're not mad or anything?"

"No." I reached out, running my fingers through her dark hair. "I only need your submission in the bedroom."

"Is that so?"

"Mmm, yes."

Not that we could be getting up to anything right now. I was injured and we had to deal with the girls. Perhaps later when all of this was sorted out.

"We should probably see those women and make sure they're okay."

I stood up and put my hand out, helping her to her feet.

"You stay here a minute," she said.

"Why?"

"I don't think it's a good idea if you go see them without a shirt on. I might know you don't want to take advantage of them, but they don't."

I nodded. She made a valid point. I waited for her to go into the bedroom and bring me back a t-shirt before pulling it on. She took my bruised hand and walked out into the hall with me. We reached the cell. The two women stared at us with wide eyes, terror evident in them.

"Hello," Avery said, letting go of my hand and stepping in. "I'm Avery, Aiden's girlfriend. I promise we're not going to harm you. We just want to keep you safe. I'm sorry Aiden put you in here."

Neither of them said anything. Avery looked back at me for a moment, her eyebrow raised before turning towards the girls again.

"Can I ask what your names are?"

"Sophie and that's Cora," said the blonde one on the right.

"Okay, Sophie and Cora. Do you want to get cleaned up? I'm not sure you'll fit in any of my clothes, but we can find you something to wear."

Sophie, the blonde girl, nodded. Avery put her hand out to them. She got to her feet, pulling Cora up with her. She took the girls into the bathroom before stepping out and leaving them to it. I followed her into the bedroom.

"We'll just have to give them something of yours for now," she said. "They're too tall for my clothes."

I went over to my cupboard and pulled out a couple of t-shirts. It wasn't like I couldn't replace these. We could get them clothes tomorrow before we took them away from here. I handed them to Avery who took them back out into the hallway. She returned, sighing as she walked over to me and wrapped her arms around my back.

"We should probably feed them."

"You're right," I replied, wrapping my arms around her. "Wait… I completely forgot to ask how it was at your parents. Did you find the paperwork?"

She stiffened in my hold.

"I did."

"Avery…"

"I'm not going to say I enjoyed it. I shouldn't have gone in the kitchen."

I stroked her hair. Fuck. I really wish I'd been there for her instead of getting into a fight with Robert fucking Bassington.

"What happened?"

"I remembered everything from that day. There's still a stain on the floor. I'm okay. It was just hard being there is all."

"I'm sorry."

She nuzzled her face on my chest.

"It's fine. Honestly, I had to face it one day. It is what it is. It happened. There's nothing either of us can do to change it. Yes, it sucked, but what they did is worse. I just don't want to go back again. Too many memories."

I kissed the top of her head. I wished she'd let me go with her, but I understood why she had to do it by herself. Avery was so strong. So fucking capable.

"Why don't you go start making some food and I'll call Chuck. We'll talk about it properly later."

She nodded, pulling away from me. She went up on her tiptoes and kissed me, wrapping her arms around my neck. When she pulled away, she smiled.

"You know, when I said you were a bad boy, I didn't mean you should go around getting into fights and coming home black and blue."

I snorted. This was not something I usually did. Yes, I'd had to rough up a few people in my time, but they rarely hit back. The idiot had brass fucking knuckles and that's what caused the fucking cuts on my body. It was lucky I was bigger than him. Knocked the fucker right out after a couple of blows to the head. Then I'd managed to hurt myself further beating the crap out of Robert. He wouldn't be going out for a while.

My parting words to him rang in my ears.

"You won't fucking breathe a word of this to Chuck or I'll be back to finish the job. And you fucking tell Rick if he ever takes Avery Daniels again, I will find him and I will fucking kill him. Do you fucking understand?"

Robert had nodded, barely able to see out of his two swollen eye sockets. Idiot. He shouldn't have fucking laughed at me like I was some kind of joke. It was his own fucking fault. Arrogant prick thought he was safe. He had no idea who he was dealing with. I'd met him on a handful of occasions. He'd always sneered at me like I was a piece of dirt on his shoe. Didn't matter that I was technically his friend's son. He thought he was better than me. I'd given him a fucking wakeup call.

"I'll try to keep that in mind."

"Please do. I don't want to patch you up again."

"Mmm, I quite liked you nursing me back to health."

She pulled away from me, shoving my chest. I winced and she immediately looked apologetic.

"I'm sorry."

"It's fine. Go check on the girls and I'll speak to Chuck."

She nodded, giving me a smile before disappearing from the room.

I pulled my phone out. It was time I sorted this shit out and made sure we had time to hide the girls before he found out I'd taken them from Robert. If this didn't work, we'd be in serious shit. As if we weren't in enough already.

I had to fix this.

Fix it so I could keep Avery safe.

And then we were going to work out our next move.

Because Avery and I were in this together.

Chapter Twenty Three

Avery

*A*iden and I ended up taking Sophie and Cora to Tina's. She'd keep them safe for the time being. Until I gained full access to my inheritance, I only had a monthly allowance along with my salary from the company. It was more than enough to live on so we could at least set the girls up with funds. I didn't like to think of it as compensation for what my family had done to them. They needed help after what they'd been through. Whatever they needed, we'd give it to them. Therapy. Medical care. Somewhere to live. All of it.

Now we'd rescued two girls, I wanted to find the rest. That meant working out where they were being housed. The biggest problem was they were being moved around all the time. Going from client to client. Whoever managed it all for my uncle, they were good at hiding their tracks and keeping everything under the radar. No matter what Aiden did, he couldn't find out where they were.

I couldn't imagine the pain they'd gone through. How much they'd suffered. Aiden and I might want to take down my family and their associates, but we also had a responsibility towards the girls too. We'd save them if it was the last thing we did.

Sophie and Cora had been with Rick's friend for six months. They hadn't wanted to tell me much about what he'd done to them. Aiden told me his name was Robert Bassington. I only knew a handful of my family's associates and he wasn't one of them. He was in his sixties according to Aiden. One of my grandfather's old friends. We hoped if Robert didn't say anything to my uncle about Aiden taking the girls, it would take him a while to discover they were gone.

When Aiden told Uncle Charlie about Robert being involved in my abduction, he'd completely lost his shit. Just as I predicted. Aiden had come into the kitchen and put the phone on speaker whilst I made food for the girls.

"That fucking cunt. I'm going to have his fucking head. How fucking dare he pull a stunt like this! I don't care who he is, no one fucking messes with my fucking family. He knows how important she is to the company. To our fucking business arrangements. If you hadn't already beat the cunt up, I would be straight down there fucking decking him myself."

"Don't worry, he knows he fucked up. I made sure of it."

"Oh, I believe you. Fucking hell. I can't believe he would be so fucking stupid. I really don't have time for this shit. I'll deal with it at a later date. I've got enough on my plate without these bastards fucking about."

"That's what you have me for."

"Thank you. Shit has just got crazier and crazier around here since Mitch died. Anyway, I'll speak to you in a few days, must get on."

At least he'd bought it for now. I was in no doubt when he found out Aiden had taken Sophie and Cora, things would be very different.

Aiden and I were sat in the living room. It was the weekend thankfully, so I finally had time to go through all the documents I'd brought home from my dad's office. I was sat by the window with some of the paperwork spread out on the floor in front of me. Aiden was lounging on the sofa with the rest of it. The documents I'd thought he would find useful.

The legal jargon in my trust fund paperwork was giving me a headache.

"Why did he have to make this so complicated?" I complained, rubbing my forehead.

He peered over the back of the sofa at me.

"I told you, I'd go through it for you if you want."

"No, it's okay. I need to do this. If anything, I should really understand how he set this up since it's my money. Not like I want it really, but if I can help the girls with it, then I will."

"John said Frazier was in the office three more times last week."

"Yeah, he spoke to Charlie a few times. He only came to see me once like I told you."

It had been the same as last time he'd ambushed me. He wanted to know if I'd made up my mind about Tristan. I'd just stalled him again. I was pretty sure he'd be in every week until I gave him an answer. I still had no idea what the rush was.

"I wish he'd stay the fuck away from you."

"Well, we can't have everything we want. Did John find out anything else about where the girls are being kept?"

"Only that the person who manages the whole operation is known as 'The Collector'. Stupid as fuck name if you ask me."

I snorted. Whoever came up with that clearly thought a lot about themselves.

"He has to be careful though. Chuck is already getting a little suspicious about why he's asking so many questions. It's fucking lucky he's so busy organising this birthday event for you or he'd have found out about Sophie and Cora."

"Did Tina say how they are?"

"They're doing okay. She's going to move them out of London next week. She has a house near Truro in Cornwall. They can stay there for the time being. I think they're just glad to be away from Robert."

I was glad we'd managed to persuade Tina to take care of them. Aiden and I weren't really equipped to be dealing with two abused, sex trafficked girls. I had a feeling they reminded him too much of his mother. He still hadn't told me what happened the night she died, but I hadn't pressed him either. It was something he needed to do in his own time.

I was well aware Rick had told me to find out, but quite frankly, he could get fucked. I wasn't about to do anything the man said. He was dangerous. Still, I was also in no doubt he'd make good on his promise to see me again. I wondered how I'd feel when confronted with him face to face. Wondered what he'd tell me. He'd promised to divulge everything.

I looked over at Aiden. I was concerned about what Rick might say. What he might tell me about the man I loved. I wasn't sure if I'd believe it anyway. Aiden had told me he'd done some bad things in his time. I mean he'd killed my parents, so it wasn't like I didn't know what he was capable of.

He wouldn't ever physically hurt me. That was the one thing I was sure of. He loved and trusted me. He'd started to let me in and that meant everything. We'd overcome so many hurdles in the past few months since I'd gone back into the world.

In the beginning, he'd found it difficult to even be in a relationship with me, but now, he was learning to let go. His outlet was the bedroom. Whenever he needed it, I let him tie me up and fuck me without mercy. I loved submitting to him as much as he loved having control of me.

Outside of the bedroom, we were forming a partnership. One where we worked together to overcome issues inside and outside our relationship.

I turned the page, settling in to read the next clause when my heart almost came to a stop. There in black and white was the reason Frazier wanted me to marry Tristan. I read through the whole clause just to make sure, but I was right. This explained everything. Aiden had been so fucking right to get me to find the paperwork. It all fell into place.

"Aiden… I think I know why Frazier is being so insistent."

He looked up, grey eyes narrowing.

"Why?"

"Come here and read this."

He hauled himself up off the sofa, dropping the document he was holding on the coffee table. He walked around and stood before me. I handed him the document, pointing at Clause 6.2.8. I watched him read over it.

"Well shit," he said, rubbing the back of his neck.

"He's not going to stop pestering me, is he?"

"No… We have to do something about it."

I stared up at him. A smile formed on his face.

"Did you have something in mind?"

He nodded, his eyes meeting mine. I saw the mischievous glint in them.

"Oh… I do. We just have to play him at his own fucking game."

Six Weeks Later

I stood in front of the mirror, looking at myself in the dress I'd got for my birthday. Dark red with a deep v running down the centre of it. I traced the outline of the new ink on my left arm. Three weeks ago, Ben had tattooed Xochiquetzal there. She matched Aiden's tattoos on his chest. She was absolutely stunning. I adored this piece. He'd spent a long time working out the details with me. Making sure we got it just right before he began inking it on my skin.

I turned my right wrist over. There sat a pair of black, highly detailed angel wings I'd designed myself. Aiden had got a matching tattoo on a free patch of skin on his stomach. Lastly, a flock of birds rested on my right shoulder. I loved all of them. Ben was so talented.

It had been nice spending time with him, Skye and baby Josh. Watching Aiden hold his nephew and tell him about when his dad and him had been in the army melted my heart. He'd told me he was crap with kids, but he'd been so good with Josh.

I wasn't sure what might be said about me turning up to a company event with all this ink, but I didn't care. Most of them knew about the A on my neck, so this wasn't really any different. It was my body and there was nothing they could do about it.

I felt two hands around my waist. Aiden's mischievous grin appeared in the mirror. Grey eyes burning with heat.

"You look absolutely fucking stunning, princess."

"You can thank Gert. She made me buy it."

He dropped a kiss on my shoulder. I'd put my hair up, securing it with pearl headed bobby pins. Make-up wasn't exactly my favourite task in the world, but I'd given myself smoky eyes to complete the look.

"I wish I could walk in there with you on my arm. Show the world you're mine."

"Me too."

I turned around placing my hands on his chest.

"Soon we'll be able to tell them all. When this is over, we'll have our future together. Just you and me."

He smiled. Hell, did I love that smile. And those grey eyes which held so many emotions. I loved everything about this man. Even the darkest parts. He was mine and I was his. We'd made sure of that.

The past six weeks had been tough on both of us, but we'd meticulously planned everything down to the last detail. We were going to take them down one by one. We knew what to do. Thinking about what would happen next pained me, but it was necessary.

"Mmm, you and me."

He leant down, capturing my mouth in a slow, sensuous kiss which had my skin tingling and my body craving his. His hands ran down my back, tugging me closer to him. He trailed kisses along my jaw.

"Fuck do I want you," he murmured.

"You'll mess up my hair and make-up."

"I don't care."

"Aiden…"

He bit down on my earlobe, his fingers tracing lines across my bare back. I shuddered, unable to help the small moan escaping from my lips.

"Let me fuck you before we both go to hell and back later."

My ability to say no to him was shot to pieces. I couldn't deny I wanted him inside me too. I needed it. Craved it. I felt him smile against my neck when I arched into him.

"Bend over for me, princess."

He knew he'd won.

"Are you sure we have time?" I asked, pulling away from him.

"Get on the bed."

He pointed at it, his tone leaving no room for disobedience. I walked over. I hadn't put my heels on yet, so I was barefoot. I tugged up the floor length dress and knelt on the bed, placing my hands down. I looked back at him as he stalked over to me. He ran his hands over my behind.

"You know what it does to me when you bend over like this?"

"No… what?"

I knew, but I wanted to hear him say it. Having him tell me how much he wanted to fuck me always did things to me.

"My cock gets so fucking hard for you."

He undid his belt. He was wearing the grey suit I loved so much. He had always been the most beautiful man I'd ever laid eyes on.

"Show me how much you want me, princess."

I shifted, sitting up slightly so I could pull up my dress further. It bunched around my waist as I set my hands back down on the bed. I heard his low growl.

"Fuck. You're such a naughty girl. Not wearing any underwear."

The thing is, I'd known he'd want me before I left. So I decided not to put any on because I knew how much it'd drive him crazy.

He was right. We would go to hell and back at this birthday event, so now, I just wanted a moment with him. One last memory I could hold onto. I needed Aiden to brand himself into my skin. Needed him to fuck me so I'd still feel him there later. So I'd know he owned me. Know he was mine forever.

"I'm aching to be filled... Fuck me."

"Mmm, do you want my cock in you?"

"Yes, please fuck me hard."

I looked back at him again. He had his cock out and was stroking it. My mouth watered at the sight of him. Shit. I shifted, very aware of the throbbing between my legs.

He gripped my hip in one hand, using the other to stroke his cock back and forth across my pussy. I moaned as it brushed against my clit relentlessly.

"Aiden, please."

"Fuck, I love hearing you beg for my cock."

"Please, I want you so much. I need you. Remind me I'm yours. Claim me."

I was rewarded with him pressing his cock inside me. He grunted, taking it agonisingly slow as he filled me up to the hilt. He felt amazing. He always did.

He leant down and kissed my shoulder, right where the birds were.

"You'll remember this later. You'll know I've been inside you. I'm going to fuck you hard and make you scream. I fucking love that sound. When we're done, you'll know your mine. You'll know it deep within your soul."

I shivered at his words. Hell, he already had my soul. He had my everything. I'd given it to him without conditions.

He straightened, pulled back and thrust into me, setting a brutal and merciless pace. He fucked me so hard, I almost couldn't take the intensity. And he really did make me scream.

My fingers dug into the covers as I held on for dear life. I cried out his name over and over. My insides clenched. My whole body felt like it was on fire.

"Fucking take it, fuck, Avery. You're mine. Mine. You hear me?"

"I'm yours. Only yours."

"You belong to me."

"Always. I'll always be yours."

His fingers dug into both my hips as he held me in place.

"Are you going to come all over my cock, princess?"

I arched back, feeling it stirring in my core. I took my weight on one hand as the other snaked between my legs.

"Yes, yes. Fuck me just like that. I'll come all over you."

He growled. I'd have to douse myself in perfume to cover up the fact that I most likely now smelt like sex. I no longer cared. All I felt was the driving need to come. To find that release with the man I loved. The one only he could give to me. The freedom we had together was unlike anything else.

"Harder, please, fuck me harder," I groaned.

I was on the edge. The sound of our brutal lovemaking rang in my ears as it all exploded at once. My blood fizzled in my veins. My skin tingled everywhere.

I slammed my hand back down on the bed so I wouldn't collapse as the waves of pleasure took me under and drowned me.

"I love you. I love you so fucking much."

"I love you too, princess."

He wasn't quite done with me. His thrusts grew erratic, letting me know he was close. He cursed, fucking me so hard, my teeth almost rattled in my skull. I felt the first pulse and his grunt vibrated across my skin.

He slowed, coming to a halt. I could hear his harsh breath as he panted behind me.

"Fuck, Avery."

He echoed my exact thoughts. Fuck indeed. It wasn't like sex with us had ever been anything but all consuming and intense, but today was a huge deal for both of us. We had a lot to accomplish. I just hoped it all paid off.

He pulled out of me, flipped me over on my back and crawled over me, capturing my mouth in his. The kiss was desperate. We clutched each other, needing that connection between us.

"I'm not ready for this shit," he whispered against my lips.

"Neither am I."

It had to happen. We had no choice but to go ahead with it. All our plans would go up in flames otherwise.

We lay there together for the longest time. Aiden kissed my cheeks, my eyes, my nose, my lips. I'd have to touch up my make-up, but I no longer cared. I needed this. He needed this. Just a few more minutes where it was me and him.

When he got off me and tucked himself back in his trousers, doing his belt up, I sat up on my elbows. He smiled at me.

"Well, looks like I did ruin your hair and make-up."

"Dick."

He laughed, pulling me up off the bed. He kissed me before I walked out of the room and went into the bathroom to clean up and sort out the mess that was my face and hair.

Twenty minutes later, I'd fixed myself up, pulled on my underwear, knowing Aiden would not be happy if I went without and slipped on my shoes.

The door buzzed. It was John. I told him I'd be down in a couple of minutes.

Aiden wrapped his arms around me, giving me one last kiss before I left. He helped me put my coat on.

"You still look stunning."

"And you scrub up well too," I said, brushing away a piece of lint from one of his lapels.

"Is that so?"

"Mmm, you're still my tattooed bad boy."

He grinned, kissing my forehead.

"I can call you my tattooed princess now."

I smiled before turning and opening the front door.

"I'll see you there."

He winked. I slipped from the flat and made my way downstairs into the waiting car. I made small talk with John on the way. He might be head of security for the event, but he was still my bodyguard.

When we reached the venue, he opened my door for me and helped me out the car. His green eyes twinkled.

"Good luck in there… Miss Daniels."

He gave me a wink. I grinned. It felt like we had our own personal in joke surrounding that name now.

"I think I'll need it."

I took a deep breath, looking up at the beautiful carvings around the front door.

It was time to face the music.

Chapter Twenty Four

Aiden

*T*onight would change everything. Our plans had to work. The groundwork was in place. Avery and I had done everything in our power to make sure they'd fall like dominoes. If we pulled this off, we'd be free. Finally free to be together without hiding in the shadows. I'd finally destroy the Daniels legacy and all its corruption and abuse.

When we'd discovered the clause in her trust fund, I'd known exactly what I had to do. Avery's safety and happiness were paramount. In a crazy twist of fate, it was me who'd insisted on this course of action when she'd been sceptical.

Whilst it might have looked like we'd done this just so Frazier couldn't get his hands on her trust fund, we knew the truth. I loved her and she loved me. Our souls were meant for each other. Who gave a fuck about timescales, about what was right or wrong? At the end of the day, all that mattered was us.

Avery had looked like a fucking goddess before she left. That dress fit her like a glove. I would have to thank her friend at a later date. Gert and James had been there for the two of us in the past few weeks and their help really was invaluable, along with Ben, Skye and John.

I knew what it was to rely on your fellow soldiers in the army, but back in civilian life, things were different. Avery taught me it was okay to trust other people when you knew they had your back. I had hers and she had mine. That made us a team. The two of us wouldn't have been able to achieve this by ourselves, which is why having our friends around us made such a difference.

I dusted my shoulder before walking out the door ten minutes after Avery left. As a valued employee, I was invited to her birthday event. Chuck had spent weeks on this. He'd coordinated the event himself.

I wasn't sure why he'd suddenly become so invested in his niece, but I had a feeling it was more to do with the publicity this event would bring than it being Avery's birthday.

Daniels Holdings had been through a string of bad press since Mitchell and Kathleen's murders. All the rumours surrounding it had done nothing but drag the company's name through the mud. Admittedly, this is what I'd wanted, but now, we needed a new narrative. A new spin on things. That's what our plans tonight would achieve.

I got in the Jag and made my way across the city. Chuck had picked a central location for it right next to Westminster. Avery had shown me pictures of the mock-ups of what the room would look like. Even though she wasn't happy about having this event in the first place, she did get stuck into helping Chuck with it.

Parking up nearby, I got out and walked to the venue. Some of the press were outside, but I imagined Chuck had invited a lot of them as guests. This was big news. The first real chance anyone would get to see Avery as the new head of the company. She'd refused so many interviews.

I nodded at the door staff as I walked in, flashing my invitation. The place was really done up. Chuck had spared no expense. There were flowers everywhere with some flowing material hanging down from the ceiling.

As I walked into the ballroom, I spied John immediately. He was standing against one of the walls, surveying the crowd. I made a beeline for him, keeping my eyes peeled for my girl. I spotted her with James and Gert towards the back of the room.

Thank fuck.

At least she wasn't with any of the other twats who'd been invited to this event. I was sure she'd be hounded all evening but for now, she was with her friends.

"You not worried someone might try steal her away from you this evening?" John said as I joined him against the wall.

"You're a funny man."

He grinned, giving me a wink.

"You sure she's ready to go through with this?"

"She knows she can back out at any time, but I don't think she will. Not now."

There was a lot at stake. In order to convince everyone, Avery had become quite the actress over the past few weeks. Still, this was going to come as quite a shock to a number of people, Chuck included.

I spied Frazier and Tristan walking in the ballroom together. Both were in tuxes, their hair slicked back in matching styles.

"You really think he's bought all of this?"

"Who, Frazier?"

"He looks very smug right now."

Frazier's eyes had fallen on Avery. The glint in them made my blood boil in my veins. Fucking cunt. I couldn't wait to make him pay.

"He thinks he has everything he's ever wanted in the palm of his hand."

John gave me a sly smile. Frazier was about to get a fucking wakeup call. Tonight was about guaranteeing our success. It wasn't easy to fool a man as suspicious of the world as Frazier, but my girl was determined. She hated Tristan and Frazier more than I did at this point.

"I never thought I'd relish the day we set the empire up to fall flat on its face."

"Well, I'm grateful you decided to switch sides."

He shrugged.

"The sooner this is over, the better. I'm done with the Daniels and their bullshit. I've seen too much."

We both had. The shit they'd made us do. No one could call John and I good men, but we were determined to make sure we made up for it in some small way.

We'd been getting closer to working out who The Collector was and where he was keeping the girls. How they were moved from client to client. We needed to topple the operation and burn it to the ground. Avery was determined to rescue all the girls before everything went up in flames.

Tristan made his way across the room towards my girl. I clenched my fists but stayed put. I couldn't do anything about that snivelling little shit. I had to keep my temper in check even though I wanted to fucking rip his balls off.

Avery gave him her brightest fake smile when he reached her and her two friends. I knew they'd all gone to school together. James' sneered at the sight of him and Gert looked like she'd rather be anywhere else. I was too far away to hear what they were saying.

"I don't know how you can stand here and watch him near her," John said.

"If I had a choice, he'd be in the ground."

"Soon all of them will be."

John didn't care if I took all of them out. I doubt he'd even care that I killed Mitchell and Kathleen. He'd become jaded with the world after spending so long around sick bastards like the Daniels and their associates. I could hardly blame him. I'd been the same way until Avery came into my life. She'd become my reason to live again.

"I keep reminding myself of that."

I scanned the room, knowing John would keep his eyes on my princess. My fists clenched again when I spied Robert Bassington talking to Chuck. Their eyes were on me. There were no longer any traces of the beating I'd given Robert on his face, but he looked thunderous. I knew what the sick fuck would be saying to him. I didn't trust him not to blab. It didn't matter now. Sophie and Cora were safe.

Tina had taken them to her house in Cornwall. She told me they were doing well. I was glad she was out of London whilst this shit was going down. I'd seen her last week and we'd talked for a long time, but she'd gone back to take care of them after that.

They were still pretty traumatised after what they'd been through. She'd found a private therapist. Avery insisted on paying for it all since it was her family who'd done this to them.

"Well, looks like I'm in for a conversation tonight."

John looked over, frowning until he noticed who I was staring at.

"You did insist on taking those girls from Robert."

"You know I couldn't leave them there."

"No, but it's going to cost you."

I shrugged. It wasn't as if I was unprepared. Chuck would have more important things to worry about before this evening was over.

"I'm sure once Avery makes her announcement, it'll be forgotten about."

He grinned, shaking his head.

"Want to bet how long it takes for Chuck to piss himself?"

I smiled. I think he'd do more than just that. Avery was about to completely turn everything on its head. I never thought she'd change her mind about all of this, but she had. We'd both come to the same conclusion. Turn everyone against each other and cause chaos. That started with her doing something she said she never would.

My eyes fell on her again. She was still talking to Tristan, who was staring at her with a disgusting leer in his eyes. James looked like he wanted to stab Tristan in the face. I couldn't blame him.

Apparently, Tristan had spent their school years tormenting the three of them for being nerds. Hardly surprising given what I knew about the fucking idiot. He was a younger version of his father on every level. Moulded to be exactly like Frazier.

Avery's doe eyes met mine across the room. The twinkle in them made my heart thump. Fuck. I loved that girl to the fucking moon and back. She was every star in the sky. So fucking bright and beautiful. Perfect for me in every single way.

"Has Chuck seen her tattoos yet?"

"No. I'm sure he'll have something to say about those. He wasn't happy when she got the first one."

"Well, we're about to find out."

He nodded at Chuck who was pushing through the crowd towards his niece. His face was a picture of irritation. When he reached her, she looked a little taken aback by what he said. He took her by the arm and pulled her away, closer to where John and I were standing.

"What the fuck are those?" he said.

We could just about make out his voice over the noise.

"What are what?"

"Tattoos, Avery. Are you determined to make sure no one takes you seriously?"

She pulled her arm away from him.

"Don't be so old fashioned, Uncle Charlie."

"This is supposed to show the company in a good light. You turning up with these is going to be headline news."

She shrugged, giving him a smile.

"Given what else might happen this evening, I don't think you have to worry too much about my new tattoos."

His eyes narrowed.

"And just what do you mean by that?"

"You'll see."

She patted him on the shoulder before sauntering away to where there was a small stage erected. She looked back at where John and I were, giving us both a wink over her shoulder. I shook my head. She was enjoying this a little too much. I absolutely hated what she was going to do next, but again, we had little choice in the matter. This was the only way.

She reached the stage and picked up the mic, patting it a little to get everyone's attention. The subtle music was switched off and everyone turned towards her. Chuck's expression grew darker. There was no going back now.

"Hello everyone, as you all probably know, I'm Avery. Firstly, I'd like to thank you all for coming. You only turn twenty one and become head of a company once in your life."

Some of the crowd chuckled. I could see the nervousness in her movements. Her fingers twitched on the mic and her smile was too big. I wished I could hold her hand. Help her get through this speech, but that would be a fucking disaster for both of us.

"I'd like to say thank you to my uncle, Charles Daniels, for arranging this event and keeping the company running after the tragic death of my parents. I have some big shoes to fill, but I'm determined to carry on in my father's footsteps. May they both rest in peace."

There was some murmuring of agreement around the room. I glanced at John who was rolling his eyes. I knew now he hated Mitchell. He'd told me working for him had been a bitch. At least when he started, he dealt with Nick who didn't mince words. Mitchell always hid behind masks.

"I don't want to keep you all for too long, but I have an announcement to make."

She looked out into the crowd and waved at someone. They made their way towards the stage and got up on the platform with her. This was it. I tried to keep my breathing steady. She reached out and took the person's hand. She plastered on the fakest smile I'd ever seen her give.

"We weren't going to make this public quite yet, but we couldn't wait. We've known each other since childhood and now we feel it is time to move forward with our lives. I'm so overjoyed. Last night, this one here got down on one knee and asked me to marry him. And well… I said yes."

The room went deathly silent before applause erupted. John looked over at me.

"Guess the cat is out of the bag."

I nodded, eying the two of them before turning towards where Chuck was standing. His mouth was hanging open. She hadn't told him anything about this.

Next, my eyes fell on Frazier who looked like he'd won the lottery. Stupid idiot had no idea. He thought he'd won, but we were going to have the last laugh. Avery had put up with a lot of shit over the past weeks from the Shaws, but this was the only way.

Chuck turned around and spied me with John. He stormed over and ran his hand through his hair.

"What the actual fuck is she playing at?"

"What do you mean?"

"Getting married to Tristan? Is she insane? I told her not to do this. For fuck's sake, she really is a nightmare."

I shook my head, shrugging, but before I had a chance to speak, he continued.

"And you, what the fuck are you about taking girls from Robert? And not only that, he told me you threatened to go after your father. What the fuck is going on, Aiden? Why is Rick involved in this shit?"

John gave me a significant look before he walked away, leaving me alone with Chuck. I'd known this was going to be a messy evening.

"I don't think you need to worry about Rick or the girls."

"And why the fuck not?"

"Your niece isn't going to marry Tristan."

"What?"

"Technically if she did, she'd be committing bigamy."

Chuck stared at me, his expression showing his complete bewilderment.

"Bigamy? What the fuck are you talking about?"

I gave him my brightest smile.

"Well, you see, Chuck. Avery is married to me."

To be continued in Revenge…

I sincerely hope you enjoyed reading this book as much as I enjoyed writing it. If you did, I would greatly appreciate a short review on Amazon or your favourite book website. Reviews are crucial for any author, and even just a line or two can make a huge difference.

Acknowledgements

Thank you so much for taking the time to read this book. Writing Avery and Aiden's second book has been quite the challenge. Having left Betrayal on a huge cliff hanger, I wanted to dive straight back in and reveal what exactly it was that Aiden asked Avery to do. What caused her to walk out on him. And the big question. Would they find their way back to each other?

These two gave me a hell of a lot of curve balls and feels when I was writing Sacrifice. Watching them navigate their relationship to the point where they decided they were it for each other was a joy.

I'm really looking forward to seeing what everyone thinks about the next part of their journey. They might not have quite got their happy ever after yet, but there's still a lot more to come. These two are near and dear to my heart. I'm so excited that the trilogy is almost complete. Revenge is coming and it's a guaranteed crazy ride!

Firstly I'd like to say a HUGE thank you to all my ARC readers for reading and reviewing Betrayal. Having your early feedback spurred me on and I'm so pleased so many of you loved the book. I'm hoping Sacrifice was worth the wait!

Thank you to my Twitter gang – #TTAF – and all of my Twitter family. You guys are amazing. Your support means the world. You all have the best banter. I loved every moment I've been in the writing community. It has given me a new lease of life and the determination to succeed.

Thank you to my family and friends. Especially my mum, who lovingly proofreads all my books. Even if she does like to make jokes about the content of them. Apparently, she only wants to visit me provided there are no butt plugs and restraints involved. And yes, this was a genuine conversation between us!

Thank you to my bestie – Sabrina. Your support is invaluable. From telling me that I can do this to listening to me rant about how much of a pain it is to write demanding characters. Slytherin Sisters for life! If anyone is going to be my soulmate, it's you. Never forget how wonderful you are and how much you mean to me.

Last but not least, thank you to my husband. You're my best friend, my partner in crime, the one who never fails to make me laugh… and creep me out on a regular basis. I love you to the moon and back.

About The Author

Born and raised in Sussex, UK near the Ashdown Forest where she grew up climbing trees and building Lego towns with her younger brother. Sarah fell in love with novels when she was a teenager reading her aunt's historical regency romances. She has always loved the supernatural and exploring the darker side of romance and fantasy novels.

Sarah currently resides in the Scottish Highlands with her husband. Music is one of her biggest inspirations and she always has something on in the background whilst writing. She is an avid gamer and is often found hogging her husband's Xbox.

Corrupt Empire

Made in the USA
Middletown, DE
13 April 2021

37510025R00215